Choosing Riley:

Sarafin Warriors: Book 1

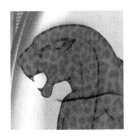

By S. E. Smith

Acknowledgments

I would like to thank my husband Steve for believing in me and being proud enough of me to give me the courage to follow my dream. I would also like to give a special thank you to my sister and best friend Linda, who not only encouraged me to write but who also read the manuscript. Also to my other friends who believe in me: Julie, Jackie, Lisa, Sally, Elizabeth (Beth) and Narelle. The girls that keep me going!
—S. E. Smith

Science Fiction Romance

CHOOSING RILEY

Copyright © 2013 by Susan E. Smith

First E-Book Publication March 2013

Cover Design by Melody Simmons

Synopsis

Riley St. Claire has always followed her own rules. When she discovers her current employer is not as law-abiding as she thought, she has to leave town in a hurry or end up buried with the dead guy she discovered. What she doesn't expect is to find herself being picked up by a passing trader from another world.

As the ruling King of Sarafin, Vox d'Rojah was expected to produce a son who would be joined in marriage with the first-born daughter of the King of Valdier. The problem was Vox had no intentions of having any sons, at least not in the near future. He was quite happy with the wide selection of females he had at his disposal. When he is captured by a ruthless Valdier royal and sold to a mining operation, the last thing he expected to find was his bride mate.

Vox isn't sure which would be easier: fighting another war with the Valdier or capturing and holding on to the human female who is unlike anyone he has ever encountered before.

Now, Vox has to escape back to his world while fighting pirates, traders, and Riley!

The King of Sarafin has met his match in Ms. Riley St. Claire from Earth. Now, he just needs to figure out a way to let her know he has chosen her as his Queen—and he has every intention of keeping her by his side forever.

Contents

Chapter 1

"Choose," the disembodied voice said.

Choose? Choose what? Riley thought, looking around her in disbelief at the rock walls. *Choose to get the fuck out of this crazy nightmare? Hell, yeah. Choose to kill the bastards who put me in this miserable spot? Oh, hell yeah. Choose...*

Riley jerked when she felt the ice-cold claw poke her in the back for the third time. Looking around, she followed the arm of the creature standing next to her as it pointed down over the edge of a small platform. She really was trying for that nice stage of being totally zoned out, but the damn creatures who kidnapped her twenty days before had an annoying habit of bringing her back to the unfortunate situation she was in.

"Choose," the nearly eight-foot-tall stick figure said again, this time losing some of the disembodied tone.

Riley couldn't help the little smirk that lifted the corner of her mouth. She really couldn't. After the first week of captivity, she had moved from being mind-numbingly terrified to just downright pissed off at life. She figured if she was going to die, she might as well do what she did best: piss everyone off around her. That was what had gotten her into this situation in the first place—her big mouth and smart-ass attitude.

Okay, maybe she shouldn't have pissed off her boss by telling him what he could do with his wandering hands when he grabbed her ass for the third time that day. Better yet, she shouldn't have broken his nose, his hand, and more than likely his nuts since he had been screaming more than an octave or two higher than a soprano. Yeah, that probably wasn't the smartest thing to do. Especially since his daddy happened to be the local sheriff. She was a bail bondsman, for heaven's sake. Any freaking idiot should have known better than to mess with her. Her line of work required she know a certain amount of self-defense.

God, she thought. *I really should have never taken that job.*

When her boss swore she would never leave town alive after she beat the shit out of him, she figured it was time to get the hell out of Righteous, New Mexico. Of course, the fact her boss owned the local bail bond company and had a somewhat lucrative business going with his daddy should have been her first warning that something wasn't right, she'd thought as she grabbed her purse and a large manila folder full of incriminating evidence against both of them. Finding out that daddy and junior were also running illegal weapons and drugs were definitely her second and third warnings. Of course, the little tidbit of information she had found that morning about the dead guy buried under the storage unit had been the real reason she figured she had made a bad mistake. That information was now safely tucked into the manila folder stuffed in her purse, and it had gone along with her as she left the small town she had been living in for the past six months as fast as her old Ford could drive.

She actually might have had a chance to live a little longer if a series of life's usual little hiccups hadn't been blessed upon her. Again. Of course, if the car had been further than one push to the nearest junkyard it would have helped her great nonexistent getaway plans. It would have been better yet if the damn car hadn't broken down just over the state line on the outskirts of the desert. She knew she should have purchased a new one last month, but she was such a tightwad she wanted to get every last mile out of it. And boy, did she!

Oh, and she couldn't forget her best idea yet—getting in a truck with a guy who had more piercings and tattoos than a model for *Prick Magazine* instead of walking the three miles to the bar she had seen a roadside sign for.

No, I had to get my fat— Riley sighed. *No, my maturely figured ass into the scum-bucket's truck.*

Riley sighed again. *I really, really should have taken those anger management classes like my sainted sister, Tina, said I needed.*

Unable to keep the grin off her face, Riley thought back to the look on the pierced, tattooed guy's face when she shot him the bird as he drove off leaving her in the middle of that godforsaken hell's beach just as it was getting dark.

Give him a fucking blow job if I wanted a ride out of the desert, Riley thought savagely. *Not bloody likely.*

She showed him! As soon as he pulled over to the side of the road she had been out of the truck cussing him up one side and down the other. Her Grandma Pearl would have been proud of her. She remembered every cuss word her grandmother ever said and a few her grandma probably didn't even know. Of course, he had left her mature ass in the middle of nowhere.

Riley thought she was a goner until she had seen all those little lights coming toward her. How the hell was she supposed to know the fucking aliens had messed up where Area 51 was and ended up in Nowhere, Arizona? Riley had thought she was about to be rescued by a dwarf biker gang riding dirt bikes, not some alien spaceship out for a Monday night cruise for well-endowed women.

"*Choose!*" the tall creature growled out loudly.

Riley cleared her throat before turning to the stick-figured alien dwarfing her. "Choose what?" she asked, unable to hold back the slightly crazed giggle that had been threatening to escape her.

She giggled again at finally making the creature's blank face break into a frustrated scowl. The creature slowly fisted its clawed hands before its shoulders actually drooped.

"Choose a male," Antrox 785 said wearily.

Riley raised her perfectly arched eyebrows at the creature before turning to look at the selection of men who had been paraded in while she had been reflecting on how her attitude *might* have played a part in her present predicament. She had been watching haphazardly as a different female—at least she thought they were female—had been led to stand where she was now. She was told—in a rather rude manner if you asked her—that she was being given the last choice because of her being so disagreeable, unpleasant, and downright ugly. She had, of course, taken it all in stride until the last comment and had to be restrained again after she'd punched the stickman guarding her in what she hoped was his balls. Whatever the creatures had under their tunics, it laid the guy out cold.

Now, she was staring at one eight-foot-tall glob of green, oozing snot, something resembling a two-foot, two-headed lizard, and three six-foot-four or more drop-dead gorgeous hunks. Riley's eyes widened. If it wasn't for the fact that she was thirstier than hell so she didn't have the capacity to produce enough spit, she would have sworn she was drooling.

She could tell by their build and their eyes and maybe the markings on their arms, chest, and shoulders, oh and did she mention their sharp teeth as they growled at the stick-alien, that they weren't human, but man-oh-man did they look yummy! Riley thought dreamily for a moment before perking up again.

"What happens to the males that aren't chosen?" Riley asked curiously, never taking her eyes off the three males.

"They will be used as food," Antrox said with a frown. "Choose! All mated males will be kept to work in the mines. Mated males are easier to control as they are protective of their female. Now choose your male!"

"What if I don't want to choose a male?" Riley asked sarcastically as she turned to face the tall creature next to her. "What if I don't *feel* like choosing a male? What if I don't even *like* males?" Riley added.

Right at that moment, she honestly believed she might not ever like any male ever again! After all, it was men who had started this whole hateful series of events starting with her no-good, dim-witted boss. Now, this overgrown toothpick expected her to just pick one of the bastards and mate with him?

That is so seriously not going to happen. Restraints or not, I will beat the shit out of any guy who tries to mate with me, she thought fiercely.

She wasn't going to mate with any alien, no matter how cute they looked. She had watched enough science fiction movies to cure her of ever wanting any alien booty! What if those things decided to do some body snatching or exploding out of her? A shudder went through Riley at the thought.

Antrox 785 looked back and forth between Riley and the men on the platform below him with a confused expression on his face. "Why would you not want to choose a male? You are female! All of our data points to you being the weaker of your species and in need of a male for protection." Antrox looked from the males back to Riley again. "Why would you not like males?"

Riley let loose a slightly hysterical laugh. Okay, maybe she was still just a little terrified. "Why don't I like males? Now, that is the sixty-four-thousand-dollar question, isn't it? How about we go get a bottle or two of your strongest booze, get good and drunk, and I'll tell you why I don't like males anymore!" Riley's voice was growing louder with each word. "Let's start with you!"

* * *

Vox looked up in surprise as he heard a husky feminine voice shouting. He growled low as he caught his first sight of the buxom female who had turned toward the Antrox male. He wanted her. He didn't understand why, but he wanted her—right now. His body instantly responded to her voice. He felt the primitive need to mate. To possess. When he saw the face and body that went with the voice, it took everything in him not to struggle against the restraints holding him captive. She was curvy, with large breasts, a small waist, and hips that made his mouth water at the thought of holding on to them. Her hair was the color of their sun and flowed in thick waves down her back almost to her lush, rounded ass.

She is built for loving, he thought in awe as he watched her.

She was wearing a light pink top that molded to her lush curves. He couldn't see what she looked like below her waist, but he could imagine it. He wanted to see her eyes. He knew they would be flashing with fire, and he wanted that fire turned on him. He snarled as another guard joined in using the stunning rods to force him back away from the edge of the platform.

He jerked in surprise, and his eyes widened as the female, who was tiny compared to the larger male, started jabbing the Antrox male in his chest and yelling at him. Vox snarled again when one of the guards pushed him back harder with one of the long rods. He ignored the sting from the shock and focused on the female's hands which were shackled in front of her. Why would the Antrox shackle a female? Females were weak and to be protected. Vox had never heard of an Antrox male using shackles on one before. He listened in disbelief as the normally impassive species roared out in a loud, aggravated voice at the female.

..*

"CHOOSE! Now, female, or I will choose for you!" Antrox 785 roared out.

He didn't know what else to do. He was in charge of the mining facility. It was not his job to question who was brought to the mines. His job was to match a female with a male to ensure the males would be more docile. He had never encountered a hostile female before and did not know how to handle a female like the one poking her sharp nails into his chest.

Riley looked at the stickman standing in front of her and let out a sniff of indignation. "Well! There is no reason for you to get so uptight!" she said, turning her back to him and tossing her heavy mane of blond hair over her shoulder. "I choose all of them," she said with an exaggerated sigh.

"What?" Antrox 785 practically shouted.

Riley turned to look at him and rolled her big, baby blue eyes. "I said, I will take all of them," she repeated slowly with a slight shake of her head showing she thought he was a dumbass.

"But…but…" Antrox 785 stuttered in confusion. He looked down at the five men looking up at him and then back at the female. "No, you must choose one."

"No, I don't have to choose just one. I choose all five," Riley said stubbornly. "Five or nothing!" she added with another determined shake to her heavy mane of hair.

"How can you have five males?" Antrox 785 asked in frustration. "All other females choose just one."

"Well, I am not all other females. I am Riley St. Claire from Denver, Colorado, and I choose five," Riley said with a stubborn tilt to her chin. "If you have a problem with that you can just get over it. I've made up my mind, so there," she added with a raised eyebrow daring him to tell her no.

She would have crossed her arms to show she meant business if they hadn't been tied together. Since she couldn't do that, she put her nose as high as it would go in the air and gave her best "that's my final answer" look. She even thrust one hip out to show she could not be intimidated into changing her mind. If she learned one thing while being a bail bondsman, it was that body language could be a very effective weapon.

Antrox 785 ground his gums together in frustration. Throwing up a hand to the guards below him, he signaled for them to take all the men to the cavern assigned to the female. With a jerk of his head, he motioned for the two guards standing back behind Riley to come forward.

"Take her to her living quarters where her mates are and bring me the trader who brought the female here," Antrox 785 said harshly.

One of the guards looked cautiously from Riley to Antrox 785 before replying. "The trader has already left, 785," Antrox 921 said.

Antrox 785 looked down at Riley who was baring her teeth at him and snapping them together. He took a step away, curling his clawed fingers into the palm of his green hands. With a nod of his head, he watched as the two guards escorted Riley out of the choosing room. Antrox 785 had already decided if it had not been for the law preventing an Antrox from harming a female—any female—he would have gleefully fed the female to the pactors, the large creatures they used to pull the ore out of the mines as food. Antrox 785 made a note to himself that the next time the trader came to the mines, he would not be leaving.

Chapter 2

Vox jerked at the collar around his neck and received another burning zap from it. He growled at the other males who watched him. He knew two out of the four. Tor was his chief of engineering, and Lodar was his medical officer. They had both been with him when he left his warship, the *Shifter*, to purchase crystals at the Valdier spaceport. All three of them had been enjoying some refreshments when a Valdier warrior approached them and said one of the members of the royal house of Valdier wished to speak with them. Vox vaguely wondered at the time if it was in reference to the tentative peace agreement they had established almost a hundred years before. As the ruling King of Sarafin, Vox d'Rojah, was expected to produce a son who would be joined in marriage with the first-born daughter of the King of Valdier. The problem was Vox had no intentions of having any sons, at least not in the near future. He was quite happy with the wide selection of females he had at his disposal.

They had sat down to drink with an older Valdier warrior named Raffvin. He said he had news for Vox that concerned the peace agreement between the two former warring species. He had already made up his mind to ignore whatever the old warrior was going to say. The male had been pestering some of his councilmen to meet with him. He was annoyed the Valdier had not taken the hint he wasn't interested in meeting with him. As far as he was concerned, if he wasn't their leader, Zoran Reykill, or Zoran's brother Creon, he really didn't give a damn what the man had to say. He had met Zoran Reykill off and on during their many years of war and respected the man for being a strong and fair warrior who fought with integrity and cared about his people. It was his friendship with the youngest royal, Creon, that had sealed the end of the war and produced a long and lasting alliance. Creon had saved his life during an assassination attempt by some of his own warriors aimed at igniting fury at the Valdier during the Great Wars. The resulting friendship had led to a collaborative effort to discover who was behind the war. A small group from the elite royal houses of Valdier, Sarafin, and Curizan were discovered to be working together to bring down the current ruling class of each star system so they could gain power.

Vox was determined to cleanse his star system of those who would betray their own people. He had gone after them without mercy, whether they were male or female; to him, a traitor was a traitor. He knew it had affected Creon badly when he found out the female he was in love with, a Curizan princess, was one of those responsible for instigating the war. They had discovered it almost too late to save their friend. Ha'ven, the ruling Curizan prince, had been kidnapped in a plot to implicate the Sarafin and Valdier and to gain important information about the location of the Curizan warships. Vox had discovered one of his warriors returning late one night after sneaking off. He and two of his brothers had confronted the man. They discovered he had met with Aria, Creon's lover. The warrior had been passing Sarafin information on to her. Vox had tortured every last piece of information from the man before he killed him and left his body on display in front of the palace for any others who thought to betray his trust.

He had approached Creon with the information he had discovered. At first, Creon had not believed him, but eventually he could not deny the evidence building up against Aria. They decided to set a trap for her. It had worked too well. Only he, Creon, and Aria knew of their reported secret mission to transport a captured prisoner. When the mercenaries Aria hired showed up at the trap, they had killed all but the leader of the group. Creon had extracted the information from him. The man's dying words were of Aria's betrayal. Later that night, Creon had the location of Ha'ven's prison, and Aria was dead. Vox never asked his friend how he got the information out of her; he knew what he would have done. They had found Ha'ven three days later in a mining asteroid not unlike the one he and his men were currently imprisoned in. Ha'ven had been tortured and was more dead than alive. It was a miracle he had survived as long as he had, considering what Aria's men had done to him.

Vox jerked back to the present when the door to the rooms he and the other men had been escorted to suddenly opened. He watched as three Antrox males entered. Two had long stunning rods, and the other had a strange-looking rectangular pink object on wheels. They were followed by the female he had seen earlier. She was talking to a fourth Antrox male who was following several steps behind her.

"Oh dear," she was saying as she looked around the room. "This place screams classic caveman! Fred and Wilma really outdid themselves this time. I'll have to be sure and send a thank you note for the lovely rock walls. Really, would it have hurt to have updated the décor by a few million years? I really am going to have to mark you down on Trip Advisor. This is simply too blasé considering today's fashions and travelers' expectations."

The Antrox male behind her was grinding his gums together as she continued to ramble on about the furniture, floors, ceiling, and everything else in the room. Vox's eyes followed the female as she tapped a slender finger on her chin when she stopped in the center of the room to look around once more. Heat filled him as her eyes swept by him. He wasn't sure at first if the heat was from irritation that her eyes kept moving by him as if he didn't even exist or his reaction to having her closer to him. One thing he did know, she was his and he wanted her now!

"Darling, you can put my luggage next to the bed. I hope you changed the sheets. I absolutely refuse to sleep on someone else's dirty linens. Oh, Sticky-pooh, be a sweetheart and take off these adorable bracelets. As much as I like them, they really do clash with my outfit and totally say 'prison inmate' all over them," the female said, walking up to the Antrox who was standing next to the one placing her suitcase next to the bed.

She smiled up at him and innocently fluttered her eyelashes. Instead of making the tall Antrox feel better, he actually took a hesitant step backward, looking at the male behind her for guidance. The one who had carried the strange large pink box looked relieved that she was focusing on someone other than him. Vox's blood heated to boiling when he saw her beautiful face glow in amusement as she watched the way the Antrox moved nervously around her. Her plump pink lips parted to show off smooth, even white teeth and a small indent appeared on her cheek. He had never thought smooth-edged teeth were sexy before, but he decided right then and there he loved the way they looked on her.

The Antrox behind her nodded once to the other male and stepped back another step. The Antrox lowered his stunning rod and held out the key to the locking device. He motioned for the female to extend her hands in front of her. She did with a wide-eyed look and a nibble to her lower lip. Vox's eyes followed the movement, and he almost groaned out loud as his cock swelled to a level of pain he had never encountered before.

The female gently rubbed her wrists and wiggled her little nose. "I hope you aren't expecting a tip," she said with a dismissive wave of her hand. "Because I have to say, I am not sure of the hospitality yet, much less the rest of the accommodations," she added as she put her hands on her hips and tapped her booted foot.

"We must leave," Antrox 264 said from behind her. "You will keep your mates calm and satisfied. They will be working the first shift so you may be near them."

"Whatever," the female said with a casual shrug. "I want clean towels brought in daily, and

I'll need a line of rope and several blankets delivered immediately."

Antrox 264 nodded at the other guards to move toward the entrance to the cell. "Why do you need these items? They are not budgeted for workers."

The female turned and glared at 264 through narrowed eyes, causing him to jerk backward another step. "Darling, put it in your budget unless you want me upset. You won't like me when I am upset, do you understand? I am *not* a nice person when I am upset," she said, taking a menacing step toward him with her eyes glittering with fury and determination. "Now go get me what I requested! Chop, chop!" she growled out with a snap of her fingers, causing all four guards to jump and hurry out.

* * *

Riley drew in a deep, calming breath to steady her nerves in preparation to meet her five new "mates." She was shaking like a leaf on the inside, but she had learned a long, long time ago not to let it show. She put her hands back on her hips, drew in another deep, steady breath, and tossed her heavy mane of blond hair over her shoulder before turning around to face the five males again.

At five feet ten inches tall, she was a big woman. When you added in the fact that she was a solid size sixteen on a good day with double-D cup breasts, she was Xena on steroids. She had learned to live with her big-boned stature a long time ago. She didn't have much choice since she practically towered over everyone she'd ever met between the ages of four and eighteen while she was growing up. She had reached puberty early and had to live through all the Amazon and she-giant jokes that any sensitive young girl would have to endure. Only other sensitive young girls didn't have Grandma Pearl raising them. Grandma Pearl showed Riley how to punch anyone who made fun of her in the nose. When the fourth school's social worker threatened Pearl that Children's Services would take Riley and Tina away from her, Pearl showed Riley how to use her mouth as the weapon of choice after that. Riley had excelled at that much better than she had the physical forms of retaliation. Over the years she had plenty of opportunity to perfect her talent, as her grandma called it.

Releasing the breath she had been holding, Riley smiled brilliantly at the five alien males staring at her. "Well, boys, it looks like Auntie Riley is going to have to set some ground rules while we are together," she said, looking at each one of the males carefully to assess how she was going to handle them.

Alien number one was about three and a half feet tall, had two heads, and looked like a combination of a lizard and ET. He was cute in his own special way. Each head had large, black eyes that moved nervously back and forth between her and the other four men. He was a dark green with areas of tan, black, and red on him running in long lines down his body. He was wearing a small leather vest and cloth, plaid-colored pants with child-size boots to match. He must have decided she posed less of a threat than the other males because he emitted a weak squeak and scurried for a corner of the room. She also decided he looked like a "Fred."

Her eyes moved to the next alien creature. He—she was assuming it was a he since the Stickman called him one—was almost eight feet tall. He towered over all of them, including the other three males standing next to him, but he just wasn't all that scary. He reminded Riley of the big tub of Jell-O in the movie *Monsters vs. Aliens*. He was green instead of blue, but he had "Bob" written all over his wiggling body. He even left a light liquid that she hoped wasn't radioactive or anything behind him. He appeared to be wearing some type of robe over most of his body. She didn't even want to think what might be under it. It was his eyes that gave her the feeling he wouldn't hurt her. They were big, round, and the color of peach gumdrops with tiny black pupils in the center. He was emitting a low humming noise that struck her as if he was terrified. She wasn't sure what he was so scared of. So far, she felt like everything was going pretty damn good considering she had been kidnapped by aliens. At least Daddy and Dudley Dip-shit back in New Mexico couldn't find her here.

Her eyes finally moved over the last three males. She felt like she needed an old fashioned fan like the women in the movies used to fan themselves to keep cool, because she could definitely feel the heat increase when she looked at them. The first one was hot! He had his long hair pulled back at the nape of his neck. It was a long, golden blond with different shades coursing through it. He had patterns on his chest and left arm that looked like spots and was wearing a black vest, black pants, and black boots. Against his lighter color they really stood out. His dark golden brown eyes remained focused on her as she assessed him. He looked more curious about her than "interested." Riley was thankful for that because she had a feeling that her mouth and her one physical ability to bop someone on the nose wouldn't stop him for long if he decided to sink those sharp teeth of his into her.

Alien number four was the same height as the first one. She figured based on her own height they were probably about six feet four inches or so. It should have been nice to finally meet some guys she actually had to look up to except for the fact they were aliens! Alien number four was looking at her with the same curiosity as number three had. He had more of a reddish-brown-colored hair and a darker tan. His hair was short and had stripes of darker reds and browns running through it. His eyes were a light greenish-tan color with specks of dark green in them. He was dressed in the same type of clothing as the other guy. Riley assumed it must be a uniform of some sort. It was kind of like a biker outfit that the guys back home dressed up in on Sundays when they put their three-piece suits up for the weekend. Only she got the feeling these guys dressed like this all the time, and this wasn't a costume to just look bad for a day. She got the impression from all the muscles on the guys that they were bad all the time.

Her impression proved correct when she finally looked at alien number five. She had avoided looking at him in the hope he was somehow less intense than the first time she saw him standing on the platform in the "Choosing" room. If she thought he was hot from a distance, he was scorching up close! It took everything inside Riley not to reach out and touch him just to see if he burnt her fingers. Thankfully, Grandma Pearl's wonderful teachings saved her from that impulsive behavior. Pearl drilled in to both her and Tina not to play with fire. Ever! Pearl explained that fire came in many different forms and most of them had two legs, one head that hung between them, and no brains to speak of. Riley thought her grandmother was like that because she and her daughter, Riley and Tina's mom, had been left to fend on their own after the loves of their lives got them pregnant and left town. It didn't take long for her to realize it happened to others, as well. Pearl pointed out to Riley and Tina just how often when their friends or just girls that lived in their neighborhood would ignore the signs. One by one, Riley saw the girls in her neighborhood fall for the "bad" boy only to be left at the first sign of another pretty face in the neighborhood, more often than not, with a baby to raise on their own. Riley decided at twelve that she was not going to be one of those girls. Of course, that was also the same time that the dirty old man who ran the grocery store on the corner propositioned her. No, she was going to have a ring on her finger before she said yes to anything. She wasn't going to get stuck raising a kid on her own like her grandma had or her mom would have if she would have stuck around. As far as Riley was concerned, the guy could put up or shut up.

It's funny, in a way, Riley thought. *That's about the only thing Tina and I ever agreed on without ending up in a major yelling match first.*

Riley looked back at the huge male glaring at her. *Alien number five is not just screaming bad-to-the-bone, but he has an international market on it,* Riley thought before a giggle escaped her. *Make that an intergalactic market,* she corrected silently as she saw his face darken at her laugh.

He was the same height as the other two but seemed taller for some reason. Either way, he still towered over her by almost six inches. His black hair was cut short, almost military style. His upper chest was visible through the same black vest the other two were wearing. He had darker spots across his chest that looked almost like a leopard's, not that she had ever seen a real leopard before. Riley let her eyes roam down the eye candy, appreciating the tight fit of his… Her eyes widened when she saw the very distinctive bulge in the front of his pants. Her eyes flew up to his in surprise, and she fought to draw in a breath.

Somebody is horny, she thought in dismay, staring into the intense, burning tawny eyes.

"Okay," Riley said, rubbing her hands together. "First rule. That is your side of the cave and this is mine. You stay on your side, and you remain in one piece. You come on my side, and I cut your dicks off and feed them to you for breakfast," she said with a small smile and raised eyebrows. "I claim dibs on the bathroom for exactly thirty minutes every morning, and one hour every night, alone," she added as she turned and walked over to where her suitcase had been dropped next to the bed.

She bent over to unzip one of the side pockets. A low, rumbling growl behind her had her reaching in quickly to grab the item she had been hoping to retrieve since she had first been taken. Her hand wrapped around the small, leather-covered device with a relieved sigh. She turned just as the huge male took a step toward where she was bent over. She looked up into the glittering eyes and swore silently. It looked like she was going to have to prove she would follow through on her instructions.

"Get back on your side of the room. *Now!*" Riley growled out, clutching the small device in her hand. "You stay! Bad alien. You are not to come on this side of the room!" she said fiercely, pointing her finger to the side where the other males stood.

"You are mine!" the huge male growled out as he took another menacing step toward her. "I claim you."

Riley's temper flared at his outrageous claim. "Last warning. Get your ass back on your side of the room, or I'll do it for you," she snarled back, straightening to her full height.

Vox grinned showing off his pearly white sharp teeth. "I'd like to see you try," he smirked, taking another step toward her until he was within arm's reach of the female he knew was his mate.

Riley smiled, and a sparkle of devious delight glittered in her eyes as she looked up at the huge male towering over her. "Oh, darling, you *really* shouldn't have said that," she said right before she pressed the device she was holding against his chest and pressed the button on the small Taser.

Vox's eyes widened briefly before a curse tore through him as his body jerked. His chest burned as the explosive shock jolted him backward where he collapsed on the hard stone floor. His body twitched as his muscles reacted to the powerful shot of electricity that it received. His jaw clenched tightly as he fought the painful effects, but it was useless. He had absolutely no control over his muscles. It was ten times more painful than the shocks from his collar or from the stunning rods he had received from the Antrox. He forced his eyes to follow the female as she put her hands back on her hips and tossed her head back with a glare at his men who were growling at her. Tor and Lodar snarled in rage as they grabbed him by his arms and pulled him away from the female who was standing back near the bed, hissing at them and snapping her teeth. His eyes flickered to hers, and he saw the brief flash of fear before she concealed it.

Chapter 3

"How are you feeling?" Lodar asked quietly.

Vox grimaced as he rubbed his chest. Twin burn marks stung as his hand moved over them. His eyes followed the female as she worked to hang a curtain wall with the items the Antrox guard brought in almost thirty minutes before. She was humming under her breath a tune he had never heard before. It had taken him almost an hour to recover the full use of his limbs without feeling like he was going to fall on his face. He tugged at the collar around his neck and cursed when he felt the small shock. His muscles reacted to it instantly as they were still a little twitchy from the heavy jolt they had received a short while ago.

"Pissed!" Vox growled out in a low voice as his eyes followed the movement of the female as she bent over again. "Guall's balls, if she bends over one more time," he swore as he felt his cock rubbing painfully against the front of his pants. "She is my mate," he muttered in a low voice to both his men.

Tor and Lodar looked at Vox in astonishment before turning to look curiously at the figure of the female trying to build a wall with blankets in the narrow room. After she had touched Vox and knocked him on his ass, she had the Gelatian move the bed closer to the wall. She proceeded to pull a piece of white rock out of the huge bag she had draped across her body. The bag had all types of different stones and images on it, and it had taken her several long minutes to find what she was looking for. After she found it, she had gotten down on her hands and knees and drawn a uneven heavy white line down the middle of the room.

She had looked so proud of herself when she finished that none of them, save Vox who was still lying on the floor twitching, knew what to say. She had proceeded to tell them who she was, and that they were to stay on their side of the line or she would rip their heads off and shove it up their asses. What was incredible was she had said it while giving them a beautiful, dimpled smile. Tor and Lodar had looked at each other and finally had to turn their backs to her so she wouldn't see them laughing silently. The thought that a line drawn in white would keep a Sarafin warrior from crossing it if they wanted to was more than they could handle without laughing, at least until they looked at Vox who was still sprawled out in a twitching mess on the floor. Moments later, an Antrox guard delivered the items she had requested with a confused frown. She had blown the guard a kiss after she grabbed the items and deposited them on the bed. The guard paled as he glanced down where Vox was lying on the floor, jerking. He left quickly after that.

"Oh, Bob, honey, can you be a sweetheart and help me for a moment again?" The husky voice called out from where she stood balanced precariously on a large rock. "Fred, baby, just hold the line for a few more minutes. I think I've got it this time."

"She is called Riley St. Claire from Denver, Colorado—wherever that is," Tor said in amusement as he watched her almost fall off the rock again. "She is…a most unusual creature."

"Do you know what she is besides being a hair up my cat's ass?" Vox snorted before he looked at Lodar who was anxiously watching as the female teetered for a moment before regaining her balance.

"No, I've never seen a female like that before," Lodar ground out through clenched teeth as she wobbled again. "Most species I know have some sort of instinct for self-preservation. This one seems to be lacking that particular trait. She has fallen off that rock three times now, and it is a miracle she hasn't broken her neck!"

Vox gritted his teeth. He was well aware of how many times she had fallen. Tor caught her once—barely—Lodar the second time, and she'd landed on the Tiliqua she kept calling Fred the last time. He had not been able to catch her because he still couldn't even stand without falling on his own face, thanks to her. Now even his jaw was sore from grinding his teeth every time she almost fell, bent over, or just thrust her— He groaned again as his cock jerked in response to her bending over and affectionately patting Fred on one of his heads.

"You are just such a sweetheart," she cooed. "Bob, you cute bowl of key lime Jell-O, can you hook the other end of the rope on the wall like you did on this side?"

The huge body of the Gelatian started to move toward Riley to take the rope she was holding out but stopped when Vox emitted a low, dangerous snarl. The huge being trembled in terror. Its head turned back and forth between Riley and Vox. Vox rose stiffly and glared at the creature in warning.

"My lord," Bob choked out. "The female— She—" the creature stuttered out before his voice faded.

"Oh, just ignore him, you scrumptious dessert. He's all growl and no howl," Riley said before she giggled. "Oh, that was so good! Do you get it? All growl, no howl? Damn, sometimes I'm just good."

"Sarafin warriors do not howl," Vox said through clenched teeth as he took a step toward the female. "Female, if you ever shock me again I'll turn you over my knee and spank your big ass until it is as red as the Brighton dwarf star."

Riley turned and wobbled dangerously for a second on the rock where she was standing. She glared at the huge figure threatening her. She was as tall as he was now. She reached her hand down along her side, easing the small cylinder she had taken out of her luggage and slipped into the pocket of her skirt into her hand. Her eyes glittered dangerously, and her lips pulled back but it was not into a smile.

Oh, like hell he did not just say I have a big *ass,* Riley thought viciously.

Her lips pinched together into a pucker before relaxing. "As you said earlier, Saraprick," she replied in a quiet, sarcastic voice. "I'd like to see you try."

Vox smiled at the challenge. He was going to enjoy getting his hands on her luscious body finally! He was going to finish the curtain wall, bend her over, and take her hard and fast.

"And as you said, you really shouldn't have said that!" He purred out as he walked slowly toward her.

"Vox," Tor murmured from behind his friend and leader. "I don't think that is a good idea," he said, getting a bad feeling from the look in the female's eyes.

She did not look like she was worried. In fact, she looked like she was out for blood—Vox's blood if he had to guess.

"She doesn't have her weapon on her," Vox responded, nodding to where the small Taser lay on the bed. "She'll be purring like a kitten once I've claimed her." Vox smiled as his eyes glittered possessively. "That's what you need, isn't it, little cat? A good fucking."

Riley's face flushed at the dark promise in the huge male's voice. "I am so going to enjoy putting your ass on the ground again!" she hissed out, trying not to give in to the desire to turn tail and run.

The problem with running was there was nowhere to go in the small room. The second problem was that she had learned a long, long time ago if you didn't stand up to a bully when you had a chance, you might never be given another one. She gripped the cylinder, waiting until he took another step closer to her.

"Last chance, big boy," Riley warned softly. "Step back over the white line and leave me alone, or I'll have to put you down again."

Vox almost paused at the soft warning he heard in her voice. There was a trace of steel that told him she wasn't going to run. She would stand and fight him tooth for tooth, claw for claw. His eyes stared deeply into hers, and he saw a resolution in them. She would not back down. His pride in her grew at her fierce determination to face him even though he could see the slight trembling in her hand as she pushed a long strand of white blond curls behind her ear. She was a worthy mate for a king.

"You are mine, little kitten," Vox responded gently. "You will accept what the gods have given you. Come to me willingly or come to me fighting, but come to me you will."

Riley shook her head and tightly pinched her lips together in determination. "Sorry, dude, I've seen enough alien movies to know that it never turns out good for the supporting actors. Since I've never been a heroine, this is a no-win situation for me. I'd just as soon go down fighting."

Vox's grin widened. "I always did like a good fight before I fucked," he said, reaching to grab her off the rock.

"Your choice," Riley muttered, holding her breath as she held the small cylinder up and depressed the button.

Vox's roar filled the small room as the pepper spray hit him in the face. Riley stood frozen on the rock, pressing her hands over her ears as his loud curses and pain-filled roar continued to echo. He fell back several steps, grabbing at his face, before he fell to his knees in agony.

"What did you do?" Lodar asked in horror as he tried to help Vox who was rocking back and forth on his knees emitting low mewing sounds of pain.

"It will stop hurting if he washes his eyes out…I think," Riley whispered. "I've never actually had to use it before, but that is what the directions say to do."

"You've never used this weapon before?" Tor said as he gripped Vox's shoulder and tried to see what was causing his friend so much pain.

"Well, I warned him!" Riley said defensively. "It's his fault for not listening."

"Female," Vox hissed out painfully. "I'm going to strangle you when I can see again."

"If you even think of it, I'll…I'll…" Riley threatened back. "I don't know what I'll do but it is going to hurt you more than me!"

"Not if I can help it," Vox groaned as Lodar laid a cool, damp cloth over his burning eyes.

Hell, he needed one for his nose, throat, and mouth as well. When she had raised her hand he had thought she was just trying to warn him to stay back. He had not expected her to have anything in it. Both of her hands had been empty except for the rope she was trying to hand the Gelatian just minutes before. He had made sure she didn't have anything in them after the first time. Where in Guall's balls she got her hands on the device she used on him he didn't know, but he was going to be damn careful the next time he got near her! Gods, his eyes, nose, mouth, and throat burned!

"Just…just keep away from me, and I won't have to hurt you again," she muttered before turning to the Gelatian and the Tiliqua. "Come on, guys, help me get this wall built before Saraprick gets on his high horse again."

Riley glanced at the green, gelatinous being and smiled when he shook and moved backward instead. "It's okay, darling. It won't take but a moment. I won't hurt you, you tub of gorgeous green."

"He is not gorgeous," Vox growled out hoarsely, trying to glare at the female through blurry, burning eyes. "You will not speak to him like that. I am your mate!"

Riley glared back at the huge, seething male who was glaring at her with watery red eyes.

She felt her pulse rocket at his deep growl, and that just made her madder. She would not let her body react to some overzealous, pompous alien, no matter how cute he was! She brought to her mind the last five alien movies she saw and reminded herself that not a one of them ended well for the humans. Just look at what happened to Sigourney Weaver. She not only had that alien bursting out of her—she became one! There was no way that Riley was going to take a chance of that happening to her.

"I don't believe I was talking to you," Riley growled back. "Now, go bother someone else for a little while. Bob, honey, get your green body over here this instant. I think I feel a headache coming on, and I want to rest in peace for a little while."

"Female"—Vox bit out in warning, wiping at his eyes—"If you need help, I will give it."

"My name is Riley. Riley St. Claire from Denver, Colorado, not female. Don't forget it." Riley sniffed indignantly and pushed a strand of hair behind her ear as she tried to balance on the rock without falling off it again. "Now, let Lodar help you. He seems to know what to do. And quit making that god-awful growling noise. It is beginning to get on my nerves."

..*

Vox lay on his back and wiped at his eyes again. They were still tearing from earlier, but thankfully the worst part of the burning had faded. He turned his head and glanced at the wall of blankets separating the two sides of the narrow cavern they had been given. Fred was curled up in a ball in the corner as far from Vox and his men as possible on one blanket. Bob was asleep standing up in the other corner. Vox, Lodar, and Tor were stretched out on the hard floor. He listened as the female rolled over on the bed behind the curtain again and released a soft sigh that tugged at his cock as if she had her hand wrapped around him. She was driving him and his cat crazy!

"How are we going to get out of here?" Lodar asked quietly. "As long as we have these collars on there is no way we can get by the guards."

"If I had some tools, I could get them off," Tor responded quietly. "Problem is, I don't think the Antrox are going to leave any tools that would work lying around."

"I'm going to kill that Valdier royal when I get my hands on him," Vox growled out softly. "The Antrox receive shipments every couple of days. We need to track when those shipments arrive. We'll figure out a way to get these damn collars off and steal a ship. Kill as many of those emotionless insects as you can on the way out. I want them to know they better not mess with a Sarafin warrior again."

"Tomorrow begins our first shift," Lodar said. "We can look for tools when they take us to the mines."

"What of the female?" Tor asked, looking over to the blankets where Riley's soft sighs could be heard. "We will need to watch her. I've heard of what can happen to females in the Antrox mines. If the Pactors don't attack them and kill them, other prisoners often try to steal them or a trader will offer credits for them. They kill the males if another female doesn't take them or another is not available."

Vox looked at the shadow of his mate as she turned over again. He watched one of her arms rise up briefly before she turned over onto her stomach. A small grin pulled at his mouth. There wasn't a part of his body that wasn't sore thanks to her. He had never been brought to his knees before, not even in battle except for the time he was poisoned. His mate had done it not once but twice in the same day.

"She is to be protected at all cost. Kill any who try to take or harm her," he ordered. "She is your new queen."

Tor chuckled softly. "I don't think she is going to be too happy with her new title," he said, fighting back another laugh.

"I don't care if she likes her new title or not; she is my mate and the queen of our people," Vox said with a grin of his own. "I have to admit I'm looking forward to seeing how she handles it. Just remind me to make sure I check her hands before I get near her again." He turned so he could stare at the curtain and imagine what she looked like lying on the narrow bed.

"You don't think she would have any tools with her, do you?" Lodar asked curiously. "She has been surprisingly resourceful so far."

Vox snorted. "She is a female! Why would a female need tools?" he said dismissively. "No, our best hope is if we can find some that the Antrox haven't accounted for."

"Like that will ever happen," Tor grunted out. "They inventory every item as the prisoners go into the mines and again coming out."

Vox bit back the curse on his lips. "I want off this asteroid. If we can't find the tools we need, then we will have to find another way to get them. Get some sleep. It will be a long day tomorrow."

Both men grunted their agreement as they rolled over, trying to get comfortable on the hard surface. Vox stared at the shadow of his mate again. He would get off the asteroid, and he would kill the Valdier royal who drugged him and his men. But first, he needed to make sure that he marked his mate in case she was taken from him. He would find her, no matter where she went, but he wanted everyone to know she belonged to him.

Chapter 4

Riley turned around to stare at the strange creatures passing their small group in the long corridor. They had been woken up way too early for her. She was not much of a morning person. In fact, until she had a decent breakfast, several cups of coffee, and it was past ten in the morning, no one even bothered to talk to her. To top it off, she had to make do with just a quick cloth bath to refresh herself. The "bathroom" was a large open area shared with other prisoners, male and female. Vox, Tor, and Lodar had stood guard in front of the door when Riley had refused to go in as long as there was anyone else in the room. Even Bob and Fred had lent a body to help cover the opening to give her privacy. She had quickly done her business and cleaned up as best she could. She decided she'd better dress appropriately if she was going to be working in a mine. She wore a pair of her favorite faded jeans that had a hole in one of the knees, a soft, long-sleeved Denver Broncos jersey, and a pair of tennis shoes. She wasn't about to ruin her designer boots working in the dusty mine. She quickly piled her hair up into a messy but chic ponytail. She touched her lips with a bit of lip gloss before quickly tossing the items she had worn to sleep in into the carry-on she had. She slid her designer handbag over her shoulder and straightened her shoulders in determination. She was NOT going to be a big baby and cry because she wanted to go home. She was going to find a way to get back to Earth, even if she had to kill someone to do it.

"Next!" Riley said as cheerfully as she could this early in the morning. "Fred, would you be a dear and run this back to our rooms? I'd hate to have to carry it all day."

Fred reached out and gripped the bag. With a muttered snort, he took off at a run. Riley couldn't help but be grudgingly surprised at how fast the little guy ran for having such short legs. She looked at Vox, Lodar, and Tor.

"Well, go on," she said. "We don't have all day!"

Lodar chuckled but turned and entered the bathroom. Tor shook his head before following. Vox stared at Riley, letting his eyes roam over the bright orange and blue top with the number eighteen on the front. His gaze moved further down to her blue jeans-clad legs before settling on her white-and-blue tennis shoes.

"Why do you dress like that?" he asked curiously. "You should be dressed like you were yesterday."

Riley sighed heavily. "I am not about to ruin my good clothes working in some nasty-ass mine! These are much more comfortable and will do just fine. Now, don't you need to take care of business?"

Vox frowned. "What business?"

"You know," she said with a roll of her eyes. "Whatever guys do in the morning. The three S's."

"The three S's?" Vox asked confused. He was focused on the shimmer of Riley's lips as she pressed them together.

"Yes! Shit, shower, and shave," she said, folding her arms across her chest. "Bob can watch me while you go do your thing."

Vox chuckled as her meaning sank in. "I have never heard of that before. I will wait until Lodar and Tor have returned before I go do my 'thing.' You can always join me while I do my business," he suggested teasingly before he remembered to glance at her hands to see if she had anything in them.

"I don't think so." She sniffed and shrugged indignantly.

Vox took a step closer to her, forcing her backward several steps until she was pressed against the rock wall behind her. Riley swallowed nervously. Her eyes darted around, looking for any type of distraction she could use. She cursed the fact that she had left her pepper spray under her pillow. She could never think straight in the morning. If she could get her hands into her handbag she could probably find something to use as a weapon. She had everything but the kitchen sink in it. Hell, she even had multiples of items like the Leatherman and Leatherman Micro that was in the bottom of the damn thing somewhere. One had scissors while the other had pliers. She was always needing one or the other. Right now, she could really use the knife on one of them.

"What are you doing?" she asked breathlessly, looking up into his determined eyes. "You need to just stay back! Remember what happens when you get close to me. I don't want to have to hurt you again."

Vox reached out and gripped her wrists in a tight but tender hold. "Then, don't," he whispered huskily. "I plan to kiss you, Riley St. Claire of Denver, Colorado. I plan to mark you so that there can be no doubt that you belong to me. And finally, I plan to claim you as my own."

Riley shook her head and pressed back as far as she could against the hard wall behind her. "No, I've seen what happens in the movies. I don't want you. I don't…" Her voice faded as Vox covered her lips with his own in a tender, possessive kiss.

His groan matched hers as he pressed deeper when her lips opened under his. The gentle kiss he planned grew heated as the touch and taste of her swept through him. He stepped closer, raising her arms up over her head so that her plump breasts were pressed against his chest. He deepened the kiss, pushing his tongue through her glistening lips and running it along her smooth teeth. He felt his cock jerk painfully in reaction to her taste. His cat purred and rubbed up against his skin, wanting a chance to rub up against his mate. He stepped closer, forcing her to open her legs for him so he could slide between them and rub his swollen cock against her. He placed both of her wrists together, holding them in one large hand and stroked her with his free one. He ran his fingers lightly over her cheek, wanting to see if her skin felt as smooth and silky as it looked. The soft touch shook him. He had never felt this deep feeling of need, desire, and the overwhelming urge to protect before.

He pulled back enough so he could look down into her dazed eyes. "I claim you as my queen, Riley St. Claire," he muttered passionately.

Riley's brain cleared as his words sunk in. She began to struggle as she realized the perilous situation she was in. She should never have let him close to her. He was an alien.

Aliens were bad. Aliens were always bad in the movies, well, most movies anyway. She also repeated her vow that she would not say yes to any guy without a ring on her finger. She decided she'd better clarify that. She would not say yes to any human guy without a ring on her finger, and she would never say yes to an alien.

Remember Aliens. *Remember* Predators. *Remember* Invasion of the Body Snatchers. *Remember Freddy.* Riley shook her head. *No, not Freddy. He was a human. Remember… remember…*

"No, no, no, no, no!" she said forcefully, focusing back on the alien holding her. "Let me go! I do not belong to you. I do not want to be a queen. I do not want to be claimed. *I do not want you!*" she added forcefully. "Now let me go, damn it! The only thing I want is to go home."

"Vox, guards are approaching," Lodar said, coming out of the bathroom.

Riley took advantage of his distraction to twist free and duck under his arm. She moved rapidly to stand behind Lodar. Vox twisted around and frowned at her in displeasure. When he moved toward her again, she squeaked and pulled Tor, who was walking out of the bathroom, in front of her as well. She stood peeking out from behind the two tall warriors, glaring at Vox.

"Go do your business so I can get something to eat," Riley snapped out from where she was hiding behind Tor and Lodar. "And I'm warning you, if you try to touch me again I'll pop you on the nose!"

Vox muttered a curse, glaring at her in frustration. He turned away in aggravation to take care of his needs. He glanced down the corridor as several Antrox guards marched down the corridor toward them, and he knew he wouldn't have much time. His observation proved to be correct. When he left the bathroom a few minutes later, ten guards holding stunning rods stood at attention waiting for him. A shiver rippled down his spine. From all the reports he had of the Antrox, this was an unusual number for six prisoners, since each prisoner, save the females, wore an explosive shock collar to control him. The Antrox normally only budgeted one guard for a group of twenty or more. If the guard was threatened or attacked in any way, one push of a button would kill any prisoner within fifteen meters. Without the right tools, if a prisoner tried to remove the collar, it would also explode. Normally, the Antrox paired one male and one female. They discarded the threat that the female would know how to help the male escape. In their case, there were five males and one female. If they could get their hands on the right tools, Vox knew Tor could figure out how to dismantle the collars.

"Darling, I really am going to write a scathing review for this establishment," Riley was telling the lead guard as he came out of the cleansing room. "Your wake-up call is far too early, your idea of bathroom accommodations is horrid, and breakfast hasn't even been mentioned! How do you expect my poor, sweet, fragile mates to survive if you don't feed them? I want the name, number, and address to your corporate headquarters. They are going to hear from me! Why, look at my poor baby. Fred, sweetheart, are you okay? You are definitely looking a little green around the gills," Riley said, pulling the struggling Tiliqua closer to her and petting one of his heads affectionately.

Vox ground his teeth together as he watched her gently stroking Fred. "He is supposed to be that color, and Tiliquas don't have gills," he bit out, feeling jealous of the attention she was giving the little two-headed reptilian pactor dung.

Riley rolled her eyes at Vox's tone, put her hand on her hip, and pointed an accusing finger at him. "You see that?" she demanded of the lead guard. "He is just a grouchy bear! He needs to be fed. How do you expect me to keep him happy if he is hungry? I want a full breakfast immediately for my mates."

Antrox 157 snarled at Riley. He had been sent by 785. It was his job to guard the Sarafin royal and his men until they received the credits promised for disposing of him. 157 had no problems following orders from his superior, but he was having problems with dealing with the bossy female who had started in on him the moment he had arrived. She was making all kinds of demands. He had been shocked to find additional supplies had been given to her yesterday by some of the newer guards. Unlike most Antrox, he did not always follow the rules governed by his people. That was why 785 gave him this position. It afforded him extra credits.

"Silence female," 157 said coldly. "You will keep your mates happy. I only have to keep one of them alive. If you are not silent, I will feed one of your mates each hour to a pactor."

"Well!" Riley growled back. "Somebody woke up with a stick up their ass this morning. You touch one slimy little green nail on one of my boys, and I'll rip it off and feed it to the pactor with the rest of you. No one messes with my boys but me, got it?"

157 looked shocked for a moment before his face became passive. He took a step closer to

Riley, trying to crowd her. "One more word and I'll silence you."

"I'd like to see you try, you overgrown piece of cow paddy," Riley snapped back in a temper.

Vox decided it would be in everyone's best interest if he silenced his mate before she got them all killed. He stepped up behind her as she opened her mouth to say something else. Wrapping his large hands around her waist, he almost groaned out loud at the feel of her soft curves under his palms. Instead, he picked her up, ignoring her squeal of indignation, and turned until she was in front of him with her back pressed against his chest.

"I think we will survive without anything to eat for a little longer," he said quietly in her ear. "I would like to keep us alive for a little longer, my fierce tiger. We do appreciate your concern for us, though," he added hastily when she opened her mouth to protest.

"So help me, if that pile of walking sticks pisses me off or messes with one of you, I'll plant my foot up his ass so far it will be coming out of his mouth," she growled, throwing a heated look at the Antrox guard over her shoulder. "You let me at him. I'll show him one more word!"

Vox could hear Tor and Lodar fighting to hold in their laughter as he fought to keep her from turning back and attacking their guards. He shook his head in exasperation. He and his men towered over the female, were known to be one of the fiercest species in the ten known galaxies, and she was ready to kick the asses of their guards because they had not been fed when she wanted them to be fed.

"Come, let us get to work so we can eat soon," Vox muttered.

* * *

Riley twisted her hair back up into the ponytail where it had fallen loose again when she bent over to pick up some of the rocks that the men were breaking through. All five of the men had argued that she wasn't supposed to work. She was just supposed to sit and watch as they worked. Like she could just sit around all day. She was already bored out of her mind. So, she ignored all of them and did what she wanted, singing in an off-key voice the song from Snow White when the dwarfs were going off to work. Fred had soon joined her, gathering the rocks alongside her and muttering under his breath.

"So, how did you end up is this delightful shit hole?" Riley asked as she dumped another pile of rocks into the bins used to haul it out.

"My older brother sold me to a trader," Fred responded with a grunt as he pushed the large rock he was carrying into the bin. "He did not want me in his way."

Riley paused in horror. "Why would he think you were in the way?" she asked as she walked back over to the ever-growing pile of rocks the men were creating. "Hell, even my sainted sister won't sell me, no matter how much I piss her off, which is about every time I open my mouth."

"I am the second oldest. My older brother is not good with our father's business. I am very good, and my father decided I should take over instead of my older brother. He paid credits to some traders to take me. Now, I will die here," he said disgruntledly.

Riley stopped from where she was lifting another large rock. "Like hell you will! I'll take care of you. You are not going to die in this shit hole. We just have to escape," she responded confidently. "Do you know how to fly one of those spaceships?"

"No," Fred replied sadly before perking up. "But the cat warriors know how. They are known for their fighting skills, and their warships are renowned for their speed."

"Cat warriors?" Riley asked as she walked back over and dumped the large rock in the bin with all the others.

"Yes, your mate is their king. I have heard about him. He is very scary. He kills those who defy him," Fred said, struggling to lift a particularly large rock over the side.

Riley frowned as she bent to help him. *Why the hell does he call them the "cat" warriors? I thought they're called Sara-something.*

She stretched once the rock was in and rubbed her aching back. She was exhausted, and they had only been at it for about two hours. She really needed some coffee. A nice latte would be fabulous right about now.

Fred must be mistaken, she thought as she looked over to where Vox, Lodar, and Tor were swinging the strangely shaped, curved pickaxes.

All three had muscles out the yin-yang, and their bodies glistened with sweat as they worked to clear another section of the cave. They didn't talk while they worked. Bob was working on another section and appeared to be having problems holding the ax correctly because his pile of rocks was miniscule compared to the others. The Antrox guards were stationed at the different exits leading into the area they had been brought to and were ignoring them.

She turned back to study all three men carefully for a moment as they worked. Each had a different pattern of spots on his upper body that ran down his chest and back before disappearing under the low waist of his pants. She felt a shiver of apprehension run through her as she remembered their eyes. All three had similar eyes, but what caught her attention the most was that their pupils were slits instead of round like a human's. A bad feeling began to sink in as she noticed other differences. They had no problems seeing in the dim corridors. She would have walked into a wall or tripped a dozen times as they were marched deeper into the mine if it hadn't been for Vox. They moved lightly on their feet just like the old cat she had when she was a kid. Half the time she couldn't even hear them walking. And Vox had roared like a wounded cat when she sprayed him with the pepper spray. He sounded a lot like that lion that came on before a movie from MGM studios. Other details came back as well. She remembered the way his chest rumbled when he was kissing her, as if he was purring.

"Shit!" she said as her eyes widened as the pieces fell into place.

Fred looked at her puzzled. "You have need for the cleansing room? I can ask a guard to escort you if you have a need," his left head said, looking at her in concern.

Riley looked down with dazed eyes at Fred. "Can they— Can they change into cats?" she asked in a hushed whisper.

Fred looked at her before turning one head to look at the three warriors working steadily. "Of course not," he said, not understanding Riley's sigh of relief.

"Thank goodness for that," Riley murmured before Fred finished his sentence.

"The shock collars prevent them from shifting. But if the collars were to be removed they could," he finished with a twist of envy coloring his voice.

Riley's sigh of relief turned to a gasp of horror. *I am stuck in a freaking science fiction-shifter-romance novel nightmare!*

* * *

Vox frowned as his mate moved her plate of food away from his and went to sit down between Bob and Fred. For the past couple of days, she had done everything she could to avoid him. She spent most of her time dancing around the huge Gelatian or keeping the small Tiliqua between her and him. Hell, she had even used Tor and Lodar as shields but only when the other two couldn't get away from her. Both of his men had noticed how skittish she had been around them after the first day in the mine. It had grown worse after they had finished their first work shift. They had been escorted to the eating room shortly after their shift ended. The skittish distance had turned into a frigid ice block by the time they were done.

On the third day Vox discovered he, Lodar, and Tor were not the only Sarafin warriors held prisoner. His best friend and cousin Titus, a member of the lead council who had disappeared over a month before, was among the prisoners, as well as his younger brother, Banu. There was also one Curizan warrior and one Valdier warrior Vox recognized. Both of them had been working undercover to bring down Raffvin and Ben'qumain's rebellion. Titus explained he had found some damning evidence of his own against several of those inside the Sarafin palace who were working with Raffvin. They were the ones behind his and his brother's kidnapping and subsequent imprisonment.

"Who are they?" Vox growled out in a low voice.

"Two are females who share your bed," Titus said quietly. "Eldora and Pursia. They were relating information to Bragnar, a male who works in the kitchens."

Vox turned to look at Riley when she sniffed loudly. He frowned when she gave him a deadly stare before turning to look the other way and focusing on what Bob and Fred were saying. He had reached to touch her hand, but she jerked it away from him before he could even get close to it.

"Who is the female?" Titus asked curiously, watching their interaction with interest. "She is much more pleasing to the eye than the one who selected me," he said with a dismissive nod toward the slender purple figure sitting on his other side.

"She is my mate," Vox said, perplexed at his mate's sudden quiet behavior.

"As in she chose you or as in you chose her?" Titus asked. "Because if I had to guess, she doesn't look any happier with you than mine is with me."

"Both," Vox said grumpily. "She chose the five of us, but I knew the moment I heard her voice she was my mate."

"What species is she? I don't think I have ever seen one like her before," Titus said, picking at the items on his plate in disgust.

"I don't know," Vox admitted reluctantly. "I forgot to ask her. We need to get off this asteroid as soon as possible," he said changing the subject. "I have a Valdier royal to kill."

"You and me both," Titus said, throwing down the few pieces of his food that were left. "Supply ships arrive every seven days. One came today," Titus murmured quickly before standing up as an Antrox guard came over to order him and his mate back to their quarters.

Vox nodded before turning his attention to the other warriors sitting across from them. They each nodded in return before rising as a guard called out to them to stand. He returned their nod. They would be off this rock in seven days if he had his way—which he always did when he put his mind to it. His eyes turned to the stiff, defiant figure of his mate sitting next to him.

Yes, he thought with a small smile at the frozen face of his mate. *I always get my way when I want something.*

* * *

Now, he wondered how he was going to be able to fulfill his promise. Over the past six days, all five of them plus Titus, his brother, and the other two warriors had zero luck in getting their hands on any type of tool that would work to remove the collars around their neck. Something was telling him that they didn't have much time left either. He paced the room. They would be escorted to their evening meal soon. Tomorrow another supply ship would arrive, and Vox's gut was telling him it would be their only chance of escape. He growled out in frustration as he paced back and forth in the narrow room.

"Those damn insects are organized, suspicious bastards," Tor said with a sigh. "They make sure there are no tools available that might work on removing these damn collars," he added with a wince as he received another small shock when he ran his fingers around the edge of it.

"I've got burn marks almost all the way around my neck from the damn thing," Lodar complained, touching his tender throat.

"Do you need some medicine for it?" Riley asked from where she was laying on the bed, reading on her iPad. "I've got all kinds of stuff."

"You wouldn't happen to have a tool kit available, would you?" Tor joked.

"Of course," Riley said without looking up. "Pliers, scissors, flathead screwdrivers, Philips head—you name it, I've probably got it. What do you need?"

She finally looked up when no one replied. All five men were looking at her in disbelief. She frowned, looking from one to the other puzzled. She didn't know what the big deal was; lots of women carried basic tools with them.

You never knew when you might need one, and it wasn't like she had a guy around with a tool bag fixing things for her.

"What?" she asked innocently.

Vox took a step toward the bed, looking down at her in disbelief. "You have tools with you, and you didn't tell us?"

Riley shrugged, looking up at him with a raised eyebrow. "No one asked."

"No one asked," Vox muttered looking at Tor and Lodar in disbelief. "We have been looking for tools for the past week! Haven't you heard us talking about it?" he asked her in aggravation.

"Well, yes, now that you mention it, but I figured when you said, 'She's a female, why would she need tools?'"—Riley said, dropping her voice to a deeper tone to imitate Vox's voice—"that it was like a guy asking for directions! I decided if you really needed them, you could ask me." And she returned her attention back to the story she was reading.

Vox bit back a curse. "Can we see the tools you have?" he asked through gritted teeth.

Riley rolled her eyes but shut off the iPad. She sat up and reached for her huge handbag at the end of the bed. After a few minutes of digging around in it, she began pulling out all the tools she had stashed in the different compartments. She pulled out her large Leatherman, then her Leatherman Micro, a folding set of Allen wrenches, a small plastic container with various sizes of screwdrivers, a pair of scissors, her manicure set, and a pair of wire snips.

"Oh, I didn't know I had those in there," she murmured. "I think I have another pair of needle-nose pliers somewhere in here." Her voice was muffled as she stuck her head further into the large bag.

"How in the names of all the gods can she have so much in there?" Lodar asked, amazed, as she began pulling more and more things out and laying them on the bed next to her.

Chapter 5

"What about this wire? Do you think it connects to the explosive pack or to the detonation switch?" Vox was asking Tor.

All five men were gathered around a partially dismantled collar. Or should she say, four of the men were gathered around one of the partially dismantled collars on Fred. Poor Fred was a shivering nervous wreck as Vox, Tor, and Lodar examined the collar while Bob leaned over their shoulders watching from a distance. They had been at it ever since they had returned from the dining area.

"I'm not sure yet," Tor murmured under his breath. "There are three sets of wires. If I cut the wrong one it could explode. I don't know enough about the Antrox to know how they do their wiring configurations."

"Please," Fred's right head said in a trembling voice. His left head was sitting perfectly still with its eyes tightly closed. "Please, c-ca-can't you do this to someone else?"

"Oh, for heaven's sake," Riley muttered, getting up from the bed where she had been trying to read. "How difficult can this be?"

She tossed her iPad down to the side. It was impossible to concentrate on what she was reading anyway with everyone in the room. Besides, she was tired of listening to Fred's soft whimpers. She walked over to where the group of men was kneeling around the small, trembling body of the Tiliqua and picked up the pair of wire snips. She studied the wires for a moment before reaching over Tor's shoulder and snipping the reddish color wire. The moment she did, the glowing light showing it was active went out.

"Problem solved," she said, dropping the pliers into Tor's open hand and returning to the bed.

Both sets of Fred's eyes rolled back in his head as he fainted. Lodar and Tor grabbed him and lowered him down to the hard floor before turning to stare at her in disbelief. Riley picked up her manicure kit, pulled out her nail file, and began shaping the chipped edges; working in the mine had made a mess of them. She finally looked up when the silence stretched into several long minutes.

Four pairs of eyes, including one blazing set, were staring at her in disbelief. "What?" she asked, looking at them in exasperation. "You guys were taking too long to make up your minds. It's not like it was that difficult of a choice, and I was tired of listening to Fred whining."

"How did you know which wire to clip?" Tor finally asked curiously.

Riley shrugged, looking at the nail she had been working on. "Everyone knows it's the red wire that you cut," she replied, working on the next nail.

"But how did you know?" Vox asked suspiciously.

He wanted to know if perhaps he had been mistaken this whole time about the female he knew to be his mate. Things were suddenly not as clear as he first thought. What better way to knock him and his men off guard than to find an unfamiliar female specimen they had no experience with? The fact that she was his mate turned out to be a bonus. He suddenly had questions he wanted answers to! Like why was she allowed to claim five mates when all other females only had one? Why did she have tools on her? How did she know which wire to cut? Was there more to her than he'd originally thought?

Vox stood up and stalked toward her menacingly. It would not make a difference that she was his mate. He would do what he had to do to protect his people, even if it meant... Even if it meant killing the one woman he knew was meant for him.

"How did you know which wire to cut?" he growled out in a low, menacing voice.

Riley stopped filing her nails and looked at him with a raised eyebrow. "I know you are not talking to me in that tone of voice," she said, staring at him through narrowed eyes.

He stopped in front of the bed and knelt down in front of her. Reaching out, he gripped her wrists in a firm but unbreakable hold. He stared deeply into her eyes, determined to know the truth even as his mind, body, and cat rebelled against the idea that she could betray them.

"How did you know?" he asked again softly.

Riley frowned back at him in confusion. Why was he suddenly so intense? Everybody knew you were supposed to cut the red wire. She frowned again, biting her lower lip.

Or was it the black one? she suddenly thought, trying to remember which wire the guys in *The Abyss* and *Speed* always said they were supposed to cut.

"Damn it, now I can't remember!" she said crossly. "I'm trying to remember if the guys in the movies said you always cut the red one or the black one." She looked at Vox with confused eyes. "I'll have to watch *The Abyss* again."

"Who is this Abyss?" he asked cautiously as Lodar and Tor came up behind him.

Riley looked up at the other two men, then over to Bob before looking down where poor Fred was still out cold. Her eyes moved back until she was looking worriedly into Vox's dark tawny ones.

"He's going to be all right, isn't he?" she asked hesitantly, glancing back at Fred before looking again at Vox. "I mean, I cut the right one, didn't I? He isn't hurt, is he?"

"Riley," Vox said squeezing her wrists gently to get her attention as her eyes drifted to the Tiliqua again. "How did you know which wire to cut?"

"From all the movies I've watched," she said looking at the other men. "I mean, I'm pretty sure it was the red wire they always cut. You see, in the movie *The Abyss*, the hero has to go to the bottom of the ocean because the bad guy was being a butthead about the aliens that came to visit them. He has to stop this bomb from blowing up the aliens that live there only he can't really see what color the wire is, and the good guys back on the underwater station are telling him to cut the red wire. Only I can't remember now if they said the red wire. It could have been the black one. Anyway, he can't really tell what color the wire is because he is using this green glow stick thingy like we used to play with on Halloween. That's when we all dress up in costumes and pretend to be monsters and stuff so we can go get some free candy, only I always dressed up as a ghost because Pearl couldn't afford costumes for me and Tina so she used some old sheets," she explained. "Does this make sense?"

"No," all four men said before Vox growled at the others to be quiet.

"No," Vox said, looking into Riley's confused eyes.

Riley sighed in frustration before remembering she had been watching *Galaxy Quest* on her iPad earlier. She tugged on her wrist so she could grab it and show them what she was talking about. Vox held her firmly for a second before reluctantly releasing one wrist. He kept his eyes glued to her while she reached for the device she had been so focused on over the past couple of days. If she tried anything, he would make her death as quick and painless as he could. Pain sliced through him at the thought of hurting the delicate beauty in front of him. His cat hissed in revolt, clawing at his insides in rebellion.

He watched as she pressed a button on the device, and it lit up. "This is a movie," she was saying as she flicked her finger along the smooth surface. "I love science fiction/fantasy-type movies. Sometimes I'll watch a good horror one, but I always get nightmares from them so I have to be careful. I had nightmares for three days after watching Stephen King's *The Mist*!" she explained as she pressed another button, and a strange creature appeared on the screen.

Vox watched it for a minute before understanding dawned. She was referring to entertainment holovids. The human on the small screen was working on an obviously fake control panel before he and a human dressed in some type of costume disappeared behind the console. He listened as Riley giggled. Her eyes were glued to the screen, mesmerized.

"God's blood," Tor muttered over Vox's shoulder before a chuckled escaped him. "She used something like this as a reference for knowing which wire to cut?" he said with a shake of his head. "It's a miracle Fred's head wasn't blown off!"

"That's okay," Riley responded absently, still watching the movie. "He has a spare one."

* * *

Fred glared at Riley again over the heads of the other men in their room. Titus, his brother, and two other men had appeared in their room a couple of hours after they had removed the other collar on Fred who finally came to in a very grouchy mood. Vox had also removed the ones on Lodar, Tor, and Bob. They had left the one on Vox but had disconnected it so it was no longer a threat. This allowed him the freedom to move around the prisoners' living quarters without attracting attention.

Tor was in the process of disconnecting the collars so the other men would not have to worry about being killed when they escaped. Riley sat curled up on the end of the bed watching everything with a wary eye. She knew she should be excited about the idea of getting off this rock, but she was still pissed at Vox. It had taken several minutes for her to finally understand the big oaf thought she was some kind of spy or something when he kept grilling her about where she got her tools from, how she had been captured, and why was she allowed to choose five mates when all the other women only had one. He had barked out one question after another, holding her wrists tightly in his large hands the entire time until she finally had enough of it and struggled to pull away. When she confronted him, he admitted he thought she was some kind of spy brought in to trick him.

He also admitted he had been prepared to kill her if she had been.

She wasn't so sure she wanted to go with him and his men when they made their escape. She was thinking she might have better luck with the next guy she chose. It didn't help that Fred was still mad at her either. Both of his heads had ripped her up one side and down the other when he woke up. It had taken Bob's calming voice and her swearing she never meant him any harm before he had sulked over to the corner where he sat shooting glares at her from both sets of eyes.

Riley decided she couldn't stand the glares Fred was giving her any longer. She had grown attached to the little two-headed lizard, and it hurt that he was shooting her such heated looks of displeasure. She scooted off the bed, trying to ignore the way Vox's eyes followed her every movement as she edged around the crowded group and went over to where Bob and Fred were huddled in the corner. She slid down the wall until she was sitting on the floor next to them.

"Fred," Riley said quietly, touching the Tiliqua who had turned a cold shoulder to her as soon as she came over to where he was sitting. "I'm sorry. I would never hurt you, you know that don't you? I think of you as a very, very dear friend," she said, running her fingers gently along the side of one of his faces.

Both heads turned to her with a scowl. "You could have killed me, Riley!" Fred bit out coolly.

"But she didn't," Bob muttered. "Be nice to her, Fred. She feels bad enough."

Riley glanced up at Bob and gave him a grateful smile before looking back at her little friend. "Will you go home once you leave here?" she asked quietly, picking up a small rock lying next to her and playing with it.

"Maybe," Fred said with a sigh. "I'd never been off the Spaceport before. I think I would like to see more before I return. It will give me time to figure out what to do should I decide to return to my father's business," he muttered.

Riley looked down at the rock. Hot tears burned her eyes at the idea of losing the small group of alien males. They were the only creatures she knew here, and she had grown attached to them. Her eyes flickered to Vox for a moment before she quickly looked back down when she saw him staring at her intently.

"I'll miss you both," she admitted quietly. "You've both become good friends. I just want you to know it has meant a lot to me."

Bob moved his big body so he was in front of her. His huge, green arms folded over his gelatinous chest. He waited patiently until she looked up at him.

"What are you planning now?" he demanded.

Riley's eyes grew large before she shielded them. She was used to losing friends. If her mouth didn't drive them away, her moving on did. It was just...she wasn't sure where to go. None of the locations she was likely to end up in were programmed into her phone.

Hell, she thought, depressed. *Even Google isn't going to be able to help me here!*

"I figured I'd stick around here for a while longer," she started to say before tears thickened her throat and she had to clear it. She forced a smile to her face before she continued. "I hope you both have a safe journey to wherever you decide to go."

"We will not leave you behind, Lady Riley," Bob said in his deep, melodious voice. "The warrior king will not leave you. You are his mate."

Riley's eyes flickered up, but she couldn't see Vox because of Bob's huge body. "Yes, well, it isn't his decision. Besides, I think I'm allergic to cats so it wouldn't work out anyway.

I'll just stick around here and see if I can't find me a trader or someone heading back toward Earth. I've got some business there I need to finish, not to mention my family is back there," she said lightly.

Bob's huge body shook as he chuckled. "Little female, you should not try to fight. It will do no good. If the Sarafin warrior king wants you, you are his. But if you do not wish to stay with him, I will do what I can to help you. I owe you a life debt for choosing me as a mate when others would have let me die."

"As do I. You know that big Sarafin warrior will kill us both if we try to take Riley away from him," the left head of Fred said with a scowl as he looked at Bob. "I don't care. I will do what I can to help you if you want to leave him," the right head added gruffly to Riley. "Let us hope if he kills us, it is quick."

"You both are just so sweet! But neither of you owe me a thing. Don't you boys go worrying about little ole me. I can take care of myself. I've been doing it for the past twenty-four years," Riley said with a watery smile. "So, when is this elaborate plan of escape supposed to take place? I didn't understand half of what they were saying. Do you need a distraction? I excel at creating distractions," she added with a mischievous smile.

"No!" a deep voice growled as the door to their living quarters opened.

Riley rose from where she was sitting. Bob slithered to one side revealing Vox. Behind him, their visitors were quietly exiting the room. Soon, it was just the three of them. Tor and Lodar had followed the men out.

"You will stay here with these two for now," Vox growled out in a soft voice. "I will return before it is time to leave. You will be ready to go with us."

Riley shrugged her shoulders and tossed a length of curly blond hair over her shoulder nonchalantly. "Yes, well, I was telling the boys I think it would be best if I just caught the next ship out with a trader who is heading toward good old Earth. You know, it would just be easier for you guys to escape without having little ole me holding you back and getting in the way," she said with a bright, fake smile.

Vox stared at Riley intently before he jerked his head at Fred and Bob. Both knew it was an order to leave. Riley watched nervously as her two friends moved reluctantly toward the exit. Fred's right head turned, and he gave her a look of apology before he stepped out of the room behind Bob.

Riley folded her arms over her chest and waited. "Okay, say what you've got to say, but it isn't going to change my mind," she said stubbornly.

Vox took a step closer, crowding her until she was backed up against the wall. "You will be ready to go when it is time," he said with a determined thrust of his chin.

She was afraid to move her arms because it would allow him to move even closer to her if she did. She frowned up at him. She was still mad at him. The big oaf was really too much! He had the nerve to think she was some kind of intergalactic spy hired by God-knew-who. He had been prepared to kill her without a second thought while he was the one sleeping with Spy One and Spy Two back home! On top of that, she'd found out that he and his friends were a bunch of alien kitty-cat shifters. And the icing on the cake was him telling everyone he was "claiming" her without even a take-her-out-to-dinner date!

Oh, hell no, I'm not going anywhere his furry ass is going. I'm going to find the first trader I can and kidnap him even if I have to threaten his ass in order to get back home, Riley thought with determination.

"No, I won't. I've decided to find me a nice little trader to kidnap. Once I do, I'll have him take me home," she replied with a stubborn tilt to her chin. "You boys go on and do your thing. I hope you find whoever it is you plan on killing. I'm sure you'll have a wonderful time. Me? I've got business back on Earth to take care of involving a few dead bodies of my own," she said with a confident nod.

Vox's hands reached out and gripped her hips, moving them slowly up to her waist. He savored every delectable inch as he slid his hands across her soft flesh under the purple top she was wearing. He pulled her closer to him, trapping her folded arms against his broad chest. He leaned into her, running his nose up along her neck as she straightened in an effort to get away from him. His cat purred in delight. Vox groaned, running his tongue along the slender column.

Riley shivered as the rough sandpaper of his tongue ran along her smooth skin. "What do you think you are doing?" she asked in a strangled voice. "You— Your chest is rumbling."

"My cat wants you," Vox whispered against her neck. "So do I. We've both been denied too long." He growled softly against her throat, nipping it gently.

"Ouch," Riley choked out hoarsely. "Well, go lick on someone else! I'm not interested."

Vox ground his hips against her, pushing his thick, swollen cock up against her. He slid one hand up to cup her chin and turned her face until she was forced to look into his blazing eyes. He studied her for a moment before a slight grin pulled at the corner of his mouth.

"Liar. I can smell your desire," he said before pressing his lips to hers in a deep, passionate kiss.

* * *

Vox had listened with half an ear to Riley, Bob, and Fred as Titus and Tor worked out how to overtake the guards in the control room. Adur, the Curizan warrior, and Titus's brother, Banu, would slip up through a narrow conduit maintenance tunnel they had discovered months ago and take out the guards in the control room. Cross, the Valdier warrior, would secure the arrival bay along with Tor and Lodar. Vox and Titus would secure the supply ship and prepare it for flight. They would need to do a fast refuel. Fred was small and fast enough to get through the tunnels unseen. His father owned a refueling station on one of the Spaceports. He would take care of the refueling before joining them. Bob would take care of making sure Riley was protected and where she was supposed to be. Vox had already warned the huge Gelatian he better make sure Riley was on the supply ship and in one piece, or he would be coming after him personally.

When he heard Riley say she wasn't going to go with them, he knew he had to convince her there would be no discussion in this matter. There would be no room for hesitation as they needed to get off the asteroid as soon as the defense shields were down. If they didn't, they would not be given another chance. His gut—and his cat—were telling him that time was running out.

He knew he had hurt her feelings when he accused her of being a spy. He could smell the hurt radiating out from her. When he had admitted he would have killed her if she had been, she had shut down on him completely. It was as if an icy wall suddenly formed around her emotions.

He pulled away reluctantly. Opening his mouth to explain to her that it was a fruitless endeavor to fight the attraction, his words froze as pain exploded through him. His eyes watered almost as much as when she had sprayed that weapon of hers in his eyes as her head connected with the end of his nose in a blow that had him stumbling back a half step.

His hands released her as he grabbed his offended nose. "What in Guall's balls did you do that for?" he bellowed out, falling back another step when she angrily pushed against him.

"You can *smell* me?" she demanded, elbowing her way around him and back toward the bed where she had her pepper spray hidden under her pillow. "You can *smell* me? Is that supposed to be a compliment? If so, that's right up there with, 'Did you use any deodorant?' or 'When is the last time you took a bath?' I do *not* stink!" She was so going to spray his ass.

"Riley, I did not mean you stink. You smell; that is different," Vox's muffled voice came out from behind his hand. "What are you doing?" he asked warily as she turned with a determined look on her beautiful but very angry face.

"I'm going to pepper spray your sorry ass," she growled, holding the small leather cylinder out in front of her. "Then I'm going to make a throw rug out of it! I. Do. Not. Smell!" she yelled out in fury.

Vox edged around her, wondering how he had gotten himself in this position. Holding his hand out, he stepped lightly to the side, heading toward the entrance to their living quarters. His cat hissed at him again for making a mess of the situation.

How in Guall's balls was I supposed to know she would take offense? he muttered to his cat in frustration.

"Riley, I smell desire," he began before he ruefully admitted, "or at least I did."

"I'll show your sorry ass desire," she said as she advanced on him shaking the cylinder menacingly. "Let's see if you can smell this!" she snarled, depressing the button on the spray cylinder at the same time the door opened.

Vox jerked to the side, covering his face in defense. Unfortunately, Tor wasn't as fast. His roar of pain echoed down the long corridor. The sound bounced along the walls, drawing others from their rooms. Several Antrox guards hurried down the corridor. They stopped when they saw Tor writhing on the floor in agony. Riley bent over him trying to pat him on his shoulder as he rolled back and forth.

785 and 157 came hurrying down the corridor. "What has happened?" 785 demanded, stopping and releasing a sigh of frustration when he saw Riley's blond head.

"Oh, baby, I'm so sorry. I didn't mean to hurt you," Riley cooed to Tor who was curled in a ball trying to rub his eyes. "I was trying to hurt the big oaf. If he would have stayed still, you wouldn't be hurting. I'm so sorry, darling," she said trying to get him to turn so she could see how bad it was.

Riley looked up and glared at Vox. "Well, don't just stand there like an idiot! Go get me a wet cloth," she demanded.

Vox nodded knowing how much pain his poor friend was in. He hurried back into their living quarters to retrieve the needed item. Riley looked up and scowled at 785 and 157.

"What do you want? Can't you see I'm busy taking care of my mates?" she snapped, glaring at both of them.

785 sighed and nodded to the guards. "If this is the way she takes care of her mates it might not be necessary to kill them. She will do a better job than we can," he said, the semblance of a smile almost curving his thin, flat lips. "Have the guards return to their post."

157 looked at the Sarafin warrior rolling in pain and whimpering on the floor while the larger one moved back and forth doing the bidding of the female. He shook his head in wonder. Perhaps 785 was right. The female was doing a better job of controlling the males than even he expected. From the reports he had read, he would have never believed the Sarafin king would be jumping to the commands of a female.

157 nodded to the guards. He glanced back once more as the blond-haired female leaned over the male on the hard floor. His mind was working numbers. With her unusual looks he calculated the number of credits he could get for her. If she could handle five mates, including three Sarafin warriors, she could handle much, much more. His flat lips thinned as an idea formed.

Yes, 157 thought. *She will bring in a lot of credits as long as I can keep her quiet long enough to sell her.*

He knew just the trader to contact. There would be no questions asked; the credits would be deposited to his hidden account, and he would have enough to buy his own mining operation. If all went as planned, the strange female would be available because by tomorrow evening her mates would be dead.

Chapter 6

"I am much better, Lady Riley," Tor said, trying to gently move away from Riley's fluttering hands. "My eyesight is almost clear again."

"Are you sure?" Riley asked, biting her tender lower lip that she had been worrying for the past several hours. "They still appear to be tearing a lot."

Tor would never admit that they still burned like the fires from the hot mountains back home or that his nose and throat weren't in much better shape. He took another sip of the cool water that Lodar handed him. He glanced at his friend and gave him a nod of thanks.

"I hope Vox took that little cylinder away from her," Lodar murmured in a low voice as Riley turned away to check on Bob and Fred, who had just returned. "I don't want to take a chance on her using it on me."

Tor wiped at his eyes with the cool, damp cloth again. "It burns like the fire moon! My throat and nose are on fire too. What did Vox do this time to upset her?"

"He said she smelled," Lodar responded with a grin. "She did not appreciate his observation."

Both men watched as Vox followed Riley around trying to get her to sit down and listen to him. It was almost comical the way he pleaded with her to just hear him out. Lodar chuckled when she swatted at their friend and leader. He had never seen anything like it before. The human female was totally oblivious to the fact she was running circles around one of the most dangerous men in the known star systems. There wasn't a female alive that he knew of who wouldn't envy her position.

"Do you think he'll be able to catch her when this is all over?" Lodar asked curiously.

"More power to him if he does," Tor said hoarsely before taking another long swig of water. "She is almost as dangerous as the Curizan and Valdier were during the wars. More so if you take into account she has no idea half the time of what she is doing."

"Do you think all females of her species are like this?" Lodar asked, admiring the way her tight pants stretched over her ass as she bent down to pack something in her strange pink case.

Tor's eyes followed Lodar's over the curve of Riley's rounded ass. He felt his cat purr. Maybe he wasn't as immune as he'd first thought. His red eyes moved to Vox who had frozen in place as he followed her, his eyes glued to the same place as the other males in the room. When Riley straightened, she reached up and tucked her mass of curly hair back up into the bright pink scrunchie. The movement pulled the thin top she was wearing up, revealing the pale skin of her slightly rounded stomach and pulling the top tight across her ample breasts.

* * *

Riley froze as she was putting her hair back up into its messy ponytail when the whole room erupted into echoes of low rumbling purrs. She turned startled baby blue eyes on the three huge cat-shifting males who had their eyes glued to her. Three pairs of eyes—one a golden brown, one a very reddened greenish color, and the other a dark, tawny color—all stared at her breasts as they thrust upward while she wound the scrunchie around the mass of curls she was holding.

She rolled her eyes. "You have got to be kidding me!" she muttered. "I swear to God all guys who aren't gay have a one-track mind!"

She quickly finished putting her hair up, trying not to turn as pink as the scrunchie as she watched their eyes follow her breasts as they bounced up and down. She didn't care how much support the manufacture promised; when you were as big as she was there was still going to be some bounce. She lowered her eyes, refusing to give into the desire to cross her arms protectively in front of her. The only thing that did was push up the watermelons she carried around. Instead, she clapped her hands loudly.

"Hello?" she snapped, shooting an evil eye at Lodar and Tor. "It's rude to stare!"

Lodar cleared his throat as Vox turned to glare at his two friends. "Yes, well... I... We... They are beautiful," he finally choked out with a sheepish grin. "And very difficult to miss."

"I wonder if they contain milk?" Tor asked, unaware he asked the question out loud. "I would love to drink from them if they did," he sighed.

Riley's mouth dropped open as what Tor said sank in. "Oh. My. God. You did not just say that," she sputtered before bursting into uncontrollable laughter. "Do they... Oh my god, that is priceless." She continued to giggle, wiping the tears from the corner of her eyes with the end of her shirt, totally unaware the movement pulled the cloth up, exposing her creamy flesh again.

Vox's loud roar ricocheted throughout the small room as he tackled Tor. The force of his shoulder hitting his chief engineer's chest knocked both of them backward through the air several feet before they hit the hard floor and slid almost to the far wall. Vox's sharp teeth gripped Tor's throat in a stranglehold while his claws dug into Tor's shoulders, pinning him to the floor.

"Bad kitty!" Riley shrieked out from behind him. "Let him go! You are a very, very bad kitty. You let go of him, or I'll neuter your ass. Vox, release him this instant. If you don't, I swear I'll go to the guards and tell them I need to borrow their stun gun thingy. I mean it. I'm out the door in three, two, one…"

Vox released Tor with a jerk and swung around to face Riley so fast she stumbled backward. Her heel caught on the uneven flooring, and she lost her balance, falling to the floor heavily with a sharp cry. She rolled over into a ball as excruciating pain exploded through her wrist as she tried to break her fall. She landed on it hard. Riley bit her lip as she pulled her left arm up against her, cradling it to her chest as she sobbed in pain.

"Riley?" Vox said hesitantly as he moved to kneel next to her curled-up figure. "Riley, I would never hurt you," he said gently as he tried to get her to look at him.

Another soft, pain-filled sob escaped Riley. "My wrist," she whispered. "It hurts so bad."

Vox turned his head, looking over his shoulder. "Lodar," he demanded hoarsely as worry engulfed him.

Lodar nodded as he stood up from where he was checking the puncture wounds on Tor's neck and shoulders. They would heal. They'd gotten worse when they were training or just wrestling with each other. If Vox had been serious about killing Tor, he would have ripped his throat out. The marks were just a warning to Tor to be careful expressing his thoughts out loud. It was obvious from the smell of Riley's fear when she saw what had happened that she didn't realize that. Now, the smell of her pain was overwhelming to the three warriors. It was a dark, musky scent that brought out a protectiveness and need to care in all of them.

"Riley, let me look at your wrist," Lodar said gently as he knelt down next to her.

Riley bit her lip and shook her head even as she looked at him with her big blue eyes swimming in tears of pain. "I don't want you to touch it. You might make it hurt worse," she whispered as her bottom lip trembled and a lone tear course down her pale cheek breaking his heart.

"*Guall's balls*, Lodar, help her," Vox demanded fiercely, unable to handle the thought of his beautiful, stubborn mate being in pain.

Lodar's lips tightened as he heard the desperate growl in his leader's voice. "Riley, I need to see how bad it is," Lodar insisted as he reached down and gently rolled her over onto her back.

Fred hurried over with the pillow from the bed and carefully lifted Riley's head so he could slide it under her. The little two-headed Tiliqua sat down next to her on the floor and tenderly brushed her hair back from her forehead, ignoring Vox's low growl of warning. His right head turned and he glared defiantly at Vox.

"You hurt our mate," Fred growled back. "You scared her!"

Vox flushed a dark red but he lowered his eyes to Riley's pale, tear-stained face. "I didn't mean to frighten you, Riley," Vox murmured softly as he reached out one of his big fingers to tenderly wipe the tears that ran down from the corner of her eye.

Riley's lips trembled as Lodar carefully lifted her arm. "You were hurting Tor," she whispered as fresh tears filled her eyes as she stared up at him.

"He wasn't really hurting me," Tor said, leaning over Vox's shoulder, oblivious to the blood covering his neck and shoulders. "We do this all the time, Riley. He didn't mean anything by it. The Sarafin often use their claws and teeth. If he was really going to hurt me, he would have ripped out my throat."

Riley's hiccuping wail filled the small room at Tor's words. "You are not making her feel better," Bob said, pulling Tor away as he moved closer to Riley. "Go clean the blood off you."

"I think it is broken," Lodar said in concern as he carefully examined the discoloration and growing swelling. "She needs immediate medical attention I cannot give her here. We will need to summon a guard."

"I will go with her," Fred said as he carefully brushed her hair to the side.

"No," Vox snapped out, glaring at the small Tiliqua. "I will go with her."

"You…You can't," Riley hiccuped. "They will see that your collar isn't working. That goes for all of you," she whispered. "I'll have to go alone."

"No," each of the five men said stubbornly.

"I will go," Bob said softly. "They do not look under my skin to see if I have my collar on. I am also the least likely to be considered a threat next to Fred."

Vox's mouth straightened into a tight line of frustration. Riley was right. They would need to reactivate his collar, and that was still no guarantee they would let him go with her. He had noticed the extra security surrounding them. Bob was the least threatening next to Fred. He stood up, growling out in frustration and anger. Closing his eyes and drawing in a deep breath, he turned to see Riley struggling to sit up.

He immediately knelt down next to her, sliding his arm around her and snarling silently at Fred who was trying to help her. He felt a moment of intense joy when she relaxed back against him before it was dashed again back down to the bottom of the mines when she turned her pain-filled eyes up to glare at him in reproach. He tried to look remorseful, but something told him she wasn't buying it.

"Stop snarling and growling," Riley snapped as pain racked her. "That's what got me in the position I'm in now!"

"Riley, you need to learn not to come up on me when I'm disciplining my crew," Vox tried to explain as he gently held her in his arms.

"I will most certainly come up on your hairy ass if you try biting one of my mates again," Riley snapped. "Only next time, I'm going to get one of those stunning rods so I can shove it up your stubborn backside, you moron! You.

Do. Not. Ever. Sink your teeth into Tor, Lodar, Fred, or Bob again, do you understand me mister?" Riley demanded stubbornly, thrusting her quivering chin out. "Do you?"

Vox stared down into her big blue eyes and felt like he was a drowning cat. He would promise her the moons, the star systems, and Tor's pelt for a rug if she asked. His head lowered on its own as he fell into the beautiful blue oceans of her soul.

"I promise," he whispered. "As long as he promises to never imagine drinking milk from your beautiful big breasts again. That is *my* fantasy."

Riley's eyes widen before she reacted out of pure frustration. She threw up her good arm and popped Vox right on the end of his beautifully shaped nose as hard as she could. It wasn't until she was connecting that it dawned on her that was probably not the best decision she could have made considering he was holding her up in the air and she already had a broken wrist. Thankfully, Lodar was standing close enough to catch her as Vox howled in pain and rage. Riley's scream of pain mixed with Vox's as her arm was jostled in the exchange. The sound was enough to draw the attention of the guards, and their door opened just as Lodar tripped over poor Fred who was trying to get out from under everyone's feet. Lodar hit the floor with a wailing Riley while blood poured from Vox's nose.

157 looked down at the sobbing female who was being held in the arms of one of her Sarafin mates before jerking to the other Sarafin warrior. The Sarafin king had blood pouring down his face while the third Sarafin warrior was sitting to the side wiping blood from his throat. 157 finally looked down at the small Tiliquan who was rubbing one of his injured feet. The only one not injured was the huge Gelatian.

"I do not even want to know what is going on," 157 muttered, shaking his head.

Lodar tucked his head so the Antrox guards couldn't see his collar wasn't glowing. "Our mate broke her wrist. She needs medical care," he said, rising with Riley in his arms.

Bob moved forward quickly, putting his larger body between the warriors and the guards. He reached out and scooped Riley into his arms and turned. Moving closer to 157 and the guards, he crowded them, forcing them back toward the door.

"I will carry our mate to medical," Bob said quietly. "The others are in no shape to do so."

157 tried to look around the massive figure in front of him but finally decided it wasn't

worth the effort. He was tired of being called down here. He would be glad when the final payment of credits was received and he could dispose of the males once and for all. By tomorrow, he would be a very wealthy Antrox. He had contacted the trader who dealt in supplying sex slaves for the pleasure houses on the nearby spaceport. He had been promised a large sum of credits and immediate pickup. By this time tomorrow, the males would be dead and the female gone.

157 turned to the two guards standing behind him. "Take her to medical and make sure she is completely healed. If necessary, keep her there the rest of the evening," he ordered.

Bob ignored the three low growls that escaped the men behind him. "I will remain with our mate and make sure she is safe. She will be returned safely," he spoke loudly enough to be heard by everyone.

"I...I need my things," Riley cried softly. "I...I can't leave my things. They are all I have left."

"I will bring them to you, Riley," Fred promised. "I won't forget."

Riley looked over Bob's head and smiled a watery smile at her little friend. "Thank you, sweetheart."

"Riley," Vox started forward, still holding his nose which had finally stopped bleeding.

Riley's eyes watered, and she shook her head gently. "Go," she whispered quietly looking at him with sorrow in her eyes. "It is better this way," she murmured before she laid her head tiredly on Bob's shoulder. "Please take me to medical. I hurt."

Vox watched as the small group left the room, the door sealing behind them. A dark emptiness filled him and his cat as both of them felt the loss of their mate. Vox's low, animalistic roar echoed through the level as he and his cat called for their mate to return to them.

"We will not leave without her," Tor said quietly coming up behind his friend and placing a reassuring hand on his shoulder.

Vox turned dark, burning eyes on Tor and Lodar. "You bet your cat we won't," he vowed.

Chapter 7

Riley felt much better several hours later. Bob had carried her up through the mines to a special lift that moved through the center of it. Riley vaguely saw the door to the control room as they passed it heading to the medical unit. The only reason she recognized it was because several Antrox guards were leaving the room, and they had to wait along the side of the corridor since Bob was too big to move past them at the same time.

The medical unit was a very small, depressing-looking room with only one bed in it. The healer was a dark red, leathery-looking man with little tufts of white hair hanging about his head in all different directions. Riley wasn't so sure she wanted some guy that looked that weird working on her, but she was in too much pain to complain when Bob gently laid her down on the small, single bed.

The healer insisted that Riley stay the night, telling her and Bob that Antrox 157 wanted to make sure she was completely healed before he was allowed to release her. Riley didn't think it was really necessary but decided it was probably for the best after everything that had happened. After the old healer put her arm in that strange looking machine it felt almost as good as new. Bob had been a darling through it all, especially since Riley didn't handle being hurt very well. The huge Gelatian had refused to leave her alone. He had held her good hand in one of his and talked quietly to her the whole time in an effort to take her mind off what was happening. Fred, true to his word, had appeared a little over an hour later with all of her things. Her large, pink suitcase and her oversized purse had been hooked together, and Riley couldn't suppress the giggle that escaped her as she watched the small Tiliquan struggle to roll it into the medical unit.

"Vox wants to know how you are feeling," Fred muttered under his breath as he sat down wearily on her suitcase. "This is very heavy, Riley. What do you have in it?"

Riley chuckled again as she watched both of Fred's heads droop tiredly. "A little bit of everything. I don't have much as I tend to move around a lot, but what I do have, I cherish. It is mostly clothes and shoes, but I also have a few mementos that I didn't want anything to happen to. You never know when you might need something so I try to be ready for just about anything that can happen."

"Vox will be very upset that I took your things. I had to sneak them out when he and the other two went to meet with Titus and Banu. The good thing is you are closer to the shuttle bay here. It will not be as far or as hard for you to get there tomorrow," Fred said quietly.

Riley lowered her head so Fred couldn't see her eyes. The incident earlier made her even more aware of the differences between her and those around her. She bit her lower lip and winced. Lip-biting was becoming a very bad habit she had picked up just since she arrived on this huge chunk of rock. If she wasn't careful, she wouldn't have any lips left by the time she got home.

No, it is better for everyone if I just find my way back home with the next trader or whoever is heading that way, Riley thought with resolve. *The last thing I need is some huge cat sticking his claws or teeth into me.*

"Fred, I'm really tired. Why don't you and Bob go on back down," Riley said, looking at her little friend with big, sad eyes. "You probably still have things that need to be taken care of before tomorrow, anyway."

Bob moved forward with a frown—at least she thought the crease between his eyes was a frown. "I will stay and guard you, Lady Riley," he insisted.

Riley rose and tenderly touched the huge, green gelatinous figure. "No," she said with a determined shake of her head. "I will be fine here. The healer said I needed to stay the night and rest. I wouldn't be able to sleep well if you stayed as I would be too worried about you. The room is too small for the two of us anyway. Go back to our rooms; the others may need you."

Bob looked down at Fred, then back at Riley for a moment. "Do not go anywhere!" he said sternly. "I will get the guards to return me first thing in the morning."

Riley gave Bob a weak smile and rose on her tiptoes to give him a light kiss. The huge green figure shook as she brushed his soft, slick cheek, and he turned a slightly deeper shade of green. Riley looked at him oddly before she turned to look at Fred, who was staring up at her intently with both sets of eyes narrowed in suspicion.

"You are not going to try anything, are you, Riley?" Fred asked quietly as she knelt down in front of him.

Riley ran her hands over both of his heads before leaning her forehead against his right one. "Now what makes you think I would try to do anything?" Riley teased lightly before she gave him a kiss on both sets of cheeks. "You be safe for me, Fred. I think you are one of the most wonderful mates a girl could ever have."

Fred turned a wide assortment of colors before he finally settled on a light shade of red. A huge grin curved both sets of lips as he stared at her with more than a slight case of hero worship. He reached out and wrapped his arms around her, holding her tightly for just a minute before he took a hurried step back.

"Don't tell Vox I hugged you," he whispered anxiously. "He might decide to take a bite out of me!"

Riley's light peal of laughter echoed through the room. "I won't. I promise. Besides, if he does I promised him a stick up his butt!" she added with a wink.

"Kitty on a stick." Bob pondered for a moment before his deep, melodious laugh echoed with Riley and Fred. "Now that I would like to see."

* * *

Vox lay on his side staring at the empty bed across from him. His cat was clawing at him to go find their mate. He could feel its damn claws slicing through his gut as if it was having fun mincing him into tiny bits.

Will you give me a break! He hissed at it in aggravation. *I can't think with you raking my insides like they are a scratching post.*

Want my mate, his cat replied with a low snarl. *You should protect better!*

May I remind you that you were the one who got all prissy when Tor mentioned drinking Riley's milk! Vox said defensively refusing to admit his own part in the desire to tear his chief engineer and close friend apart.

Mmmm, milk, his cat purred, lapping its long tongue out over its sharp teeth. *I bet it is warm and sweet and tasty. I would drink and drink and drink all day at our mate's milk.*

Guall's balls! Vox groaned out loud as he felt his own balls draw up to the point they were throbbing at the idea of lapping sweet, warm milk from Riley's huge breasts.

His cock was so hard he couldn't even sit up without extreme discomfort with the way it was pressing down the inside of his thigh. There was no way he was going to make it without getting some relief. The images his cat created were enough to make him come in his own damn pants! That was something he had never even come close to imagining, much less it becoming a real possibility.

"Vox, are you all right?" Lodar's quiet voice sounded in the dark. "You don't sound good."

"I'm fine!" Vox bit out in annoyance. "I need to relieve myself."

Vox rolled up onto his knees on his hard bed and stiffly got to his feet. This would be beyond embarrassing if his men knew he was having hot dreams of Riley on all fours, her big breasts hanging down over his face, full with the milk from his child.

Will you fucking have mercy on me? Vox begged as he stumbled to the door and out into the silent corridor.

Warm, sweet, yes... His cat hummed in pleasure.

Vox cursed as he felt the first spurt of cum leaking out of his cock, wetting the front of his black pants. Turning into the wall, he quickly undid the ties on the front of his pants until he could pull his cock free. He gripped it in his right hand tightly while he leaned his forehead against his left arm, pressed against the wall. He bit down on his forearm as he stroked the hard flesh of his cock. He only had to pump it three times before his whole body tensed and his orgasm hit him like a vicious blow. His body shuddered as he spent himself all over the wall. His loud pants mocked his loss of self-control. He leaned his head against his arm and drew in a shuddering breath. He tensed, turning slightly away from the door when it opened behind him, and Tor walked out, followed by Lodar.

"Leave me be," Vox gritted out hoarsely, not turning around.

"I, uh, I…" Lodar began before he stopped and drew in a deep breath.

"Oh hell," Tor muttered darkly. "You might as well kill us. Our cats are dreaming of drinking milk, and it isn't from some damn bowl! I need to go relieve myself before I explode," he grunted out, moving rapidly down the corridor.

"Sorry, Vox," Lodar said, slapping Vox on the shoulder. "Your mate… The image is just…" His words died out as he disappeared down the corridor as well.

Vox groaned out loud, letting his head drop back so he could stare up at the ceiling. He could feel his cock growing hard again as he pictured what Tor and Lodar were thinking about. If it was the last damn thing he ever did in all his long lives, he was going to get his mate with cubs and he was going to enjoy the damn milk with them. The thought of Riley rounded with his cubs sent him into another climax.

* * *

Early the next morning, Riley was thinking very unkind thoughts about the healer when he came in to check on her. It was the first time since she had been abducted that she had been able to sleep in, and Mr. Spooky Madman decided he needed to check her arm out. He wanted to check out a little more but decided against it when Riley kicked him in the balls. She was so not in the mood to be playing doctor and patient with someone who creeped her out. When short, squat, and red leather decided he wanted to do some touchy-feely to her breasts, she had sent him to his knees.

"Yes, sir," Riley said with a grin as the creepy old man wobbled out of the room. "Reflexes are in perfectly good working condition." She hopped down off the bed. "Now, time to do a little exploring. You never know if Dr. Dreadula might have something in here that could come in handy for when the boys decide to escape."

Riley thoroughly searched the small room. There was a medicine cabinet that wasn't even locked on the far wall that she decided might come in handy. She pulled it open and looked at a wide selection of small injection guns and tiny glass bottles. She tilted her head, but she couldn't read what the vials said. She pulled all of them out and placed them in her handbag with a shrug.

You never know when you might need something, she thought as she continued searching.

She sat down at the battered desk the man used and opened the top drawer. There was a strange-looking device that looked like some kind of fancy scanning wand and a laser pistol like the one the trader had been wearing when he shot her ass when she tried to run. Her eyes lit up when she saw it. Being a fully qualified bail bondsman, she was required to have a permit to carry a concealed weapon. It was true that she wasn't much of a fighter, but she was one hell of a shot! All those years playing the first shooter games at the bar her dear Grandma Pearl worked at paid off big time at the shooting range.

Riley pulled the bottom draw open and discovered a slim disk. She pulled it out and slid it into the slot on the desk for viewing video. It was a video of some sort. Her eyes widened when she saw Vox. They narrowed into deadly slits when she saw two nude women walking up to him and beginning to undress him. With a hiss, she quickly ejected the disk. She stood up and raised her arm to throw the damn thing against the wall but had second thoughts when she thought of where else she would like to shove it.

Right down his arrogant, lying, deceitful throat and I hope he chokes on it as it goes down, Riley thought viciously.

The video silenced the little voice that kept saying maybe she should go with him. Maybe she would be the heroine in this movie and not the supporting character that got knocked off. Maybe there was a happily ever after out there for her in the shape of a big sexy cat.

Maybe, my ass, Riley thought bitterly. *The only thing out there for you, girlfriend, is heartache if you begin to think things might be different here than back home. Guys are the same wherever the hell you go. They only want one thing, and it isn't a ring on my finger but one through my nose.*

Riley slid the disk into the zippered pocket of her purse. Maybe they had intergalactic email, or better yet, Intergalatictube. She would post the damn thing on it and let him be the star of his own porn movie. One thing was for sure, she didn't want any part of his...

"Don't even go there, Riley St. Claire! You will not think of his stupid you-know-what!" she muttered under her breath as she worked herself up into a fine fury. "It is time for them to get their asses off this rock so I can find me my own spaceship heading back home."

Riley slammed the drawer shut and walked over to her bright pink suitcase. She tucked the strap of her oversized purse over one shoulder, grabbed the handle of her rolling suitcase with the other, and firmly gripped the pistol she had found in her right hand. It was time to liberate the prisoners of this stupid mine! Riley raised her hand, tossed the massive wave of blond curls over her shoulder, and marched out the door, laser pistol blazing at anything that moved.

* * *

Vox cursed as he worked beside not just Tor, Lodar, Bob, and Fred, but alongside Titus and the others as well. They had been rounded up earlier than usual and marched to a different part of the mine than they had worked in before. Vox had known something was wrong immediately. First, the guards had refused to let Bob go back up to be with Riley. Second, they had been rounded up not only early but not given the normal tools for work. Finally, he knew they were going to be terminated when he saw the others already waiting for him and his men. All their carefully laid plans were worthless in the face of the twenty Antrox guards surrounding them. The only thing that gave them half a chance was the fact their collars were deactivated.

Vox dropped the large rock he had picked up when he saw Antrox 157 walking toward the group. He flexed his shoulders as rage poured through him. He was going to kill every one of the damn insects on this asteroid, and then he was going to kill him a Valdier royal. Vox's eyes narrowed on the smug expression of the normally passive face of the Antrox.

"Where is my mate?" Vox growled out menacingly.

157 raised his hand to stop the guards who took a step toward Vox with their stunning rods raised. 157 looked Vox up and down with a look of pure enjoyment. He was looking forward to explaining exactly what would happen to the Sarafin king's mate.

"She is in the process of being acclimated to her new position. She is an unusual species, and I was fortunate enough to acquire a large sum of credits for her. She will not be quite so demanding in her new position, but I am sure she will be in quite a lot of demand," 157 said, actually snorting at his own joke.

"What have you done with her?" Vox demanded tensely.

He would rip the Antrox apart, limb by limb, if one curly, blond hair on Riley's head had been touched. He would slowly gut the slimy bastard and listen as he begged for his miserable life. Then he would shove the credits the creature loved so much down his throat and watch him choke to death on them.

"She has been sold to a trader who supplies for the pleasure houses on the Grigillian Spaceport. It was decided if she could handle three huge Sarafin warriors and those two, she could handle even more. The trader has assured me she will bring prime credits," 157 added gleefully, his eyes glowing with greed at the idea of the number of credits he would shortly be receiving.

Lodar and Tor reached out and grabbed Vox by the arms when he roared out in rage. "You'll never live to see those credits, you miserable insect. I am going to rip off your fucking head and shove it up your ass," Vox snarled, fighting as Titus, Banu, and the others moved to help restrain him.

"No, you will be dead," 157 said with a smug smile. "That is where my other credits will come from. If it was not that I am a businessman, I would have offered to kill you for free. But, I am a businessman first. Your lives have been terminated per the Valdier royal Raffvin Reykill."

Vox felt the change sweep over him as the others tried to get him to calm down. He watched even as his vision began to change as Antrox 157 lifted a long slender palm for the device that would kill them all. The Antrox was so focused on pressing the button on the device in his hand that he did not pay attention to the ripple of fur running up and over Vox's arms, chest, and shoulders. He didn't notice Vox's face as his teeth began to elongate and his facial features shifted and transformed into that of the power cat that he was. It was only when 157 glanced up with a look that changed from triumph to horror in one heartbeat to the next as he pressed the button and nothing happened that he realized all was not as it should be.

157 pushed back, grabbing the guards around him and shoving them in front of him even as he screamed for them to use the stunning rods to hold the males back. It was too late. Vox was already clamping down on the skull of one guard while Tor, Lodar, Titus, and Banu did the same. Adur spun around, grabbing one of the long stunning rods and began using it just as Cross shifted into his dragon form and blew a long stream of condensed blue flames at the retreating figure of 157 and several of his guards.

Vox spit out the remains of another guard just as the alarms began blaring. He quickly shifted back into his two-legged form, turning in a confused circle for a moment as the red lights swirled around him. Loud shouts, followed by screams, could be heard in the distance.

"What in Guall's balls is going on?" he snarled out, turning to look at Titus and Banu.

"That is the emergency release system. It deactivates all the systems, including the collars," Titus said in shock. "Do you think our people found us?"

"Or perhaps the Valdier lords?" Cross said hopefully.

"Hello. Can everyone hear me? Hel-lo! Vox, Tor, Lodar?" Riley's husky voice came over the sound system. "Damn it! How do you turn the alarms off? The damn things are giving me a headache. Oh no, you don't, you nasty little insect!"

Vox jerked when he heard the loud sound of a laser pistol firing. "Riley?" he whispered hoarsely before his voice faded again in shock.

"Take that, you son of a bitch! Who's your momma now, asshole?" Riley crowed into the mic. "Fred, Bob honey, if you can hear me, I have all the doors open. I have to tell you, you'd better hurry. Those spaceship thingies are really flying out of here fast. I don't know if there are going to be any left if you don't get your asses up here now. Uh-oh, I don't think those two know how to drive one. Oops, nope. They didn't."

Tor shuddered as the loud sound of screeching could be heard followed by an explosion. "She must be in the control room. Let's get out of here!"

Vox didn't wait for his second in command to repeat himself. He turned and took off as fast as he could. He could hear Fred encouraging Bob to hurry. The little Tiliquan could keep up with them, but the Gelatian were not known for their speed. Vox yelled out a tense order for Banu and Cross to stay with Bob. The two warriors nodded, falling back to cover the large male who was struggling to follow them.

"Go," Bob groaned out. "Go, I will remain here."

"We have our orders, my friend," Cross laughed as he swung around to watch as a group of Antrox tried to escape several former prisoners who were not in the mood to let them go. "Besides, something tells me if you are not on board the spaceship there is no way that we will get the female on board it."

Bob thought of Riley's beautiful sad eyes last night and knew she didn't plan on being on the same ship that they were on. His huge body shuddered as determination swept through him. She was a remarkable female! She had chosen him even though she didn't have to. She had befriended him and cared for him when even the females of his own species wouldn't have thought twice about casting him aside for a stronger male. And she had set not just him and her other mates free but every prisoner on the mining asteroid. If she could fight for what she wanted, could he do any less for her?

"I have a mate to get out of here," Bob mumbled out, picking up speed ever so slightly.

The sound of an automated voice suddenly sounded around them. "Self-destruct has been activated. Countdown is set for ten-point-two-nine and counting. Evacuation of all personnel is recommended immediately."

"Then, I suggest we do not let her wait, my big green warrior," chuckled Banu. "Onward to freedom before she kills us all."

Chapter 8

Riley shot two guards the minute she exited the medical unit. The leathery, red-skinned healer had been coming down the corridor from the control room. The second he saw her shooting, he turned his wacky self around so fast he actually fell down. Riley took off as fast as she could, pulling her big, pink suitcase, and shot his ass as he was entering the control room. She had quickly disposed of him and the three guards inside. Normally she would have had second thoughts about killing anything. Hell, she was known for rescuing and nursing the injured lizards back home before releasing them back into the wild. Since she had never had to save a praying mantis before, she decided those miserable creatures didn't count, and the healer was just too freaky to let live. Those thoughts helped ease her conscience so she could concentrate on trying to figure out what in the hell to do next.

"One of these days, girl," she muttered out loud to herself. "You are going to have an actual plan before you start shooting."

Riley's nose turned up in disgust as she shoved the last of the dead bodies outside the door. There were some things she could handle; being in a room with dead guys was not one of them. She cursed again when she couldn't figure out how to close the door to the room, so she stood back and shot the panel out. Her loud moans filled the air when instead of closing, it remained frozen opened.

"Oh, for crying out loud!" she groaned in frustration. "It worked in the movies, damn it all to hell!" There was nothing she could do about the door except shoot anything that tried to come through it now.

She turned and looked at all the lights flashing on the console with a confused frown. Glancing out the huge section of windows that overlooked two separate landing bays divided by a huge wall of rock, she figured she could at least watch as her guys took off. Since she couldn't see them down there yet she figured they might need a little help. She had absolutely no idea what to do but figured if she started pushing enough buttons something was bound to work sooner or later.

"Well, I told them I was great at causing a distraction," she muttered darkly as she began pushing as many buttons as fast as she could. "Oops, maybe I shouldn't have pushed that one," she whispered under her breath when the lights flashed on and off in the landing bay.

Riley pushed another button and realized she could hear herself breathing over the PA system. She could warn the guys they needed to get their asses up here toot sweet if they wanted a spaceship. At the rate the other prisoners were leaving, they were going fast.

"Hello. Can everyone hear me? Hell-lo! Vox, Tor, Lodar?" she called out, hoping they could hear her over the stupid alarms that had gone off when she was pushing buttons. Unfortunately, she couldn't figure out how to turn them off. "Damn it! How do you turn the alarms off? The damn things are giving me a headache," she muttered before she turned to see one of the Antrox guards trying to sneak up behind her. "Oh no, you don't, you nasty little insect!"

Riley let loose with several shots, adding to the growing pile of dead bodies. "Take that, you son of a bitch! Who's your momma now, asshole?" Riley crowed before she realized she still had the communication system open. "Fred, Bob honey, if you can hear me I have all the doors open. I have to tell you. You'd better hurry. Those spaceship thingies are really flying out of here fast. I don't know if there are going to be any left if you don't get your asses up here now. Uh-oh, I don't think those two know how to drive one. Oops, nope. They didn't," she croaked out as she watched the dark night of space light up when two departing ships exploded.

* * *

Several Antrox guards turned, startled, and looked up at the control room as the lights in the landing bay flashed on and off. Antrox 785 looked up in disbelief when he saw the strange female standing at the controls instead of his men. Riley glanced down at him at the same time as he turned all the way around to stare in disbelief. Antrox 785 watched as if in slow motion as she gave him a huge smile and raised her hand, her middle finger pointing straight up, before blowing him a kiss. He could feel the deep flush of shock and outrage that his mining operation was no longer under his control.

"Get me the guards on Level Five," he growled out at the same time the alarms sounded, stating all systems had been deactivated. "Wait!" he ordered sharply. "On second thought, get my personal ship ready immediately. It is time I retired," he muttered to his personal guards.

"Antrox 785, what of the others?" his guard asked stiffly.

"The prisoners have been released," Antrox 785 stated coolly, looking at the guard. "Do you wish to search for the others?"

The guard looked back up at the female in the control room who was currently firing a laser pistol at someone. He looked back at Antrox 785 and bowed his head. Turning, the small group hurried to one of the tubes leading up to Antrox 785's personal space craft.

Antrox 785 turned before he walked up to the tube to look one last time at the strange female who had brought an end to his sixty years of profit. Luckily, he had always known that something like this could happen and had prepared for it. He shook his head as he turned to follow his guards. Before he retired, he first would have liked to have killed the trader who brought her here. A small smile curved his thin lips as he thought about how much Antrox 157 wanted to be promoted. He hoped he enjoyed his new position.

* * *

Riley screamed as two more guards fell. This time not from her but from one of the escaped prisoners who decided he wanted to take her with him. She raised her arm and fired on the huge orange man again. He grunted but continued to creep toward her even though he was bleeding from several places including where she had just shot him in the shoulder.

"Oh, for crying out loud!" Riley snarled as she aimed the pistol between his eyes. "Will you just fucking die already!" she snapped out as she fired again. The huge orange figure flew backward landing on the growing pile of bodies outside the door. This time, he didn't get back up.

Who the hell needs a door when I can just make one out of dead bodies, she thought in disgust.

Riley turned to slam her hand down on the last button in frustration and anger. This one had been hidden under a huge clear lid. The little nagging thought in her head that maybe it was covered for a reason didn't go off until the voice of the automated system announced that the self-destruct had been activated.

"Well, shit a brick!" Riley groaned in despair.

Tears filled her eyes as she watched another spaceship depart. There was only one left, and it looked like it had been left behind for a reason. She wasn't even sure if it could fly. Her hand pressed against the glass, her fingers spread as she watched Cross, Banu, Bob, and Fred hurrying across the landing bay toward the last spaceship. A moment later, she saw Adur and Titus making their way up the tube as well. She must have missed Vox, Tor, and Lodar. She was sure they had already escaped in all the confusion.

"Good luck, my strange friends," Riley whispered sadly as she watched them disappear. "I'm glad you are getting away."

She pulled away from the glass. The sounds in the background of the countdown seemed to match her heartbeat. Riley stepped away, pulling her purse and big, pink suitcase with her as she moved over to the wall, where she slid down until she was sitting on the floor. She pulled her knees up to her chest and smoothed her huge purse down against her side.

Riley rolled the laser pistol in her hands absently before taking a deep breath. She wasn't going to wait until the place exploded around her. If she was going to die, it wasn't going to be by having her head explode from decompressing in space. No, she would take her own life in the last few seconds. A quick blast to the heart and she wouldn't feel the dark emptiness that would become her tomb.

"Hell, Riley girl," she whispered as tears coursed down her cheeks. "You are really getting morbid. At least it is better than being buried in concrete under the shed in Righteous, New Mexico." She giggled, on the verge of hysteria. "Here floats the body of Riley St. Claire from Denver, Colorado. She forgot that the self-destruct button is always covered. The idiot! So much for twenty-four years of good B-rated movies. This totally sucks!" Riley groaned as she pulled the pistol so it was pressed tightly against her chest. "I can't believe with my family history that I am probably the only female in the history of the St. Claires to die a frigging virgin!" She sniffled sadly.

She closed her eyes and drew in a shuddering sob. She could do this. *Just don't think about it.* Instead, she thought about the things that brought a warmth to her heart and calmed her. Images shimmered into her mind as she thought back to the things that really mattered to her. A wobbly smile curved her lips as she remembered her Grandma Pearl laughing and wiping down the counter at the bar as she listened to Riley telling her about her latest retorts to the bullies at school. She thought about her sainted sister Tina rolling her big blue eyes at her when their Grandma got called to school again because of Riley fighting or mouthing off. She thought of Vox's beautiful tawny eyes glaring at her with hot desire as he tried to get her to rest instead of working alongside them down in the mines. Her body began to shake uncontrollably as her finger tightened on the trigger; then she jerked in shock as pain exploded through her.

I didn't think dying would hurt so much, she thought as the breath exploded out of her.

* * *

Vox let out another loud snarl as he slashed at anything in his way. Tor and Lodar were right beside him clearing a path. He didn't care who it was. If they were in the way, they were dead. His only thought was to get to Riley, his mate, his everything. How he ever thought he could kill her if he had to made him realize just how stupid he really was. The thought of her being in danger was enough to drive him insane. He would never have been able to kill her. He would have had to lock her up somewhere if she had been a spy. Hell, he might do that anyway after this crazy stunt of hers. He was damn sure going to whip her delicious ass for scaring him so badly.

He had roared for the others to go secure a ship for them while he, Tor, and Lodar shifted into their cats and went after Riley. They could move faster and clear a larger path in that form. Vox burst down the corridor that housed the medical unit and control room, his sharp claws digging gouges into the stone floor. He slowed as he saw the pile of bodies outside of the control room door which stood open. He pulled back on his cat, slowing it down. It hissed at him, fighting for control as fear threatened to overwhelm caution.

Vox moved silently toward the door. Tor and Lodar had shifted behind him and were moving up the sides, checking each room for any guards that might remain. His ears twitched back and forth as he picked up Riley's husky, tear-filled voice. His cat picked up speed at the sound of its mate. He jumped over the pile of dead bodies and froze, his eyes narrowing on where Riley was sitting with the laser pistol pressed against her chest. Time seemed to stand still as he watched her draw in a deep, shaky breath. A silent curse tore through his mind as he realized what she was about to do. With a burst of speed he hit her sideways, whipping his huge paw out and knocking the pistol out of her hand as he stumbled over her, rolling as the pistol fired mere inches from her.

He knew he hit her hard enough to knock the breath out of her, but he had been so frightened he could barely restrain himself. Gods! He had almost lost her again. He didn't know if his heart would ever beat calmly again. He shifted, rolling until she was trapped underneath him. His hands were framing her face as he frantically looked down at her.

"Riley," he croaked out desperately. "Where are you hurt?"

Riley opened her mouth as she stared up in a daze at the huge figure above her. She couldn't breathe. He had her pinned under his huge body and had knocked the frigging wind out of her. She finally drew in a huge breath as dark spots began dancing around the edges of her vision.

"You aren't supposed to be here," she said confused. "You were supposed to have already escaped."

"Are you hurt?" Vox tenderly growled out again as he ran the palms of his big hands down over her hair and cheeks.

"No, I don't think so," Riley said before she let out a loud squeal as she found herself flung over Vox's huge shoulder as he jumped to his feet.

"Good! Once we know for sure, I'm going to tan your ass for this little stunt, female!" Vox growled out turning back toward the door.

"My suitcase! Don't forget my purse either!" Riley cried out looking over at her big, pink suitcase from upside down. "I need it!"

"I'm on it," Tor said, hurrying into the room and grabbing the huge case and heavy handbag with a grunt. "Damn, Riley, this is heavy. What do you have in it?" Tor asked as he jogged down the corridor behind Vox.

"Can we talk less and run faster?" Lodar asked coming up the rear. "We have less than two minutes to get far enough away from this rock we don't get blown up with it."

"Sor…ry…ab…ou…t-th-tha-that!" Riley finally got out as she bounced up and down.

"I…hit…the…wronnnggg…butt…on. Damn it, Vox. Will…you…quit…bouncing…me!"

Vox's large hand tightened around Riley's legs while his other one landed on her ass with a satisfying whack. He couldn't help the grin that lit up his face at her outraged yelp followed by a long string of colorful curses and threats. He let his hand rest there, enjoying the soft, heated flesh under his palm.

Gods, but I love this female! he thought, almost tripping as he bolted down the steps and charged across the landing bay. *I love her!*

He never thought he would feel this emotion for a female, but he realized he did. His cat rolled deep inside him in disgust as the revelation spread warmth to every inch of his huge frame. He never expected love to feel like this! He felt wonderful and terrified at the same time. He, Vox d'Rojah, ruling king of the Sarafin was terrified of a little alien female from a species he had never even heard of before. She scared him to the marrow of his bones, and he loved it. She drove him nuts, was totally oblivious to just who he was and the power he had, and he never knew what in Guall's balls she was going to say or do next. He was also terrified that something might happen to her. He and his cat needed to protect her, even if it was from herself. Speaking of which—

"What in the hell did you think you were doing?" Vox growled out as he charged up the loading tube to— "What in the hell is that?" he croaked out in dismay as he got his first good look at the dilapidated freighter.

"It is the only thing left," Banu snarled out. "Move your asses. Titus and Adur have the engines primed as much as they could without blowing them. We have less than a minute to get as far from this place as possible."

Vox's curses echoed as Banu sealed the door behind them and barked out to Titus to get them the fuck out of there. Vox reached out and grabbed the bar along the side of the passageway as he felt the old freighter groan and shake as Titus and Adur pushed it to the maximum.

"Go! Go! Go!" Lodar muttered under his breath as he hung tightly to the bar next to Vox.

"I'm going to go see if I can't get this rusted piece of dragon dung to move faster," Tor snarled, holding onto the bar as he worked his way down the corridor.

"Ah, hello," Riley said, blowing her hair out of her face. "Is it possible to be put down now? The blood is, like, flowing to my head, and I am definitely getting a headrush here. Not to mention, you have a very uncomfortable shoulder considering how much meat you've got on you. Let me tell you, muscle is not soft!" she complained.

Vox snarled at Banu who had his eyes glued to Riley's ass. "Mine!" he snapped to the younger Sarafin warrior.

Banu grinned at Vox. "If we are about to die at least give me something nice to look at," he said with a shrug.

Cross grinned at Banu. "I couldn't agree with you more, my friend. If I have to die I wouldn't mind having her in my arms."

"What are they looking at?" Riley said, trying to walk herself up Vox's back with her hands. She turned and looked at Banu and Cross who were grinning mischievously at her. "What is nice?"

"They are staring at your big ass," Vox snapped in irritation. "It is mine!"

Riley's eyes widened before they narrowed to dangerous slits. "I know you did not just say I have a big ass, you hot-headed, no-good, two-timing piece of kitty-litter trash!" she snapped. "Put me down right this minute."

Vox slid Riley's succulent body down along his own solid form with a loud purr. Gods, she had curves on top of curves and was so soft he could feel his hands sinking down into the creamy flesh as his hands slipped under her shirt. His cat rumbled in delight as her sweet scent overwhelmed his senses, and his eyes actually rolled back in his head when her huge breasts caressed his cheeks.

"Gods, female, you are potent," Vox purred against her ear as he leaned into her.

Riley opened her mouth to let him have it, but before she could the entire freighter shuddered violently, creaking and groaning as the asteroid exploded. Her arms flew out, wrapping around his neck at the same time as she tried crawling back up his huge frame. She had too much to live for to die now. She had to find a way home, she had to lose her virginity, she had a big, gorgeous-smelling lummox to kill.

Vox turned, pressing Riley's shivering figure between his body and the wall. She had her long legs wrapped tightly around his waist, and her face was buried in his neck. He didn't know whether the groan that escaped him was because he could feel the old freighter struggling to move through the shockwave or because he could feel the heat of his mate's pussy pressing against his cock which decided it didn't care that they were in mortal danger right now. He pressed her against the side of the corridor as his arms strained to hold onto the metal grip bar.

"Brace for impact!" Titus's voice came over the communication system. "Adur, see if this piece of crap's shields can be increased to the stern. We have debris coming at us."

"Shields are at ninety percent. I'm rerouting power from life support to give it additional power," Adur muttered tensely.

"I've got the engines primed," Tor's voice came in. "Give it full thrust, Titus. She can handle it for a short period. Just get us the fuck out of here."

"Hang on," Titus yelled as he pushed the freighter past its specifications.

Banu cursed as he was jerked almost off his feet as the freighter lurched before surging forward. Cross reached out and grabbed Banu, pulling him upright at the last second. Banu muttered a quick thanks under his breath as he grabbed for the bar again. Vox whispered quietly in Riley's ear as she whimpered. His heart beat heavily against his chest as he turned his face into her silky hair and pressed his lips against her.

"It will be all right, Riley," Vox promised in a soft, husky voice. "I promise I won't let anything happen to you. It will be all right. I'll keep you safe."

Riley didn't answer. She just closed her eyes and held on as tight as she could to the anchor holding her. She could always kill him later, but for now she needed his strength and calming presence to keep her from having a complete meltdown.

Riley pressed her lips against his neck, hoping for that plane of total oblivion until the wild ride they were having was over. She had always hated roller coasters. She never understood why anyone wanted to go on something that scared the shit out of them and think it was funny. That was why she kept the damn old Ford she had. It couldn't go faster than fifty miles an hour without shaking apart. Slow was good; slow was safe.

Vox chuckled as he listened to Riley whispering. That was something else he loved about her. She was totally open, there was no deceit in her. But most of all, she could make him laugh even in the face of danger.

"Yes, my sweet mate," Vox murmured. "Slow can be very, very good. But I still want to show you how wonderful fast can be as well."

Chapter 9

Vox muttered another curse as he wiped the sweat from his eyes. He and Tor had been working on the engines for the past two days. He had to hand it to his chief engineer, the man knew his engines. He had rebuilt the main engine while Adur and Cross worked on the defense systems with a little help from Bob and Fred. The damn Curizan was just as impressive when it came to his knowledge of electronics. He knew the species loved their toys. Hell, Ha'ven, the Curizan prince, and his brother, Adalard, loved to show off the damn things they had invented. They had a racing bike he really wanted, but Ha'ven refused to give him another one after he crashed the first one into a tree less than an hour after Ha'ven gave it to him.

"So, is Riley talking to you yet?" Tor asked as he walked up to where Vox was working. He was wiping down another sleeve that needed to be fitted into the new cylinder that attached to one of the boosters.

"No," Vox grunted out as he slammed the cover closed on the panel he had been working on. "Why she is upset that I said she had a big ass I'll never understand. I love it, but she won't listen to me when I try to tell her that I like her being big and soft," he complained as he looked up in frustration at Tor.

"Well, Adur is having to adjust the environmental systems to handle the extra power he needs for the shields and weapons systems. It is going to get chilly in here. We can handle it since we run hotter, but our mate will need to be kept warm. Maybe she will be more receptive to some cuddling," Tor said turning away with a grin as Vox snarl at his use of the words "our mate."

"She is *my* mate," Vox responded in a low voice. "I will be the only one to keep her warm."

Tor grinned at his friend and leader. "I am not the one you have to convince." He chuckled as he worked the sleeve onto the booster module and tightened it down.

Vox ran his hand over the back of his neck tiredly. Once they had made it far enough from the exploding mining asteroid to be sure they would be safe, Riley had demanded that he release her. She had smacked his chest and informed him with an inelegant sniff that she did not have a "big" ass, she had a maturely figured one and he better never forget it! She had then grabbed her large pink case that Tor had dropped and marched off to find her a room of her own. He hadn't seen her since as Tor needed assistance trying to keep the damn piece of dragon dung they had appropriated from falling apart around them. Banu and Titus were working on the system controls, while Adur, Bob, and Fred worked on the weapons. Lodar was working on the single replicator that was malfunctioning and inventorying the medical supplies.

"Well, I think I have the replicator working temporarily," Lodar responded tiredly as he walked into the engine room. "Just don't order anything elaborate. There is no telling what the damn thing might do. Oh, and don't get hurt. The equipment on this piece of shit is downright barbaric. I wouldn't operate on my worst enemy with it. There isn't even a stolen Curizan portable regen machine—which, by the way, I would give my right arm to appropriate—and all the medicine is out of date by at least twenty years."

Vox grimaced. "Have you heard if Titus or Banu were able to get the communications system up yet? I want to contact the *Shifter*."

Lodar shook his head and lean back against the wall. "Not yet, but Banu thought they should have it fixed in another couple of hours. They are having to dismantle some of the non-essential control panels to get the parts they need to fix it. We are going to be operating on the bare minimum until we get off this death trap."

"Have you seen Riley?" Vox finally asked reluctantly.

Lodar laughed. "Yes, she has been like a small storm sweeping through the upper living and dining quarters. The only thing that works on this bucket of rust is the laundry unit. She has washed every piece of cloth on this thing. We all have nice clean linen on the beds that are available, any clothing she found was also washed and neatly hung up for our use, and she has refreshed all her clothing," Lodar added, raising his eyebrows up and down with a wicked smile.

Vox's eyes narrowed. "Why did you do that?" he demanded.

"Do what?" Lodar asked innocently.

"The eyebrow thing," Vox growled in a low voice. "What did she wash that makes you smile like that?"

Tor stopped what he was doing so he could hear what Lodar had discovered. It had to be good if Lodar got that look in his eyes. It really took a lot to get a reaction out of his friend.

Lodar leaned forward excitedly. "She has these undergarments she wears that are all lacy and sexy. I've never seen anything like it before. There was this one set that looked like your cat's coat, Vox. It had the same coloring and spots. I would kill to see her in it. There were two pieces to it. The top had these sheer cups that molded to her breasts, and they were like…" Lodar held his big hands out with his fingers spread wide. "I swear they would overflow both my hands easily! The piece that she wears over her mound was like…" His voice faded as his eyes glazed over.

Vox rose to his feet, grabbing the front of Lodar's shirt in one of his fists. "Like what?" he growled out in frustration.

Hell, he was too damn aroused to care that it was Lodar telling him what his mate wore under her clothing. His curiosity was about to kill both him and his cat. The idea of his mate wearing something that looked like his cat was enough to make him want to hunt her down and strip her to see for himself. His cat was panting, wondering what Riley would look like in cat form.

"Lodar, tell us! This is killing me," Tor muttered.

"It is this little thing with two pretty little bows on each side and one long thin strip of material up the back. I asked her what it was for, and she told me it was called a thong. She liked to wear them because they didn't leave panty lines under her clothes. I asked her if she would model it for me, but she just rolled her eyes and told me to get out or she was going to put me in the laundry unit so she could clean my dirty little mind." Lodar chuckled as Vox's face turned dark with envy.

"Damn, my cat and I have been dreaming every night about drinking milk," Tor muttered as he turned away to hide how aroused he was. "Now we are going to be dreaming about her wearing nothing but those little pieces of cloth." He threw a pained expression at Vox who turned to glare at him. "Sorry, Vox. It's been too damn long since my cat or I've had sex."

"Well, quit thinking and dreaming about my mate," Vox ordered roughly. "Dream about another female."

Lodar barked out a resigned laugh. "Yeah, like Titus's purple mate?"

Tor shuddered and felt his desire cooling at the idea of the slender purple female. There was just nothing sexy about making love to a stick. Now, after meeting Riley, he wondered if even the females back home could stir his cock the way they used to. The Sarafin females were attractive, and they were definitely always in the mood for a sexual romp, but they were hard and muscular due to their cat. Now he wanted something he could actually cuddle up to without getting bruised. He looked at Vox, barely hiding his grin. Vox's nose was still a little swollen from where Riley had boxed him yesterday. Well, there might be some bruising involved, but it would definitely be worth it.

* * *

Riley shivered. She was freezing her ass off. She needed to talk to the guys about working on the damn heater. She pulled her suitcase out from under the bed and unzipped it. She didn't unpack her things. The biggest reason why was she was afraid they might have to evacuate the old tub they were on in a hurry, and she wouldn't have time to repack everything. She dug around until she felt the soft fur lining of the jacket she had bought herself for her birthday two years ago. It would have cost her a pretty penny at that boutique where her sister worked if it hadn't been on the seventy-percent-off rack. Even with Tina's employee discount it had still cost her a small fortune, but she loved the damn thing. It was gaudy to the point of being chic. The rich, dark purple dyed rabbit fur offset the glittering silver sequins all over it. The damn thing practically glowed in the dark, and when she wore it to the bar with a pair of her black leather pants it screamed "unavailable rich bitch." Of course, the one and only time she wore it to the bar, Pearl had threatened to shoot the damn thing. She'd said nothing that ugly should be allowed to live.

Riley had ignored her dear grandmother and put it down to jealousy that Tina had shown it to her instead of Pearl who seemed to only like black leather and metal. Riley had drooled over the damn jacket every time she picked Tina up after work for almost a year. Tina must have hidden it so that the owner would finally mark it down from the twelve hundred dollars it had originally been marked at because she knew how badly Riley wanted the damn thing.

She gave a thrilled grin as she slid the quilted jacket on, rubbing her cheek against the soft rabbit fur. Yes, she was an animal lover, but she figured if she convinced herself that the damn thing died of old age or something similar she wouldn't have to feel guilty about where it came from. Hell, as far as she knew it could have been roadkill. The only thing she cared about was that it was soft, flamboyant, and hers!

Riley zipped the jacket up and pulled the collar up until it covered her ears. The fur lining practically covered her face, and she was able to bury her nose in it to keep it warm too. She couldn't wait to see how the guys reacted to it. The men in the bar had just stared at her all night like they thought she was some movie star or something. Of course, her grandmother said they didn't know whether she needed help from the alien attacking her or if she was the newest hooker on the street. Riley had blown her grandmother the middle-finger kiss and told her that her john had given her the night off. Tina had groaned, mortified, while Pearl had laughed so hard she had to excuse herself so she wouldn't piss all over herself.

"Some grandmother I have," Riley muttered as she walked down the corridor to the dining quarters. "She pisses her pants because she knows her granddaughters are virgins! Most grandmas would be proud of that."

"Hi, Riley," Fred said, coming up behind her. "What is attacking you? Did it come off the ship?" he asked, frightened, looking at the glittering silver and purple jacket she had wrapped around her snugly.

Riley rolled her eyes at Fred. "Yes, there are thousands of them on board. You better not lie down for too long or one of them will take over your body as well!" she grumbled, not looking at him as she turned to continue on her way. "Is it attacking me? He's a freaking comedian, and I didn't even know it!"

She sighed as she entered the dining quarters and found no one was there. Maybe she could just fix herself something quick and take it back to her room where she could bundle up in the nice, clean blankets that she had piled on her bed. Shit, she could see her breath now. What was their frigging problem? Did they forget to pay the damn heating bill or something? Riley shrugged her shoulders, just thankful she had something to keep her warm. She plugged her earbuds into her iPhone, adjusting the ear pieces so she could listen to Enigma as she fixed herself something to eat. She was totally oblivious to the fact that Fred had disappeared.

* * *

"How long before you can meet up with us?" Vox asked his younger brother, Viper, who was commanding his warship, the *Shifter*.

"It will take us two, possibly three days to get there. We have been raiding every damn Antrox mine we can find. I didn't realize the greedy insects had so many. We've been to four star systems so far looking for you and have raided at least two dozen," Viper said, leaning back and grinning. "So, how did you escape? I would love to have seen the Antrox's expressions as you gave them hell."

Vox flushed, not wanting to explain to his brother just yet that his new mate had been the one to save them, even if she had blown the damn mining asteroid to smithereens in the process. He shifted uncomfortably, wondering how his parents and brothers were going to react to Riley. His parents had recently reminded him that he was destined to mate with a Valdier princess. That had been part of the treaty his father and the old Valdier king had signed to ensure peace between the two species. Now, he was about to blow the treaty to hell because he had no intention of mating with anyone other than Riley.

"Remind me to tell you about it when you pick us up," Vox muttered in frustration. "Just meet up with us as soon as possible. I'm not sure how long this piece of dragon dung will hold up. We have it patched together with our piss and sweat."

Viper laughed. "There is a Valdier warship closer. I'll notify them that you may need assistance before we can arrive. It is Creon's warship. They could be there within a day."

Vox nodded in resignation. "That might be best. I need to speak with Creon Reykill about a personal matter anyway," he muttered. "I will contact you later."

"Gods be with you, brother," Viper said, signing off.

"I hope they will be," Vox said as he thought of how he was going to approach the youngest Valdier royal and ask for his help in breaking the treaty between their people without it causing a war.

Vox looked at Titus and Adur and rubbed the back of his neck wearily. Gods, he was tired.

He hadn't slept well since he was captured, and with trying to keep the damn freighter from falling apart, he hadn't had a chance to even think about it in over two days. He sat back in the chair near the communications console and was listening as Titus and Adur talked about what still needed to be done when he heard the sound of Fred's little feet scurrying toward them.

"Vox! Vox! You have to help! Riley! Help her! She has been attacked!" Fred said breathlessly as he skidded onto the bridge where Vox, Adur, and Titus were. "A strange creature! It has Riley in the dining quarters!"

Vox's loud roar shook the room as he shifted into his cat. He sent Fred flying into Adur as he rushed through the door. His claws clattered against the metal flooring of the old freighter as he rushed down the long corridor. He vaguely heard Titus yelling for Lodar and Tor to meet them in the dining quarters, that Riley was being attacked. Bob heard the loud roars as it echoed through the old freighter to where he was working on sealing off another section of the ship so they would not have to maintain its environmental system. His huge body shook with rage when he heard that something was attacking Riley in the dining quarters. He turned quickly and moved as fast as his big body would let him through the narrow corridors.

Vox's blood boiled at the thought of some unknown creature attacking his beautiful, vulnerable mate. He would tear it to shreds. He would teach whatever creature it was that no one messed with his delicate, fragile mate. He rounded the corner leading to the dining quarters, skidding around it so fast his shoulder left a deep dent in the wall where he hit it. He slowed as he saw Riley coming out of the room. She had a tray in her hands, but that was not what caught his attention. It was the mass of purple threatening to strangle her. The thing had glittering scales all over it. Vox's heart skipped a beat when he saw the purple tentacles embedded in her ears. The thing was trying to take over her mind!

Vox leaped to rip the thing off Riley at the same time she looked up. Horror and fear flashed through her eyes as she screamed. The tray in her hands flew through the air over her head at the same time as Vox hit her chest, knocking her backward and down to the hard metal floor. He used his teeth and claws to slice the creature off his mate, tearing and slashing in desperate fear that it might be too late to save her.

He shifted when he had most of the creature torn apart enough so he could use his hands to finish pulling it from her body. Riley's screams of panic continued to tear a hole through his soul. Grief and rage made his fingers clumsy as he pulled the last bit of purple fur away from her face and neck. With trembling fingers, he gently pulled the remains of the tentacles from her right ear, the other had already fallen out.

"Riley, speak to me," Vox whispered hoarsely. "My *lumi*, please speak to me. Tell me if it is still hurting you."

* * *

Riley breathed in the scent of the hot soup she had programmed into the replicator that Lodar had shown her earlier how to use. She had decided she'd better stick with something simple like he suggested and decided on a broth and hot tea. Anything hot to warm her up since she was beginning to shiver even with the jacket on. She tugged on the fur lining, pulling it up around her ears and adjusted her earbuds so they wouldn't fall out before she picked up the tray she had found.

Yes, sir—she thought as she lifted the tray to her nose to smell the fragrant soup—*something hot for the belly and a bunch of nice, clean blankets piled high waiting for me in my own room. Now all I need is a good movie or book to go with it.*

She was humming along with the song she was listening to, her eyes focused on the tray so she wouldn't spill any when a low rumbling sound made her eyes jerk up. Her mouth opened in surprise and horror as she saw the biggest damn cat in the universe glaring at her in rage. A high scream worthy of any *King Kong* heroine burst from her lips as it launched itself at her. She jerked her hands up, throwing the tray over her head as she tried to protect her face from the massive teeth in its mouth. She closed her eyes and screamed even louder and longer the second time as the huge cat hit her square in her chest, knocking her backward until she was lying on the floor. She could feel its teeth and claws as it ripped into her jacket. She continued to scream, unable to stop as the huge cat tugged and pulled until the material of her jacket fell away from her body. A final quick tug pulled the remaining earbud out of her ear. Riley felt the change in the body above her at the same time as she felt the freezing air of the freighter.

"Riley, speak to me." Vox's husky voice resonated through her at the same time as frantic fingers kept pulling at the tattered remains of her beloved jacket. "My *lumi*, please speak to me. Tell me if it is still hurting you."

It took a minute for his words to process in her stunned brain. What the hell was he talking about? If what was still hurting her? She slowly opened her eyes to stare into the frantically worried tawny color eyes above her. A shiver coursed through her as the icy metal under her seeped into her already chilled body. Huge warm hands pulled her up into equally huge and warm arms. One big palm pressed her head against his chest as the other pushed the remains of her jacket away from her. Riley's heart began to slow even as the heart under her ear beat with a thundering roar, as if he had just run a marathon.

"Please, my love, please be all right," Vox whispered cradling her against him fiercely. "It will not harm you again. I promise."

"Vox, let me look at her," Lodar said urgently coming up behind him. "I need to see what damage the creature may have done. It was wrapped all around her."

"Adur, Cross, and Banu can help me search the freighter for any more of the creatures," Tor said harshly. "We should have done that in the first place," he added with disgust.

"Perhaps that is why no one else wanted this ship," Fred whispered, looking up at Bob who was standing behind him.

"I have sealed off the two lower levels," Bob said. "If there are any there, they will not be able to get to us and with the environmental systems shut down they shouldn't be able to survive for long."

"I have not seen any other purple and silver creatures, but if I modify the scanners I might be able to pick them up on it," Titus added.

"I can help you," Cross said, looking down at the remnants of the beast that had attacked Riley. "I have never seen anything like this before," he murmured as he pushed a piece of the purple fur with the tip of his toe.

Riley listened as the men talked back and forth between each other. Each piece slowly fitting together in her brain to make the puzzle clearer until the image of her jacket, totally shredded, loomed like a beacon in the mass confusion. At first, just a little giggle escaped as she thought about Fred's reaction when he first saw it. His comment and her offhand, sarcastic response floated through her memory. The more she thought about it, the more she realized that they actually thought her jacket had been alive. That it was some type of alien creature that ate aliens! A little hiccup escaped her as she fought the surge of adrenaline-laced hysteria at having the shit scared out of her all because of her beautiful but dead birthday present.

Vox stroked Riley's back tenderly as he felt her beginning to shake. He looked at Lodar with wide, worried eyes. Lodar nodded as he moved in closer so he could examine her without having to pull her too far from his friend.

"Riley, it will be all right," Lodar said calmly. "We won't let anything happen to you. I just need to take a closer look at you. Can you tell me about what happened?"

Riley turned her face into Vox's chest and burst out into uncontrollable laughter. It was just too much! They were totally freaking out over a gaudy piece of cloth. She shook her head, knowing she wasn't going to be able to speak rationally yet. She was too busy having a hysterical moment.

"Just… just…a…moment," she breathed out in a muffled voice against Vox's warm skin. Hell, he was ten times warmer than her jacket! She snuggled closer and was rewarded when Vox's arms wrapped even tighter around her, pulling her so close she was practically molded into him. "You… You… You…killed my…my…jacket," Riley giggled.

"I killed your what?" Vox asked, confused, looking at Lodar to see if he understood what she was trying to say.

Lodar shrugged and touched Riley's wild wave of curly hair. "What did you say, Riley? We couldn't understand," he asked gently.

Riley tilted her head back until she was looking up at both men. Her eyes danced with merriment as she fought back the uncontrollable laughter threatening to escape her. Her face warmed as she saw the other men looking on with concern.

"Vox, you dolt, you killed my favorite jacket!" Riley burst out laughing. "This is priceless! You thought my jacket was attacking me, and you killed it! My Grandma Pearl was right. She said that it looked like an alien attacking me and threatened to shoot it the one time I wore it to the bar. But hell! I never really thought that would ha-ha-happen!" Riley crowed before she buried her face into Vox's warm chest again as her body shook with glee.

* * *

"Not one damn word," Vox growled out, looking down at Fred. "Do not say one damn word!"

Fred tucked both of his chins down into his chest and nodded before scurrying away. Vox watched the little Tiliquan move rapidly down the corridor. He was probably going to go apologize again to Riley for getting her jacket killed.

"You should go easy on the little guy," Adur said, trying to keep a straight face. "After all, we all thought the damn thing was alive."

Banu and Titus turned around quickly, trying to hide their grins. Cross didn't even bother turning around. He just grinned. He couldn't wait to see what happened next. He had to admit, ever since they had been introduced to the young female, life had been very, very interesting.

Vox growled darkly at all of them before he got up and strode off the bridge. Why, oh why, did he continue to screw up whenever he was around Riley? He had always been so in control, so commanding, so not an idiot before he met her. Hell, others trembled in fear of him! Riley trembled, but it was because she was either madder than hell at him or laughing her ass off at the idiotic things he did.

Vox paused and took a deep breath. Well, that was about to end. He was going to show her that he was not some idiot! He was the Sarafin king! He ruled over some of the fiercest warriors in the known star systems. He was a male that females from numerous different species begged to make love to them. It was about time that Riley realized that. She was his damn mate, his queen. It was time he claimed Ms. Riley St. Claire from Denver, Colorado and showed her he wasn't going to take no for an answer any longer.

Chapter 10

Riley snuggled down into the thick pile of blankets trying to get warm. She could swear ice was beginning to form on the inside of the walls. She understood they needed to have shields and things like that, but none of that would do a damn bit of good to them if they were all dead from hyperthermia. She hated cold weather! That was why she had left Colorado and stayed to the south as much as she could. She should have just gone to live back in San Diego where her Grandma Pearl and Tina lived, but she had wanted to see if she could make it on her own.

Tears pooled in her eyes and overflowed as she thought about what a mess she had made of her already crazy life. Was it too much to ask for just one thing to go right in her life? She pulled the covers over her head and turned her cellphone on. She was going to have to talk to Tor about recharging it and her iPad again. She didn't know how he did it, but she was grateful that he had figured out a way to keep them charged for her. It was the only link she had to her life back on Earth.

She pulled up a video of her sister and Pearl at the bar. She had recorded it on Tina's birthday several months ago. Her Grandma was relating some silly story that happened the weekend before when a bunch of biker wannabes encountered the real thing. They had sat around laughing, drinking beer, and having a good time. Tina and she had been getting along better lately. Riley had a feeling it was because they had confided to each other that they were terrified of ending up being like their mom and Pearl. All either one of them really wanted was to fall in love, have a happy home, a couple of kids, and the mangy mutt that would come along and adopt them.

"Pearl, have you heard from momma lately?" Tina was asking Pearl.

"Now don't you be asking about that wasted piece of fluff," Pearl said gruffly. "She made her decision when she left you girls and decided not to come back."

"But," Tina started to say.

"She's gone, Tina," Riley heard her videotaped voice say. "Let her go."

Riley bit her lip now as she looked at the sadness in her baby sister's eyes. Tina was only two years younger than she but had never given up hope that their mom would one day come home. Riley and Pearl knew that would never happen. Riley had used her contacts at the bail bond company she had been working for to look up information on their mother. She found out their mom had died when she was ten and Tina was eight, of a drug overdose in Los Angeles. Riley had traveled up to the City of Angels to visit the grave. Pearl had their mom cremated and her ashes placed between her great-grandparents.

Riley had confronted Pearl, wanting her to tell Tina, but Pearl had been adamant. "Your momma has caused enough pain and sorrow. Let your sister have her dream for a little longer. She will find out eventually. I'm just not ready for her to find out yet."

Riley had reluctantly agreed simply because it was Tina's twenty-second birthday, and she didn't want her sister to remember finding out their mother was dead on her special day. Tina had always been the more sensitive of the two of them. Riley wasn't really sure who Tina took after, but it was probably her dad. Riley had never found any information on him or her own father. Riley knew she had Pearl's smart mouth while Tina just became quieter when she was confronted. Riley figured she took after her father in size. There was no doubt about that. Tina was petite like Pearl and the pictures they had of their mom when she was a little girl, and had their mom's straight, dark hair.

Tears poured down her cheeks as her iPhone finally cut off. She sniffed and let them come; quiet sobs poured out of her as she thought of her small family back home that she would more than likely never see again. She figured she deserved a good cry every once in a while. No one could blame her for that. She drew in a deep breath when she felt the bed she was lying on suddenly sink down. The covers were pulled free from around her head until she could feel the freezing air on her damp cheeks. She looked up into dark, tawny eyes filled with concern.

"Can I hold you?" the deep voice asked quietly.

Riley's eyes filled with more tears, she bit her lip and nodded slowly. She pulled the pile of blankets back so Vox's huge figure could crawl under them with her. She waited as he pulled his boots and vest off. He tossed them onto a nearby chair before he crawled under the covers with her. She didn't care that she had promised herself that she would stay away from his ornery ass. She didn't care about anything but feeling safe, protected, and warm for a little while. She needed to be held and he was offering. She would have been the biggest fool in every known star system if she turned down a heater better than any electric blanket, not to mention she was just feeling very fragile and lost right now and needed something she could hold onto. She would kick his stubborn butt out after she had a good night's sleep and was feeling better.

Riley curled up as close as she could next to Vox's warm body without actually pulling him on top of her. She let out a deep sigh of contentment as he wrapped his strong arms around her waist, pulling her even closer. Her head rested on his broad shoulder, and she rested her hand over his heart.

Vox held her close. After a few minutes he noticed her breathing had slowed down, and her body had melted against his as she slipped into a deep sleep. A chuckle shook his body slightly. This was the last thing he expected. Why he should be surprised or have expected anything less was beyond him anymore. He had planned to claim his mate. He had expected a fierce fight, followed by some new bruises, before he would wrestle her down and make love to her so much she would have to concede that she was his mate. Instead, he had entered the room she had claimed only to hear her muffled sobs. They had broken through his fierce determination and replaced it with something inside him he had never experienced before—tenderness. When he had drawn the covers back and she looked at him with her big, baby blue eyes shimmering with tears and sadness, his heart had actually hurt. It had melted into a mushy puddle when she gazed up at him with such heartfelt need when he had asked if he could hold her. He bit back a silent groan as he felt her soft, plump flesh melt against his body. Her hand moved up to curl in the hair at the base of his neck just as she rolled over enough to bury her nose contently against his chest, a soft snore escaping her. His body pulsed for a moment before he felt it relax as his own tiredness overwhelmed him. He turned his head so he could rub his cheek against her hair.

It feels so good to hold her, he thought sleepily. *I'm never going to sleep without her against me again.*

Vox gave up on trying to stay awake. He would claim her when they were both well rested. It would be more fun anyway. A smile curved his lips as he realized this was the first time he had been able to hold her without getting hurt. He was making progress after all.

* * *

The violent shudder of the freighter woke Vox before the sound of the alarms did. He paused for just a moment before he jerked into a sitting position and looked around in confusion for a moment. He ran his hand through his hair as he felt the freighter groan again.

"Vox!" Titus's voice boomed out over the communications console. "Get your ass up here! We're under attack by two fucking Marastin Dow pirate ships! The shields are failing."

A soft moan sounded next to him, and a slender, pale arm reached out and grabbed for the covers. "Tell them to come back later, I'm still sleeping," Riley muttered before she rolled over, dragging the covers over her head.

Vox's chuckle turned into a loud laugh as he surged to his feet. His mate was not a morning person. He would have to let the fucking purple pirates know that if he let any of them live. He pulled his boots and vest on before he turned around to his mate who was snoring away under the covers.

"Riley, you have to get up," Vox growled out as he felt another shudder before the sounds of hooks scraping against metal resonated through the freighter. Shit, they were about to be boarded. "Riley, get your ass up now! We are under attack."

Riley jerked into a sitting position, fighting to drag the blankets off her head and push her wild mass of curly hair out of her face. She scowled deeply in irritation at Vox. She grabbed one of the blankets and dragged it around her shoulders.

"Well, you are the stupid warriors! Go kick them off. I am not in the mood to deal with anyone until after ten o'clock in the morning, a good breakfast, and three pots of coffee. You go on, I'll follow in a bit," she said before she started to slide back down under the pile of blankets again. "Besides, it's too damn cold to fight. Tell them the heater is broken."

"Vox, we could really use your help," Adur barked out. "They have breached one of the lower levels that wasn't sealed off."

Vox let loose a long stream of curses. The damn purple bastards were only a level below them. He had to get Riley out of there now! Those bastards always killed anything that wasn't of value. If they saw Riley, they would know she was very valuable. They would kill everyone else to get to her.

Vox leaned over and ripped the pile of covers off Riley, flinging them across the room with a flick of his wrist. His breath slammed out of him, and his eyes widened as he gazed down at where she lay glaring up at him. His throat worked up and down as he fought to get a sound pass the lump in his throat. His eyes glazed as he took in her lush figure in the sheer blue lacy cloth. The front had a deep V that went all the way down to her softly rounded stomach. There were slits on each side that parted, leaving her legs bare and only a narrow length of the fabric lay between her legs. His eyes roamed her full figure, noting the darker rose color of her nipples that poked up, lifting the sheer material and leaving very little hidden from his view. He could see the slightly darker patch of curls between her legs.

It was official. He was an idiot. He was the biggest, stupidest male in all the known star systems. He had fallen into her bed, wrapped her in his arms, and slept like a baby while she was wearing… He swallowed again as she rolled over onto her hands and knees in an effort to get out of the bed. His cat went nuts. Before he even realized it, he was draped over her back molding his groin to her ass and rubbing his pulsing cock against the shadowed line while his hands kneaded her hips. His loud purr rumbled through the room as he rubbed himself back and forth against her.

"What in the hell?" Riley's voice faded as she looked over her shoulder at Vox's glazed eyes. "What do you think you are doing?" she demanded hoarsely as she felt his swollen cock pressing against her.

"Mine!" he purred in a deep, low voice.

The door opened behind them, and Lodar stuck his head into the room. His eyes widened when he saw Riley pinned on her hands and knees with Vox's hands glued to her hips. From where he was standing all he could see was creamy flesh and a hint of sheer blue lace.

"Aw, gods, Riley," Lodar groaned out loud. "You are killing me! Vox, you are going to have to wait. The Marastin Dow have broken through the first door, and they are heading this way."

"Gods! She is gorgeous," Cross murmured in a low voice, peeking over Lodar's shoulder with wide eyes at Riley's lush figure. He could feel his dragon sitting up and taking notice. It was a good thing his symbiot was back on Valdier with the Hive. If the damn thing reacted the way the man and the dragon did, Vox might be in trouble.

Vox jerked back to the fact the alarms were blaring around them and glared at Lodar and Cross. His eyes narrowed when he saw the glazed look on their faces as they stared at the sheer cloth covering Riley's breasts as she turned and sat down again on the bed. He stepped in front of her so he was blocking her.

"Get out!" Vox roared in outrage.

Lodar jerked back, running into Cross, and nodded. He turned to leave but couldn't resist one more peek at Riley sitting on the bed with her hair all disheveled and wearing an outfit he would never forget for the rest of all his lives. He shook his head and hurried out when Vox took another threatening step toward him.

"Vox—" Cross started to say in a deep, husky voice.

"Get out before I kill you both," Vox snarled.

"Just hurry," Cross muttered before he turned and followed Lodar with a shake of his head.

Vox turned and glared at Riley. "Get dressed. We don't have much time. I need to get you somewhere safe."

Riley glared at him and pointed to the door. "You get your happy little ass out of here, and I will. I'm not getting naked with you watching me!"

Vox growled out a warning in a low voice. "This is not the time for modesty. Get dressed now, or I will dress you."

Riley stood up and walked over to where she had laid out her clothes the night before. "Turn around and I will," she said stubbornly, putting her hands on her hips and glaring at him.

Vox swore loudly before he turned so his back was to her. He had to quit looking at her or neither one of them would be dressed in another two seconds. He closed his eyes, but that only made the image of Riley standing proudly in front of him in that damn sheer outfit with her huge, perky breasts pointing daggers at him and her creamy flesh begging for his touch.

Drink milk, his cat purred.

Guall's balls. Vox groaned, forcing his eyes open and his mind to start reciting every damn training procedure he could remember from his youth. *If I don't claim her soon I'm going to explode.*

"I'm ready," Riley's voice sounded breathlessly behind him.

Vox turned to see Riley dressed in a long, heavy dark green skirt, a pair of knee-length black boots, and a thick white sweater. Her hair was still a mass of wild curls that begged for him to twist his hands around the silky strands while he fucked her until he and his cat were totally sated. He watched as she pulled that damn huge bag that she carried everywhere over her shoulder.

"Well, are we being invaded or not?" Riley snapped, annoyed. "I haven't even had a chance to brush my damn teeth. This is really pissing me off," she said running the tip of her tongue along the edges of her smooth, pearly white teeth.

Vox muttered the entire rite of passage ceremony speech each Sarafin warrior was required to say before he finally gave up and decided he needed to get her out of here before he just said to hell with everything and fucked her. He turned with a sharp nod and strode out of the door at the same time as a blast flung the heavy metal door at the far end of the corridor open.

"Run!" Vox snarled as he felt the change coming over him. "Get to the bridge!"

Riley looked at the faces of the purple creatures swarming through the door, turned, and hauled ass for the bridge. She could hear the screams as Vox roared out and charged into the group. Riley decided this was definitely not the way she wanted to be woken up in the mornings. Her heart felt like it was about to explode as she raced through the corridors and up the short ladders until she was on the same level as the bridge. Fred was at the top of the ladder motioning for her to hurry.

"Vox!" Riley cried out as she let Cross reach down and pull her the rest of the way up. "Those purple people eaters are going to get him! Someone has to help him."

"Tor and Lodar are with him. Come up onto the bridge," Banu said gently as he wrapped his arm around Riley and pulled her toward the bridge. "The damn door won't close, so we are going to have to do what we can to keep them out."

"Do you have a gun?" Riley asked, looking with frightened eyes at the other men who were working frantically on a control panel.

"Here, you can hold this one," Banu said, pressing one into her hands. "Don't worry, it is not activated."

"Banu, I don't think giving Riley a laser pistol is a good idea," Fred's left head started to say before his voice faded at the glare she sent him. "Riley, you know you have a tendency to do things…" His right head decided he'd better not finish the sentence when she pointed the pistol at him and glared.

Vox, Tor, and Lodar tumbled through the open doorway, snapping and snarling. Tor and Lodar shifted back into their two-legged form, but Vox remained in his cat form. He had blood splattered all over his coat and along his muzzle. He turned dark eyes on Riley before he shifted.

He strode over to her, gripping her arm and seating her in front of the communications console. "You will sit there and not move! Do you understand?" he snarled.

"But what if—" Riley began, pushing her hair back behind her ear.

"No!" Vox snapped, turning to place his hands on each side of the chair, caging her in.

She was forced to sit back when he leaned forward, menacingly. "You. Will. Not. Move!"

"Well, fine!" she snapped back in frustration. "I wouldn't want to have to save your sorry ass anyway!" She sniffed indignantly.

Vox leaned forward looking deeply into Riley's eyes. "I will not let them take you."

"Vox?" Titus asked as he stepped forward in concern.

"They want Riley. We heard several of the bastards stating she was to be captured unharmed," Tor answered for Vox who was still glaring at Riley.

"They have a buyer for her," Lodar said quietly moving to stand next to the door.

"That will explain why there are two of their damn ships," Adur said coolly. "They don't normally waste two ships on a freighter this old. Someone must have known Riley was on it."

Vox turned his head, finally breaking eye contact with the stubborn female glaring at him. "When I find out who, I am going to kill him."

Riley rolled her eyes and released a loud sigh. "Come on, guys. Get real! Who would want me? I'm about as pleasant as fingernails on a chalkboard."

Bob moved forward and looked over Vox's shoulder. "I would want you, Riley," he said quietly.

Riley looked up, startled, and blushed. A surprised smile curved her lips at her big green friend's words. In truth, it was the nicest thing anyone had ever said to her.

"You are such a sweetheart," Riley replied shyly. "Some Jell-O girl some day is going to be very, very lucky when you come calling."

"I don't believe this!" Vox exploded as a wave of jealousy swept through him. He looked back and forth in frustration between Riley's glowing face and Bob.

"Vox, I think you are going to have to wait to tear Bob apart," Tor said gruffly trying not to laugh at his friend and leader's unfortunate luck where Riley was concerned. "We have more company heading this way."

Chapter 11

Vox gave Riley one more warning glance before he pulled away. He had erupted into uncontrollable fury when he heard the command from the Marastin Dow leading the raiding group to get Riley. His comment that a king's ransom worth of credits was at stake told Vox that they would stop at nothing to get her. The damn purple species lived for murder, mayhem, and credits. The only difference between them and the Antrox was that the Marastin Dow enjoyed killing for the sake of killing. Their young were often encouraged to try to kill each other. Both species' philosophies were definitely survival of the fittest. It was amazing any of them survived long enough to grow into an adult. The adults who did survive were forced to commit to twenty years aboard raiding ships. Life aboard was not much better. If a position came open for advancement it was usually due to someone murdering their commanding officer.

He, Tor, and Lodar had taken out the first ten members of the boarding party before the others fell back to regroup. He knew a larger wave would be involved in the next onslaught. He rolled his shoulders, ignoring the sting from the numerous blasts from the lasers. In his cat form, his fur was very thick. It was almost impossible for a laser pistol to penetrate it.

Laser swords were a different matter. He had received several deep cuts along his side as he sliced through the group that was surging onto the lower level.

"Whatever happens, do not let them get Riley," Vox snarled before he shifted back into his cat form.

Riley scooted back in her seat when the huge cat turned its tawny eyes to her. It trotted over to her, staring at her intently. If she didn't know better she would swear the damn thing was challenging her! The look in its beautiful eyes was one of amusement, desire, and possession.

It's official, Riley thought as she leaned forward, tilting her head to the side as she fell into the shimmering yellow depths. *I've lost the last of my sanity if I think a cat thinks I'm desirable.*

Her pulse jerked as the huge head lowered to rub its muzzle against her leg. She reached out her hand and gently touched the thick fur. She bit her bottom lip to keep the smile from showing when she felt the massive chest rumble with a purr.

Leaning forward, she couldn't help but whisper in its twitching ear. "You are pretty cute for being a big hairball."

The huge cat jerked its head up and shook it back and forth as if denying it was merely "cute." Vox's eyes narrowed dangerously before he let his long sandpaper tongue stretch out and run the length of Riley's cheek, drawing a startled shriek from her. His lips pulled back, showing his long fangs as he reacted to her outrage.

"Vox, here they come," Tor called out, looking down the corridor as Marastin Dow poured from the upper and lower levels.

Bob turned a pale green as he watched what looked like hundreds but was more than likely fifty or more of the beings converge on the bridge. "I will protect Riley with my life," he stammered out.

"Let's give them hell, boys!" Riley said with false bravado as she stood up to look down the corridor at the mass of purple flesh rushing for them. She let out a squeal when Vox moved back over and pushed her back down into her seat forcefully.

"You will not move!" he snapped out.

"Will you quit changing back and forth!" Riley snapped back, startled. "First you are a man, then you are a cat, then you are a man, then you are a cat. Now you are a man again!

Do you have a frigging personality disorder or what?"

Vox opened his mouth to snap back a reply, but he never got a chance before the first group burst through the door. He turned, raising his laser sword, and rushed forward with Banu, Tor, Lodar, Adur, and Titus right beside him. An emergency hatch near the far wall blew upward with enough force the lid sealing it flew through the air, barely missing Fred who had been standing to the right of it. The fact he was so short was probably the only thing that kept him from being killed. Even so, he fell backward. His hands shook as he fired on the purple male coming up through the hole.

"Fred, look out!" Riley cried out as another male popped up behind the one Fred shot.

Riley didn't think twice, she lifted the laser pistol in her hand, flipped the activation button, and shot, hitting the male between the eyes. She stood up to go help Fred when Vox turned with a loud roar. She froze when she saw his face twist in a savage rage.

"Riley! Sit your big ass down in that chair and don't move, or so help me I'm going to smack it," Vox roared out over the noise of battle.

Riley fell back into the chair in shock and disbelief. He had done it again! He had told her she had a big ass. Tears of anger and hurt pooled in her eyes before she settled to burning fury. That was it. His ass was toast as far as she was concerned. He had told her she had a big ass at least three times if not more. She knew her ass was big, but there was no need for him to rub it in her face every chance he got. Not only that, he had said it so everyone, friend and enemy, could hear. So help her, she was going to shoot his hairy alien ass the first chance she got. Let him see what it felt like to be on the wrong side of Ms. Riley St. Claire! She would show him.

Riley turned in her chair and crossed her arms, refusing to watch what happened. She would shoot anyone who came near her, and if the battle ended badly—well, she would figure out what to do then. She stared down at all the glowing lights on the panel in front of her. She started when she saw one suddenly light up. Reaching to push it, her mouth dropped open when a deep, sexy male voice came over the line.

"This is the *Horizon*—do you need assistance?" the deep voice asked as soon as the communications link button was pushed.

Riley glanced behind her at the mayhem of bodies flying through the air. Luckily, it looked like the only ones doing the flying, or falling, appeared to be purple. She shrugged her shoulders and turned back to the console panel. It looked like the guys had things under control, at least for now.

"I'm sorry we can't come to the phone right now, but if you would like to leave your name and number after the beep we'll be happy to return your call as soon as possible. *BEEP*." Riley replied.

Vox's head turned when he heard Riley's husky voice talking to someone on the communications console. With his luck, she was probably having a conversation with the Marastin Dow letting them know that they were vastly outnumbered. His gaze turned to a female Marastin Dow as she slipped past Fred, who was battling two of the damn creatures. He pulled a knife from the chest of one of the dead warriors and threw it, striking the female in the chest.

"Riley, who in the gods are you talking to now? You are just supposed to sit there! You aren't supposed to be touching anything," Vox roared out as he swung his fist and connected with the jaw of another male.

"It's someone called the *Horizon*," Riley replied with a wave of her hand.

"Who in the hell is *Horizon*?" Vox asked as he sliced through the stomach of another male. Guall's balls, how many more were there going to be? They were having trouble moving around the bodies piling up.

"How the bloody hell am I supposed to know who the hell the *Horizon* is? You just ordered me to sit here and not move, damn it!" she yelled back.

"Well, stop pushing buttons! The last time you did that you blew up the asteroid we were on, and we ended up on this piece of dragon dung!" Vox huffed out as he ducked when a blade flew at him.

"Well, if you don't want me pushing the fucking buttons, then don't put me where I can reach them!" Riley said, turning around and glaring at Vox before she stuck her tongue out at him for added measure.

Laughter sounded from the console behind her reminding Riley that she had never cut the transmission. "I repeat, this is…" the deeply amused voice started to say.

"I know who in the fucking hell you are," Riley bit out in frustration. "I heard you the first time. We are just a little busy at the moment, and there's a big pussy pissing me off right now. Will you just leave a frigging message, and I'll have him call you after I declaw his ornery ass?" Riley said before she cursed in rage as Vox sliced through the throat of one of the purple guys who was just a few feet from her. It was so close, blood flew through the air, almost getting on her handbag. "Vox, I swear you need to be neutered! If you get blood on my handbag I'll do it with the first dull knife I can find. Do you have any idea how much I paid for that damn thing?" She had almost forgiven him for ruining her ultra-expensive jacket, but she would never forgive him if he ruined her handbag. She had paid almost three hundred dollars for it just days before she moved to New Mexico.

Perfect, now the big hairball has shifted into his kitty cat again, Riley thought, peeved. She was about to make another derisive comment when she saw a huge purple guy trying to sneak up on Bob through the hatch in the floor. She twirled around to line up a shot, but Bob was in the way.

"Bob! Look out behind you, sweetie. There's another ugly purple guy coming up through the hatch." She turned to see who could help him since that guy appeared to be twice the size of the others. "Fred, be a sweetheart and give Bob a hand." She cursed when she saw that Fred had a deep cut on the brow of his right head. "Lodar, baby, I think Fred might have a little cut on one of his heads. There is blood all down the side of it. When you get a chance, can you look at him?" Riley called out to Lodar who was fighting two others on the far side of the bridge. "Tor, darling, why can't you just zap their asses out into space? I thought you knew how to do things like that," Riley called out, pushing a wave of hair back when it fell into her eyes as she swung back and forth in the chair. She swiveled back around when she heard Lodar's muffled voice. "What did you say, Lodar? I couldn't hear you because a certain hairball was making too much noise when you spoke," Riley replied, ignoring Vox's loud roar at her criticism of him. "Oh yes, dear, I'll tell Fred you'll see him as soon as you finish fighting," she replied before swiveling again so she could locate Fred in all the chaos going on. "Fred, honey, Lodar is busy, but he'll see you as soon as he is done killing the bad guys," Riley called out cheerfully. It looked like there were fewer purple people eaters than there had been just minutes earlier. Her cheerful mood evaporated when Vox sliced his claws across the back of one of the purple bad guys. Blood flew through the air again, this time landing in a splattering along her thick, green skirt. Dark stains appeared, and Riley shuddered in horror. "Vox, damn it, you are totally on my shit list! You got blood on my skirt, you jerk! Go kill someone on the other side of the room. I can shoot the bastards near me! I don't need your help!" she yelled angrily as she reached into her purse to get a Tide pen out to see if she could get rid of the blood before it stained her skirt. It was the only heavy one she had with her. All the others were too thin to wear since the guys didn't believe in turning on a damn heater.

Riley's frown turned to amusement when she heard the laughter from numerous voices coming from the console. She heard the deep voice speaking to someone else on the other end. "I think we have found our missing hairball," the man said between chuckles. "I'm just not sure who he needs rescuing from, the Marastin Dow or the female who is manning the communication console.

"I heard that, honey," Riley replied with an exaggerated Midwestern drawl. "I would place all bets on that bossy, arrogant, demanding…" Vox's loud roar of rage interrupted her descriptive response. She turned and glared at the huge cat that was glaring back at her in fury. "Well, if you don't like what I have to say about you then you can just dump my *big* ass back on my planet!"

Riley refused to back down. She was royally pissed at him, and he was about to find out just how *unpleasant* she could be when she was pissed. She had enough self-esteem problems without him broadcasting to half the solar system that she needed to lose weight. She was happy with the way she was, and he could just shove it up his hairy ass if he thought she was going to let him put her down. She had to deal with that from enough people when she was growing up.

She turned when she heard the voice of a woman on the other end of the console. Her face flushed when she heard the woman introduce herself as Carmen Walker from Wyoming. She clenched her jaw as a wave of emotion swept through her. Tears stung her eyes before she forced them back. Her chance to go home might just be on the other end of this console, and she was going to grab it with both hands. If Vox didn't like her the way she was, well, that was probably for the best. It was better to stop these annoying feelings coursing through her before things went any further, anyway.

Riley was just telling Carmen she hoped she'd had a better time of it than Riley had when Bob's deep melodious voice spoke out in protest. He was asking her if it had really been all bad. Riley released a resigned sigh before explaining to Bob he had been a dear. "…I was referring to that annoying pile of cat…" This time her voice faded because Vox had shifted back into his two-legged shape again and was walking toward her with a look that promised retribution.

"By Guall's balls, Riley, I'm going to spank your ass until it is bloody red if you don't stop giving me a hard time," Vox snarled out impatiently as he thrust the dead body of a Marastin Dow away from him and headed for her.

"Don't you mean my *big* ass, you moron?" Riley replied sarcastically, determined to make him more than willing to toss her ass on the nearest spaceship heading toward Earth.

Her eyes widened when his face darkened and a low, dangerous snarl escaped him. His eyes glittered with determination. Riley could have handled it if the determination written on his face promised he was tired of her smart mouth. Instead, the look smoldered with a deep passion that scared her more than any amount of anger could have.

"Female, I am going to…" Vox's voice faded in disbelief when Riley raised her arm pointing the laser pistol Banu gave her at him. She remembered at the last minute to flick the charge to the lowest setting before she aimed it at his arm and pulled the trigger. Vox's loud curses filled the air. "You shot me!" he roared out in astonishment, freezing and looking at her as if he couldn't believe she had really pulled the trigger. If it wasn't for the burning on his arm, he wouldn't have thought she had it in her.

"But not where I was aiming for," Riley snapped back defensively. "So help me, Vox, you better stay away from me until my temper has cooled or I won't miss where I'm aiming for the next time I shoot you."

"Vox, do you need assistance?" a different male called out from the console.

"Yes! I need you to come and…" Vox growled out, taking another menacing step toward Riley, his mouth set in fierce determination. He was going to whip her ass good for this little stunt! He groaned when she aimed and fired at him again as he took another step toward her, almost grazing him in the leg. "Come on, Riley. I didn't mean anything when I said you had a big ass. I like big asses." He stopped when he saw her standing up and taking aim between his legs with fury glittering from her eyes. Shit, she was really pissed off at him this time. "I…" he started to say before he jumped to the side when she fired again. "…Shit. Will you quit shooting at me!" he yelled out, moving behind a chair before he finally took refuge behind Tor and Lodar who were too busy laughing their asses off to move fast enough to get away from him.

Vox peeked out from behind his chief engineer and his medical officer with a low moan. "I thought you two were my friends," he muttered as he looked at Riley who was busy adjusting the charge on the pistol in her hand.

"We are, otherwise we wouldn't let you hide behind us," Lodar chuckled. "I think this is a fitting payback for the hell we've been going through knowing Riley is your mate. You have no idea the effect she has had on all of us, including Fred and Bob! I need a good fuck so bad I'm about ready to take a Marastin Dow female as a captive."

Vox ducked back behind Tor—who was shaking with laughter—when Riley looked around the room to see where he was hiding. "I would kill you two for that comment if it wasn't for the fact I need you two standing so she doesn't kill me!" he snapped out ruefully.

Tor chuckled again. "Well, you have to admit you can't complain about being bored anymore."

Vox glared at the back of his friend's head wishing he could smack it but knowing if he did that Tor might move and give Riley a clear shot. He opened his mouth to make a smart-assed comment, but the freighter gave a horrendous groan at that moment. The lights flickered on and off before finally staying off. Vox had no trouble seeing in the dim lighting, but he knew Riley would. He made his move, pushing Tor and Lodar out of the way and springing for his aggravating mate. His large hand wrapped around the laser pistol, pulling it to the side where it fired into one of the control panels. Smoke rose and alarms sounded as an automated voice came on announcing that the life support system was in critical failure, immediate evacuation was recommended.

"Oh hell," Riley huffed out, blowing her hair out of her eyes. "Not again! How many frigging things can go wrong in my life?"

"That's all right, Riley," Fred said coming over to where Vox had his arms wrapped tightly around her. "I'll get your pink case for you."

"You might want to let me get it, Fred," Tor said with a deep sigh. "It's heavy."

Riley smiled at the guys, happy that everyone appeared to have survived the attack. "Thank you, guys, for protecting me and everything."

Vox listened as Riley's voice softened when she talked to the other males. His cat hissed angrily, blaming him for the mess they were in. All he wanted to do now was to get back home so he could have Riley in an environment totally controlled by him. He hoped if he was at least on his home turf he could finally quit acting like such an idiot where she was concerned.

"Come get us off this piece of worthless Trillian shit," Vox snarled out to the *Horizon*. "There are ten of us on board. You can kill any number over that," he added as he pulled Riley closer to him.

"A shuttle will be dispatched immediately," the male responded with a chuckle. "It is good to hear your voice, my old friend."

"Yeah, well, your uncle isn't going to like to hear it. That piece of royal Valdier ass is mine! He'll wish he had never messed with this Sarafin prince," Vox bit out harshly as he recognized Creon Reykill's voice.

"Yewww, the big puddy-cat is hissing again," Riley's sarcastic voice grated out. "Watch out—the next thing you know you'll be shooting hairballs," she snapped out in a drawl as she stomped down on his instep and darted away from him when he jumped back with a startled yelp.

"Riley, so help me I'm going to wring your neck when I catch you!" Vox snarled out as he watched her jump over a pile of dead purple bodies as he stomped after her.

"Tor!" Riley called out loudly as she hurried down the corridor after Titus, Adur, Cross, and Banu who were laughing loudly. "Vox is being mean to me again."

"Don't you listen to a thing she says. I am not being mean to her! What did I ever do to deserve a mate like this?" Vox groaned out before the communications link blinked out as the emergency power failed.

Chapter 12

Riley nervously smoothed down the robe over her nightgown as she stared out the viewport at the darkness of space. She had always been a sucker for sexy lingerie. It was the one thing that made her feel all girly and not like an oversized cow in a china shop. She had to admit, she thought she looked good in the stuff. She had a full figure with an hourglass shape. She was big on top and had wide hips which made her waist look small. She shook her head when she remembered what one boy told her when she was fifteen. She had gone to an afterschool dance; it had been the first and last one she ever attended. She had been standing awkwardly to the side, watching as one girl after another got asked to dance. The night was almost over when one of the football players, Todd Patterson, came over and asked her to dance with him. It was a slow song, and she had been thrilled. Sure, she stood a couple inches taller than him, but it wasn't that bad. He had placed his hands on her hips, and they had rocked back and forth for a couple of seconds before he squeezed her, pulling her closer.

"You feel good," he had murmured in her ear.

Riley had felt an excited shiver run down her spine. She wondered if he would kiss her. A part of her hoped that he would. She often listened to the other girls talk about what it was like when one of the boys kissed them. The lights had been dim with the flickering of a disco ball lighting up the area, making it kind of romantic. She could hear other couples talking quietly over the music the band teacher was playing.

"Thanks," Riley had replied shyly. "Uh, you do too," she added nervously.

"You know, with hips like this you were made for having babies," he whispered in her ear. "Do you want to go out back for a little while? I could show you how it's done."

Riley flushed as her Grandma Pearl's warning came back to her. "You've got big boobs and a big ass, Riley girl. Every guy between the ages of twelve and eighty are going to be wanting a piece of you. You need to decide if you are willing to give it away for nothing, and if you do, are you willing to pay the price for giving away your body to someone who only wants to use you."

Riley had pulled back and looked down into the smirking, know-it-all face with a sinking feeling. "What did they bet you to dance with the Amazon?" she asked in a deceptively quiet voice.

Todd had flushed before he glanced over to his friends along the wall. They were watching them and laughing. "Twenty bucks if I get to fuck you. Ten if I get to cop a feel of your big tits."

Riley smiled sadly down at the flushed face. "Thank you for the dance," Riley said, pulling out of his arms. "I won't humiliate you because you were honest about why you asked me. May I give you a bit of advice, though?" she asked as she stared down at his shocked face.

"Uh, sure," he said awkwardly.

"Even Amazons have feelings. Think about that the next time you want to use one of us as a whore. Now, I think your friends need to pay up. It's the least they can do for forcing you to have to dance with me," Riley said as she turned to look at the three football players lounging along the wall. Her eyes glittered with fury.

She had gotten a three-day suspension and told she wouldn't be allowed to attend any more after school functions, but it had been worth it. She had taken the punch bowl and poured it over the three guys who thought it would be fun to pick on the big girl. She had then proceeded to relate a long list of observations about the guys to the entire sophomore through senior class. She never got asked to dance again. Hell, she never even got asked out on a date. She had focused on her school work and started dual enrollment the next year. The unfortunate consequence was Tina was also punished for what Riley had done. Her little sister had been ostracized for simply being related to her.

She started and turned around when the door opened to the living quarters she had been shown to earlier. She bit her lower lip as Vox strode into the room as if he owned the place. They had been rescued earlier in the day from the old freighter and brought aboard the *Horizon*. There were several different alien species on board this ship—warship, Riley corrected herself. There were quite a few that looked like Adur and Cross and a few that looked like Vox, Tor, and Lodar. She hadn't seen any others that looked like Bob or Fred, though. What did surprise her was when she saw two other human males. They had been with two of the same purple creatures that had attacked the freighter, only they didn't appear to find the purple females unattractive.

"What are you doing here?" Riley asked nervously, looking at Vox as he stopped to stare at her intently. "You know it's polite to knock or something before entering someone's room."

Vox's lips curved and his eyebrows rose at the nervous wobble in her voice. "I am here because this is my living quarters, therefore there is no need for me to ask for permission to enter," he said quietly.

Riley could feel her throat moving up and down as she tried to say something smart but nothing came out. Her mind went blank as her eyes focused on Vox's fingers. He was undoing the hooks on the front of his vest. Her eyes followed the movement as he slowly pulled the black leather apart, then slid it off his broad shoulders. Her tongue came out, and she licked her suddenly dry lips as his hands moved down to the front of his pants. She groaned softly when he paused to toe off his boots. Her gaze flickered up to his briefly before moving back down to his fingers. She trembled as he slowly undid each button.

"I need you, Riley," Vox said softly. "My cat and I want you so badly we can taste your sweet cream on our lips."

"You can," Riley replied faintly. "I mean you shouldn't. I can't... I'm... This is a bad idea," she stammered, looking up into Vox's dark tawny eyes.

They were darker than before, the yellow containing more gold than before. "Why can't you? Why would you think this is a bad idea when I can smell your desire every time we are in the same room?" he asked. "I know you want me."

Riley looked up into his eyes again. "You'll just use me, like the other men wanted to. Once you get tired of me, I'll..." Her muttered words faded as he closed the distance between them and pressed his lips against hers in a savage kiss that left them both shaking.

"Does this feel like I'll just use you? I'll never get tired of you, Riley," he said, pulling back until his lips barely touched hers and ran his large hands up over the silky fabric of her robe to her shoulders, drawing her closer.

"I promised myself I wouldn't give in to a man unless he put his ring on my finger and promised me forever," Riley tried desperately to explain. "I don't want to end up raising a baby on my own."

Vox's dark groan filled the air at the thought of Riley rounded with his cubs. A fierce wave of need, stronger than anything he had ever felt before swept through him. He closed his eyes in an effort to regain control of his slipping hunger. If he didn't, he would take her hard, fast, and often. His hands slid back down along her arms, and he gripped them tightly as he tried to breathe deeply. He knew that was a mistake the moment he drew in the heady scent of their combined arousal.

"You will not raise our cubs alone, Riley. I will be there for you always," he growled out in a deep voice.

"Vox?" she choked out as her eyes widened at the dark possession reflected in his.

"You are mine, Riley. I claim you," he purred out in a rough voice as he gripped the silky fabric in his hands and tore it from her body. "I have waited too long for this. My cat and I must mark you, claim you."

"But..." Riley cried out, startled, as the fabric of her robe tore under his hands. "I can't—"

Vox's mouth descended again, blocking her words of protest. His hands caressed all thoughts of resistance out of her mind as they ran up and down her back until he pulled her against his swollen cock. Riley raised her hands shyly up, touching his stomach and feeling the muscles tighten under her fingertips. A shudder ran through him, giving Riley a heady sense of power that her touch could draw such a reaction out of so powerful a man. She opened like a flower to the sun under his skilled lips, moaning as his tongue swept into her mouth. She tentatively returned his caress with her own. Her hands moved up to his chest where she ran her thumbs over his distended nipples as she flicked her tongue along his sharp teeth. She ran the tip along one of his slightly longer canines and was rewarded with a reverberation of a purr.

"Gods, Riley," Vox pulled back and choked out in a strangled voice. "You fire my blood."

* * *

Vox was fighting a losing battle with his control. He wasn't kidding when he said she fired his blood. The feel of her soft, sweet flesh under his hands and the taste of her lips ignited his blood to a raging fury. He could feel his cat pacing back and forth, determined to mark his mate with his essence. Her hands running up over his stomach to his chest tore at him. The soft, sweet hands moved slowly, as if unsure of his response to her tentative touch. How any male could resist her was beyond comprehension. He believed Tor and Lodar when they said it had been killing them. Riley had an innocence about her that brought out the protectiveness in him and his cat, and her natural sensual nature was enough to cause both of them to want to pounce on her. The sway of her hips, the flash of humor in her baby blue eyes, and the way she nibbled at her bottom lip when she was nervous all played havoc on his system.

Vox deepened the kiss, sliding his arm down under her knees so he could pick her up. He silenced her objection with his kisses, holding her tightly against him so she would know there was no more protesting. He would take her. He carried her across to the large bed. Bending, he gently lowered her onto the soft covers, never releasing her lips. He didn't want to give her a chance to change her mind. The way his body and his cat were reacting at this point, he wouldn't have stopped anyway. It may have been wrong, but he knew she was his even if she wasn't sure. There was absolutely no doubt in his mind.

He had talked privately with Creon Reykill. Creon had been very receptive, even amused, and if Vox wasn't mistaken, relieved when he had explained he would not be able to fulfill the requirements of the treaty between his people and the Valdier. Creon had laughed and slapped Vox on his shoulder and told him there was no need to worry, he was positive Zoran would have no problems with the changes. Creon had explained that each of them had taken a human female as a mate and could appreciate the effect the species had on a male. Vox had to admit after he met Creon's mate, Carmen, he was thankful she had come into the young lord's life. He could see the difference in his friend and thanked the Gods for sending the female to help Creon heal.

His fingers trembled slightly as he gripped the thin straps of the gown that Riley was wearing. He pulled them down as he continued running kisses along her swollen lips and down along her neck. He drew in a deep breath as her large, plump breasts brushed seductively against his chest. His cat was in heaven. The only thing that would make it completely happy was when it could mate with the she-cat that was about to be born. He would give a part of himself to his mate, allowing her body to change. His cat couldn't wait to see what its mate would look like. The thought of her silky fur brushing against his male was enough to make him want to bite her and release the chemical regardless whether she was ready or not.

Riley's gasp and loud cry spurred him on as he sucked one of her succulent nipples between his teeth. He nipped it gently, purring as she arched up into him in response, her body flushing in response to his touch.

"Vox," her husky voice panted out. "Oh God!"

He chuckled and sucked deeply, pulling and tugging on the swollen nub until her legs fell apart and she tried to wrap her long legs around his in an effort to draw him down to her. He sighed deeply as he realized there was no saving the delicate fabric of her gown. It didn't matter anyway. After tonight, she would not be wearing any type of clothing to bed again. He wanted to feel her silky flesh against his without a barrier between them. He doubted she even heard or realized he had ripped the thin silk away. She was muttering hoarsely as she unconsciously kneaded her fingers against his shoulder, her nails digging into his flesh as he became more frantic.

"Please!" she wailed. "I need you."

He released her nipple with a loud pop, then pulled away far enough to shuck his pants and kick them away. He knew he would take her hard and fast this first time. He would have loved to be able to take her at a leisurely pace, but he was beyond that. He would take his time when he made love to her again. Vox reached down and gripped Riley's thighs in his large palms, pulling them apart and bringing them up to his waist. Aligning his cock to her slick, heated core he gazed down at her. He shook his head as he realized he was having problems catching his breath. She was magnificent! Lodar was right, her breasts were going to overflow his hands when he cupped them. The rounded globes with the dark roses of her areolae drew a groan of pleasure out of Vox as he rocked his hips forward, sliding his thick cock into her tight vaginal channel. The hot, smooth walls surrounded him, calling to him to claim her in the primal ways of a male. His arms shook as he tried to hold himself still long enough for her to adjust to his hard length.

"Vox?" Riley's frightened gaze turned to him as she felt the sudden fullness invading her body.

She squirmed as he pushed in another inch, his thick cock resting against the barrier she had protected. "You are mine, my beautiful mate," he groaned as he fell forward, burying his face in the curve between her shoulder and neck at the same time he buried his cock all the way to her womb.

He felt her stiffen in surprise at the sudden intrusion. Her cry of pain tore at his soul even as he let his teeth sink into the tender flesh of her neck, releasing the mating chemical that would forever bind her to him. His large hands moved to pin her wrists to the sides by her head when she started to struggle. He pulled his hips back slowly, allowing the feel of his cock to stroke the sweet, sensitive lining of her vagina before he drove it back in. He repeated the movement over and over until her hips were rocking in rhythm with his. He continued sucking her sweet blood into his mouth even as he allowed his cat to release his essence into her blood in return. The exchange was even more erotic than he had read about. Thin threads wove between them, connecting their souls together as one in both two-legged and four-legged forms. The snarling hunger and restlessness of his cat calmed, rubbing and purring as the hunger that ate at him was sated for the first time.

He could taste the difference in her blood as her body accepted the gift from his cat. His body picked up the increased heat coursing through her as the chemicals mixed with her own genetic makeup, shaping and changing her even as he fucked her harder and faster. They both groaned loudly when he finally released her, swiping over the mark on her neck with his rough tongue. He would have to show her just how good his tongue could feel against other parts of her body.

He pulled back far enough so he could look down into her eyes as he took her. Damp paths still glistened near the corner of her eyes where tears had fallen from his possession of her. There was no pain reflected in her eyes now. The beautiful clear blue eyes were glazed with desire and need. Her swollen lips parted as the essence of him and his cat swept through her body in a ferocious wave, taking, molding, and changing her into their perfect mate. Vox rode Riley hard and fast, his need to claim her overwhelming him.

Her shattered cry exploded as her body convulsed around his. Her fingernails dug into his back as she bowed into him, her body milking him as her orgasm held her in its grip. A loud roar ripped from his soul as he felt his cock lock into her and his seed burst from his body in wave after wave of delicious ecstasy unlike anything he had ever felt before. Vox's arms strained as he tried to hold his upper body off Riley so he wouldn't crush her. It was an impossible feat. The power of his orgasm sucked every ounce of strength from his body, leaving him weak as a kitten. His head fell forward until it rested in the curve of her shoulder where he had bitten her just a short time earlier. He rubbed his nose along the vivid mark he had left. He could feel the hot walls of her vagina still pulsing around his cock as he remained locked to her. He gently licked his mark; a deep rumble of contentment coursed through him as he gathered her closer.

* * *

Riley shivered as she felt the rough tongue lapping at her neck. Goose bumps formed as her body reacted to the rough texture. She kept her eyes closed, trying to piece together how on Earth she was going to handle this new development.

Earth! She groaned silently. *How could I forget he was an alien and it never, ever works out good for girls like me,* she thought in despair.

Everything had turned hazy after he started kissing her. She would have liked to have blamed it on a momentary lapse of consciousness, some alien pheromone, or even insanity, but she knew it had been something else entirely different. He had, without question, knocked her upside down and inside out with just his touch. Her eyes popped open, and her breath escaped her in a sudden panic. She wasn't on birth control thanks to there being no pharmacies available, and he hadn't worn a condom. Just the thought of being knocked up scared all the desire right out of her. Riley began to struggle, pushing against Vox's shoulders to get him to move.

"Get off me, you big oaf!" Riley snapped out in panic.

Vox rolled off Riley but kept his arms wrapped tightly around her. A satisfied smile curved his lips as he realized he was still locked to her. It would take several more minutes before he could safely pull out of her. He was already thinking of how he was going to take her next. His gaze slid down to her huge breasts as she pushed up against his chest. He released her hips and cupped both globes in his hands, curious to see if they really would overflow them. Hot desire burst through him causing his cock to swell again when they did. He growled softly when he felt Riley trying to lift off him.

"Do not move yet," he hissed out in a deep voice. "I am still locked to your womb. I do not want to hurt you."

Riley froze above him, looking down at him in horror. "What do you mean you are locked to my womb? You need to get out," she said in panic.

Vox looked up at her, startled. "I cannot pull out of you until my seed and my cat have finished."

"What do you mean your seed and your cat?" she asked, licking her swollen lips. "I really need you to let me go."

Vox sighed in regret as he released her breasts so he could cup her face gently instead. "The tip of my cock swells, locking me to you. This is to make sure that as much of my seed as possible is released into your womb, increasing the chance of cubs. Since this is our first mating, my cat is also releasing our essence into you," he explained tenderly.

Riley began to tremble as the sinking feeling in the pit of her stomach began to grow. "What in the hell are you talking about?" she demanded hoarsely.

Vox grinned in triumph as he felt his cat stretching and rolling over inside him. The mating was complete. Riley had been marked on the inside and the outside. She was bound to him forever. There was no going back and no way she could escape him now. She belonged to him.

"You have been claimed!" Vox declared with a satisfied grin. "My cat and I have released our essence into you. Soon, you will be able to mate with both me and my cat. You are also close to your heat. When you go into it, we will both fuck you every which way we can and as often as we can. We can't wait to see you rounded with our cubs," he growled out again before reaching up and hungrily latching onto her breasts.

Riley jerked as a combination of pleasure and pain exploded through her. Her body heated up, fire coursing through her from where Vox was feasting all the way down to where they were still melded together. Moisture pooled, making her slicker than before. She felt Vox's cock swell again as he began the incredible rhythm that had shattered her before. Her mind blanked as pleasure seared her from head to toe. Her fingers kneaded his shoulders where she still held herself up, giving him access to her aching breasts. She whimpered as he drove into her over and over until she couldn't hold back any longer. Throwing her head back as another climax shattered her body and soul, she cried out his name over and over as he devoured her.

Chapter 13

Riley whimpered as she stepped into the hot shower. Vox had been insatiable last night. For a girl who had held onto her virginity like it was the Olympic torch, she really knew how to drop the damn thing at the worst possible time. There hadn't been one damn word in any of the magazine articles that she had read that said a guy could keep it up as much as Vox did. Once was the average, twice if they were lucky, three if they were fucking Hercules—but Vox had taken her at least that many times in an hour! Not only that, he had done it every hour on the hour until she had finally passed out in exhaustion. Now, she was so sore it hurt to think, much less move. She blushed as she ran the soap over her tender breasts and down between her legs. She was going to either have to neuter his ass or drug it because she really didn't think she could survive another night like last night. Not that she planned on there being another one.

He had thankfully been called to a meeting with the new guys she had met when they were brought aboard. Creon Something or other and Ha'ven the Dark. That was about as much as her brain could remember. She did remember the blond-haired human female she had been introduced to, Carmen. Riley felt like crying when she saw the other woman. She didn't know if it was because there was a chance the woman could help her get back home or because it meant she really might have a way of escaping the big lummox that had her so totally messed up in the head.

Riley let her head fall forward as she thought about what had happened. "I am so totally screwed," she whispered out loud. "I have to get away from him before I become a total schmuck. A dead schmuck at that, Riley girl. Remember, you are just the supporting character. They always get killed before the end of the movie."

She turned off the shower unit and stepped out. A blast of hot air circled her, drying the moisture from her skin and hair. She looked in the mirror, staring at her huge blue eyes for a moment before her gaze narrowed on the symbol of a leopard's paw on her neck.

"There's nothing you can do about what has already happened, but you can prevent it from happening again. It was only one night, Riley girl. Make sure you keep it to that. He wasn't wearing a condom and you aren't on birth control, but he *is* an alien so that has to count as a natural contraceptive. His DNA and mine are totally incompatible. Just think positive. Don't think about what happens to the poor schmucks in the movies. The aliens did all kinds of weird shit in them before they could get the girl pregnant. He didn't do anything except bite you...and...lock his you-know-what inside you...and said some weird shit about essence and claiming and heat..." Her voice faded as she began to shake. "I am so totally screwed!" she whispered again as tears formed in her eyes.

* * *

Several hours later, Riley felt like she had her life back under control as she sat down at a table in the dining quarters. She had scrubbed at the mark on her neck repeatedly, trying to get it off but nothing she did worked. So she did the next best thing, she pulled out her makeup bag and hid it. Then, she put on a soft pink angora turtleneck sweater and matched it with a flowing white skirt. She decided a pair of silver slip-ons would be better than wearing her boots. Fluffing her hair once more time, she decided she was ready to at least face someone other than herself. Taking a deep breath, she left her soon-to-be former living quarters and set out to complete the second part of her plan. She needed support—female reinforcement—so she hunted down Carmen. It turned out fate was finally working in her favor as Carmen was heading down to see her.

Carmen had taken one look at Riley and tugged her down to the dining quarters. Riley hoped that didn't mean she looked as bad as she felt. Heat flooded Riley as she sat down gingerly in the seat. She glanced at Carmen to see if she noticed that she had slid into the seat a little more carefully than was normal. Riley released a relieved sigh when Carmen didn't appear to notice anything amiss.

"Would you like something to eat and drink?" Carmen asked as Riley settled into the seat across from where she was standing.

Riley pushed her heavy mass of curls behind her ear and fought the urge to fan herself as the furnace inside her increased another couple of degrees. "Ice water and something light, no seafood," Riley said with a forced smile.

"They actually have a pretty good replicator. How about a ham and cheese sandwich and chips?" Carmen asked.

"That sounds wonderful," Riley replied as her stomach gave a loud growl.

Carmen laughed as she turned away. Riley watched Carmen walk over to the other side of the room where the replicators were located. She glanced around noticing with relief that there was hardly anyone else in the room. The warship was a lot different from anything else she had been on to date. Between the trader's small ship, the asteroid, and the old freighter, Riley had been anything but impressed with the idea of space travel slash alien worlds. This ship could make her change her mind, though. Everything on the inside gleamed. There were over a dozen silver round tables with matching swivel chairs bolted to the floor. The flooring was a polished black offset by the white walls. On the far wall were a series of replicators inset into the wall. In the far left corner was an opening where dirty dishes disappeared into a cleansing unit. Riley sighed and rested her chin on her palm. She wondered if she could fit one of the replicators in her suitcase. She would love to never have to cook again. That was another thing that she didn't excel at. She loved to eat—out. Her cooking skills were basic at best.

There were probably only about a dozen men in the room. Riley was surprised that there weren't any women. She would have thought, with all the *Star Trek* episodes she had seen, that the crew would have been about half and half. She was so deep in thought that she didn't even notice the shadow that fell over her until the sound of a clearing throat drew her attention from her thoughts.

Riley turned and smiled up at the handsome young man staring down at her. She sat up straighter, raising an eyebrow in amusement as she observed that he was focused on her curly mane of hair. She reached up and twirled a few of the strands around her finger before she said anything to the silent figure standing over her.

"Yes, I am a natural blonde," she drawled out in her best Midwestern accent. "But don't try any of the blonde jokes if you want to live," she added with a dimpled smile.

"Can I touch it?" the man asked hesitantly.

Riley chuckled as she held out her slender hand. "I think we should at least introduce ourselves before you start feeling me up," she replied with a grin. "My name is Riley St. Claire, and I'm from the mile-high city of Denver, Colorado."

"I am called Mondu," he replied. "I am from the Curizan star system. You are the female from the freighter, the one with five mates?"

Riley blushed and looked over at Carmen who was talking to another male. Riley frowned when she realized he looked like the same guy who had been shadowing Carmen last night when they first came on board, but there was something different about him. Whatever Carmen was saying to the guy, he didn't look like he was very happy about it.

She looked back at the male who had slid into the seat next to her. She leaned back a little in surprise when he moved into her personal space. She opened her mouth to respond to him, but the words died as he wound his fingers in her hair, pulling it closer to his face.

"It was the only way to prevent them from being someone's dinner," Riley said with a slight squeak in her voice. "I mean, it wasn't real or anything. Besides, those stickmen really pissed me off. It was worth saying I'd take the guys just to see the expression on their faces."

Mondu smiled down at Riley. He was enjoying watching her nervousness. He had been captivated by her the moment he walked into the room. Some of the other men had been talking about the beautiful female with the white hair. He wanted to see if she was anything like Lord Creon's mate. Few things surprised him, but this female had definitely done that. He was expecting her to be slender like Lady Carmen, but this female—this female had curves that a male could hold onto. If she was not truly mated to any of the males then he would make his move.

"So you are not mated to any of them?" Mondu asked with a satisfied curve to his lips.

Riley nervously pulled her hair away from him and scooted over as far as she could without falling out of her seat. What was it with these guys? Sure she got the occasional stare or comment back home but these guys were like in your face, here I am—not the nice wolf whistle she could shoot a bird at.

"No, I'm not mated to any of them," Riley said in exasperation, waving her hand at him. "Listen, do you mind—like—sitting back. You are crowding me, and I don't like it when people get in my space and all."

Mondu chuckled but leaned back in his seat. "What do you like?"

Riley looked over to where Carmen was picking up a tray full of food. "I like food that I don't have to cook, warm beaches, good movies, and"—she paused to look at Mondu with a dimpled grin—"shopping for great deals."

Mondu's chuckle turned to a laugh as he picked up one of her waving hands. "What do you not like?"

Riley tilted her head as she tugged unsuccessfully to remove her hand from his grasp. "Spending my own money, liars, murders, and cheats, but most of all," she said with a pointed look in her eyes, "pushy men who don't know their places."

"Like me?" Mondu asked with a lazy grin, while he caressed the back of her hand with his thumb.

"Like you, if you don't let go of my hand," Riley replied with another tug.

"What if I don't want to let it go?" he asked, raising it to his lips.

"Then you die." A dark snarl sounded behind him.

Riley looked up startled to stare at Vox's dark face. Dark wasn't the word for it. Truthfully, she didn't know a face could be that frightening. Mondu slowly released her hand and stood, turning to face the furious ruler of the Sarafin. He appeared to be relaxed, but Riley could tell from his stance that he had moved into a defensive pose. Vox must have realized it as well because a menacing growl escaped from him as he focused his narrowed eyes on the huge male standing between him and Riley.

"Move away from my mate, or I will kill you," Vox demanded, flexing his fingers.

"The female says she has no mate," Mondu replied calmly.

Vox's eyes narrowed, and he took another step closer. "I have claimed her. She wears my mark."

Mondu glanced over his shoulder at Riley, who was looking back and forth between the two of them with huge, bright, wary eyes. "Show me his mark," he said.

"What?" Riley asked, puzzled.

Vox glared down at Riley. "Show him my mark before I kill him, Riley."

Riley stood up and glared at Vox. "Which one? You frigging left bruises all over me, you big ape! I am not in the mood to deal with your mangy ass right now, especially if you think you can talk to me in that tone of voice after what you did to me."

"What did he do?" Carmen demanded, dropping the tray on the table with a loud bang. "Did he hurt you?"

Riley's eyes brightened with furious tears. She was so not having this conversation with everyone staring at her. This was worse than the high school dance because this time she had been the idiot who said "yes" to going behind the building instead of remembering her dear Grandma Pearl's words of wisdom. She angrily brushed a tear that escaped down her cheek, turned on her heel without another word, and strode out of the dining quarters.

Vox took a step to follow, but Carmen stepped in his way. "I don't know what you did to her, but you need to step back now before I put you on your ass," she hissed out in a cold voice.

Vox looked down in surprise at Creon's mate. Her eyes glittered with a deadly promise of retribution if he should try to move around her. "She is my mate," he explained quietly. "I will see to her needs."

Carmen shook her head. "Right now what she needs is a little breathing room." She looked over his shoulder at Calo, who was glaring at her. "You guys don't realize we Earth girls aren't used to all this claiming bullshit. It can be a little overwhelming. Just back off for a little while and give her time to collect herself. She would not appreciate you breathing down her neck right now."

Vox swore darkly under his breath. He nodded briefly to Carmen before looking at Mondu. He would only tell the Curizan male once more that Riley was his. If he saw the male near her again, he would kill him.

"Stay away from my mate," Vox growled out in a low, cold voice. "Let the others know she has been claimed and that I will kill any who touch her."

Mondu studied Vox for several seconds before bowing his head in respect. "Your claim will not be challenged by me, my lord."

Vox turned back to Carmen with a frown. "You will go to her?"

Carmen raised an eyebrow and stared at the huge male in front of her. Nodding her head, she couldn't resist making a jab at Calo. Creon had assigned the twin brothers to be her shadow despite all her protests. Calo was on duty today. She had a feeling Riley might be able to help her figure out a few phrases she had missed calling them. If nothing else, it would give her something else to think about.

"Yeah, me and Fido will make sure she is okay," Carmen said before grabbing the tray she had dropped. "Come on, boy. That's a good boy, come on."

"One of these days, Carmen…" Calo muttered darkly as he followed her out of the dining quarters. "One of these days…"

Vox listened as Carmen laughed at the huge male following her. He shook his head in wonder that such a small, delicate creature could be such a big pain in the ass. He couldn't help but marvel what his family was going to think of his mate. Or what his mate was going to think of his family.

"Do you think there might be more of them?" Mondu asked, coming to stand next to Vox.

Vox gave a dry chuckle. "Gods, I hope not. I'm having a hard enough time with the one I've got. I can't imagine what would happen to our worlds if there were more of them."

..*

Riley stared out the viewport without really seeing anything. Her mind and her body kept drifting to a certain irritating fur ball that had gotten not only under her skin but into her heart. Every movement of her body reminded her of his touch. She had to admit it had been an incredible night, but it would have to be the only incredible night. She couldn't take a chance of letting herself fall any further.

"Are you all right?" Carmen's soft voice asked as she entered the small conference room she had been directed to thanks to Calo's inquiries.

Riley wiped at her face to make sure her cheeks were dry and quickly put on her I-don't-give-a-damn mask. She had learned a long, long time ago how to perfect hiding her feelings. No one cared anyway. Even her Grandma Pearl said feelings were for drunks, weak men, and wimps. None of those were allowed in their house when she was growing up.

Riley turned with a grimace and a shrug. "Yeah, hate it when I'm PMSing."

Carmen set the tray down on the table near the viewport and sat down. "We never did get a chance to eat. I don't know about you, but I'm starving."

Riley gave a short laugh and nodded. "Me too. So, how did you end up in the *Twilight Zone?*"

Carmen looked around and shook her head in amazement. "My sister and my best friend were piloting a client of the Boswell's back to California along with another friend who was a mechanic for the company. I hitched a ride. The client, Abby, was kidnapped by the local sheriff who had the hots for her. Trisha, Cara, my sister Ariel, and I took off after them with the hopes of rescuing Abby. Turns out her boyfriend was not only hot but out-of-this-world hot," Carmen explained with a grin. "I don't remember much. I had been stabbed a couple of times and was pretty much dead by the time Zoran and his brothers got there. They transported me and the others up to their ship after toasting the bad guy. I woke up, and the rest is history," she muttered before taking a big bite of her sandwich. "What about you?"

Riley picked at her sandwich, not really sure she was hungry anymore. "I found out my boss and his daddy were running drugs and guns among other things. When my boss made a pass at me, I clobbered him," she smirked at Carmen.

"He probably will never be able to give himself a hand job or have kids. Anyway, I had found out they also had a dead guy buried under the shed out back. I decided it was in my best interest to get out of town before I ended up joining him. Needless to say, my car broke down, I got in a truck with a major asshole, and the lights did *not* belong to the dwarf biker gang as I had hoped."

Carmen choked at Riley's vague explanation of events. "So, how did you end up with five mates?" She sighed heavily when Riley lifted her eyebrow at her. "I promised Creon I'd find out."

Riley chuckled. "You lose?"

Carmen nodded. "I never should have taught him how to play poker," she said before a rosy blush swept up her cheeks.

Riley sighed before she looked up at Carmen. "Will you help me get back home?" she asked nervously.

Carmen stared into Riley's eyes for several minutes before she nodded. "If that is what you want, I will do my best to see that you get back home."

Riley looked away as tears burned her eyes again. She didn't know what was wrong with her. Between the sudden hot flashes and the emotional roller coasters she was about ready to go postal on someone's ass. She was too damn young for menopause.

"I have family back home," Riley said clearing her throat. "I have a grandmother and a baby sister. Not much, but it is all I have. Plus, I need to stop Dudley Dipshit and Daddy Dumbest from killing anyone else. I took the files and photos that would put them away, but it doesn't do a damn bit of good up here."

"I'll talk to Creon and see what I can do. By the way, I love your descriptions. You wouldn't have a few you could share on a couple of Bobbsey twins that have been practically parked up my ass, do you?" Carmen asked humorously.

Riley's eyes glittered. "Darling, you are talking to the Queen of Mean. The mouth from Denver. The Bitch Extraordinaire. Give me a little background, and we can make them beg for a transfer."

Chapter 14

The next several days passed in relative quiet, at least after the first night. She had talked Carmen into helping her find a temporary place to stay until she could sort out her feelings and deal with what had happened. Vox had not handled the new sleeping arrangements very well. He had left deep gouges on the outside of the door when she refused to open it. According to Carmen, he had gone ballistic when he returned to their living quarters and found her things gone. He had roared, hissed, and snarled for over an hour before he realized that she was not coming out and he was not going to be allowed in. Riley shivered as she thought about his parting words. He had vowed that when he got his hands on her, she would never get away from him again.

Lucky for her, she had a few hidden resources he wasn't aware of, namely a couple of guys who were having way too much fun at his expense. Thanks to them, she had gotten really, really good at hiding from him. If she didn't know better, she would think they were enjoying his discomfort. The first clue she had was when Creon's face lit up with a huge grin as he showed her to her new living quarters, then proceeded to show her a half dozen times how to override the system so she could seal it from the inside. The second clue was when Ha'ven had come trotting up to her early the next morning with a cool little device that showed Vox's exact position at all times on board the *Horizon*. He had even shown her how to switch to a map that would display ways to get away from Vox should he get too close. She had eyed the two men with a cynical look, but all they did was grin and slap each other on the back a lot. She had even approached Carmen about it, but all her new friend did was roll her eyes and mutter something about little boys and payback.

She spent most of the day with Carmen or exploring the ship. Her favorite time was when she and Carmen went to visit with Mel and Cal, two other humans on board. They had been abducted in much the same way as she had been and sold to the Antrox as well. The biggest difference was Mel turned out to be Melina. Riley just shook her head in disbelief that no one else appeared to see through the oversized clothes and the grandson references. One look at the way Melina walked and the soft sound of her giggle was enough for Riley to figure it out.

She had been relaxing with Carmen and Cal when she put two and two together. She finally answered Carmen's question as to how she had ended up with five mates instead of the one. That was when Melina had given herself away.

"So, who is the scarecrow?" Riley asked Cal.

"Scarecrow?" Cal repeated confused.

Riley jerked her head toward the cargo crates where Melina spent her time hiding whenever anyone came into the repair bay. "Yeah, little miss Priss. Does she think I have cooties or something?"

Carmen's soft gasp told Riley she had let the cat out of the bag. "Granddaughter," Carmen murmured. "That is why she stays hidden and doesn't talk."

Cal had called out to Melina to join them and slowly explained why they had decided to continue the ruse. Cal mentioned that Creon promised that he would return them to Earth with the understanding that they could never tell anyone about what happen to them. Riley's brain froze on those softly spoken words. Cal and Melina were going to be returned to Earth, so that meant she would be going as well.

Riley listened absent-mindedly to the conversation going on around her. A part of her was interested as Cal relayed story after story of the past four years of their lives on the mining asteroid, but it was only a small part. She was overwhelmed with sorrow at the thought of never seeing Vox again. Sure she had been avoiding the big pussy cat, but she always knew where he was thanks to Ha'ven's neat little device. She casually slid it out of the pocket of her skirt and glanced down at the mark showing Vox was back in their living quarters.

His, Riley reminded herself. *His living quarters*, she thought sadly as she watched the tiny speck on the screen. *I wonder if he misses me as much as I miss him.*

She was just sliding the device back into her pocket when the door to the repair bay opened and the other twin who protected Carmen walked in. Melina jumped to her feet and scurried back between the crates before he had taken more than a few steps inside. Riley's eyebrow rose in wonder as she saw the dark hunger and confusion in the male's eyes before he shielded them.

Somebody is not happy, Riley thought with a curve of her lips. *And somebody doesn't realize that Mel is really Melina if the confused look is any indication of his feelings.*

Life, it would appear, was about to get very interesting for Melina if Riley had to make a guess. She had seen the same expressions on the other twin's face. She wondered how long it would take before they figured out Mel was a girl. She also wondered if they would discover it before Cal and Melina made it back to Earth.

"My lady, your mate wishes to see you," Cree said in a low voice to Carmen before he cleared his throat and looked carefully at Riley. "Your mate as well, Lady Riley. Lord Vox said, quote, 'Tell her to get her beautiful ass to our living quarters now.'"

Riley snorted and tossed her heavy mane of blond hair over her shoulder. If he thought trying to be sweet while still bossing her around was going to work, he had another think coming. It didn't matter anyway. Now that she knew for sure they were heading back to Earth, she would do whatever she had to resist. Deep down, she admitted that if Vox ever got his hands on her again, she might not let him take them off.

She shivered as another wave of heat started flaring inside her. She was already wearing lighter clothing. Ever since Vox had made love to her she had been having blasted hot flashes. They were getting worse, especially at night. Not only that, she felt like there was something weird going on with her skin. She could swear something was moving underneath it. It was really beginning to freak her out. If it didn't stop soon, she might have to ask Carmen for help again.

No, Riley thought dismally. *I need to stick with my plan. Staying away from him is definitely still the best for everyone, especially me.*

Her mind might rebel against the idea, her body might protest it vehemently, but it was the safest plan for a supporting character like her. That was one reason why she had made herself watch all the science fiction movies she had on her iPad again. She was not about to take a chance of having anything exploding out of her or morphing her into some disgusting creature that ate people.

Riley drew in a deep breath before she responded to Cree with a determination born out of desperation. "Tell him, quote, 'My beautiful ass is quite comfortable where it is, and he can shove his…'" Riley almost broke off when Cree made a choking sound during one of her really descriptive-filled sentences. She finally took pity on him when she realized there was no way he could remember everything she said anyway. "Oh, never mind. Tell him I'll be there when I'm damn well ready," she muttered instead, in resignation.

* * *

Vox ran his hands through his hair and groaned as he bent over. The pain he was feeling was not just mental anymore but had manifested in the physical as well. His cat needed his mate as much as he needed his. The fact they were one and the same didn't matter. His cat was clawing at his insides until he felt raw. The one night that he had with Riley would never be enough. He couldn't sleep, couldn't eat; he could barely function. He knew Creon and Ha'ven were having fun at his expense. He would have done the same thing to them if given half a chance. The problem is they didn't understand how devastating it was for a Sarafin male to be separated from his mate, especially during the transformation. Riley would have begun feeling the changes almost from the very first. The problem was that the symptoms she was experiencing would gradually get worse. It could become dangerous to them both if he was not there to support her.

Go get mate, his cat roared furiously, slashing at him again. *You should have kept her with you.*

Vox grimaced at the fury in his cat. *How in Guall's balls was I to know she would get a hair up her butt and hide from us?*

Need mate. Can feel her, his cat hissed back, pacing inside him.

Gods, he probably should have told her about the transformation. In all honesty, he hadn't thought about it since he didn't think it was going to be an issue. Now, he wasn't so sure that had been a good thing to keep from her. With his luck, she would finish shredding him to pieces once she found out what he had done.

That's what you get for thinking, his cat angrily snarled back.

Will you just go lie down? Vox snapped back. *And for the sake of all the gods, quit using my insides as a scratching post! It is not helping me.*

Vox breathed a sigh of relief when his cat finally settled down in a sullen heap inside him. He tiredly ran his hands over his face. He straightened up when the door sounded to let him know someone was there. His heart jumped for a moment, wondering hopefully if maybe Riley had finally come to her senses and returned to him before he remembered that this was *Riley.* She never did anything that he expected—or wanted, for that matter. He gave the command for the door to open and let out his breath when he saw Cree standing outside of it alone.

"She's not coming, is she?" Vox said more than asked.

Cree's lips turned up in a slight tilt at the corners before he replied. "No, my lord. I have to admit I've never heard so many colorful and descriptive ways for body parts to be placed. She said to inform you she will join you when she feels like it. I would not expect her anytime soon."

"Thank you, Cree," Vox said wearily. "I would just like to know how in the gods she is able to avoid me."

Cree's eyes lit up with amusement. "I couldn't say, my lord. Though I believe the tiny device she carries around that Lord Ha'ven gave her might have something to do with that," he offered.

Vox's eyes narrowed. "Thank you again, my friend. If you ever get tired of hanging with the Valdier, you could always come to Sarafin. Who knows, you might find your mate among our females."

Cree's face smoothed into a blank mask, but Vox saw the slight tightening around his mouth before he replied, "I appreciate the offer, my lord. I may take it under consideration."

Cree nodded to Vox before he turned and strode down the corridor. Vox stood at the door, watching. So, Creon and Ha'ven were behind Riley's successful escape. He needed to find out what Ha'ven gave her. That damn Curizan was a wizard when it came to creating useful and annoying devices. It was about time he took some of his aggravation out on a couple of royal pains in the asses.

"Computer, what is the location of Ha'ven and Creon?" Vox called out.

"Lords Ha'ven and Creon are currently in the training area," the automated voice replied.

"Perfect." Vox grinned as he headed out the door.

* * *

An hour later, all three men sat on the padding covering the floor. They were drenched in sweat and a small amount of blood. Creon lay back, staring up at the ceiling, drawing in deep breaths while Ha'ven checked out a new wound he had on the back of his arm. Vox sat with his arms draped over his knees, panting.

"That was interesting," Ha'ven said dryly. "Could you keep the claws in next time, Vox? This stings like a Sargum's piss."

Vox looked up with a nasty grin. "You help Riley again and it won't be your arm that feels my claws."

Creon chuckled from where he lay on the mat, exhausted. "So that was why you felt the need to kick our asses. I haven't had to fight so hard since the wars."

Vox glared at Creon. "Don't think I didn't figure out that you were the one to help my mate relocate," Vox grunted out. "You two owe me. You have to help me capture her."

"What the hell fun is that?" Ha'ven grumbled.

"I need her," Vox replied quietly. "She will be going through the transformation."

Creon sat up and stared at Vox. "I thought all your females could already transform into cats."

Vox looked at Creon before he turned his gaze down to the floor in front of him. "Sarafin females, yes. As you know, Riley is human. If a female is of a different species and is our mate, a warrior and his cat can share his essence, giving a part of himself to her." He looked up at his two friends who were now focused on what he was saying. "This leaves us vulnerable. Because we have given a part of who we are away, we must be near them, or we suffer great distress."

Creon stared intently at his huge, spotted friend. "Define distress."

Vox grimaced as a wave of pain swept through him. "It is much like you and your dragon," he said. "We feel intense pain, need, and anxiety. Riley will have already begun the transformation. I did not tell her about it. I was afraid if I did she would not be very happy," he grinned briefly. "Riley can be very difficult when she is not happy."

Ha'ven threaded his fingers through his hair and looked at his friend in sympathy. "Gods, Vox, if I had known it would be this difficult for you I would never have given her that damn locator. I was just playing around."

"I know. That is why I didn't beat your ass into the ground," Vox replied. "But, I will if you ever help her to get away from me again. You know, she is pretty good at that on her own. She put me on the ground twice already."

"If you tell us how she did it, we'll help you catch her," Creon laughed. "I would pay good credits to hear how she was able to put the mighty king of the Sarafin down on the ground. You know, she is not the most coordinated female I have ever met."

* * *

Carmen came to see Riley later that evening. She explained Vox's warship, the *Shifter*, had arrived. If anything, that made Riley want to stay locked in the living quarters even more. All she wanted to do was sit and cry. In fact, that was all she had been wanting to do since she moved into the stupid room. She had thought being away from Vox would have helped her put things in perspective. She was human and returning to Earth; he was an alien and would go off and kill other aliens. Instead, she was suffering from PMS, menopause, and newly discovered sexual frustration on top of feeling like she was about ready to pop out of her own skin when anything brushed against her. Hell, even her clothes were driving her crazy. This morning when she had gotten dressed she had actually hissed when she put on her bra! Who the hell hissed about a bra?

"Are you okay?" Carmen asked as she took in Riley's flushed face. "You look like you might be running a fever."

Riley's eyes teared up. "Ever since Vox made love to me I've felt funny. I don't know what is going on. I'm having hot flashes, my skin is so sensitive I want to scream, and it...it..." Her voice hiccuped as she tried to talk over the lump in her throat. "I feel like something is crawling around inside me," she wailed.

Carmen's eyes grew round as she listened to Riley's choked explanation. Her mouth tightened as she remembered Creon forgetting to tell her about a vital piece of information when he had claimed her. She suspected what Riley was going through was very similar. Carmen put her arm around Riley and guided her over to a chair. Pushing her friend down, she sat across from her.

"I didn't understand what it would mean when Creon claimed me," Carmen began. "I don't know what it is like for the Sarafin species. I can only tell you what happened to me. When a Valdier warrior and his dragon claim a female they release something known as the dragon's fire into the female. It changes her. I didn't understand at first. It felt like there was something moving under my skin." Carmen smiled in understanding when Riley brushed her damp cheeks and nodded. "Then, I heard another voice inside me. It turned out to be my dragon. I suddenly remembered seeing scales rippling across my skin when Creon and I were making love. When I heard the voice, everything fell into place. Creon had changed me somehow. I was now able to transform into a dragon as well. I was his true mate," Carmen said before she looked over to stare out into the darkness of space. "It is still unbelievable to me how much my life has changed." Carmen looked back at Riley with sad eyes. "I was waiting to die. My only focus was to return to Earth to do it."

"Do you still want to go back?" Riley asked, sensing there was a lot to Carmen that she didn't know.

"A part of me does," Carmen admitted softly. "I need closure for my life before. My husband…" Carmen paused and took a deep breath, laying one of her hands across her stomach. "My husband was murdered in front of me. I was pregnant and had been shot several times. I lost them both. I wanted—needed—to kill the man responsible. I knew that I would die as well." Carmen looked at Riley with a haunted expression in her eyes. "I wanted to die before. Now I have Creon, and I'm expecting again. I have a chance at starting over."

"What about your family? Do you have anyone else back on Earth who will miss you?" Riley asked, pushing her own fears and problems aside as she felt the depth of pain in Carmen's words.

Carmen shook her head. "No. Well, except for Trisha's dad. My sister is mated to Creon's older brother. She is all the family I have left."

Riley bit her lip and looked warily at Carmen. "Do you think that Vox did something to me? I know they can turn into a big pussy cat, but surely that doesn't mean he did anything to make me turn into one."

Carmen chuckled reluctantly as she looked at Riley's pensive expression. "Truthfully, I don't know. Vox, Titus, and Banu are the first Sarafin warriors I've ever met. It is just the things you are saying you are feeling sound an awful lot like some of the things I was feeling before I turned into a dragon for the first time."

"Great! So what happens when I get home and turn into a big hairball? I really don't see the local humane society as being a great place to visit," Riley growled out as she started heating up again. This time not because of the changes but because of a certain something a soon to be dead hairball forgot to mention!

Chapter 15

Riley let out another stream of curses as she bounced on Vox's shoulder. The huge moron and the two traitors had tricked her. Ha'ven had reprogrammed the device he had given her, and Creon had tricked her into coming down to the dining quarters on the pretense Carmen wanted to meet with her. Instead, Vox had been waiting. He had lived up to his promise that if he got his hands on her again he wasn't going to let her go. He had snuck up behind her. The next thing she knew, he had twirled her around so she could see the determination in his face before he bent over and tossed her struggling, cursing body over his broad shoulder.

"Let me go!" Riley yelled out as she clawed at her hair to get it out of her eyes. "Damn it, Vox, I am not talking to you!"

"You could have fooled me!" He chuckled. "You have threatened me with every possible means of dismemberment. I did not know a female could even think of some of the ways you described."

"I can easily think of a few more," Riley snapped in irritation. "Let me down, you moron. This is totally messing my hair up and I'm wearing a skirt, you creep. I don't want everyone seeing my underwear."

Vox's chest rumbled with a purr as he ran his hand up her leg and under her skirt to touch the soft skin of her ass. He grinned in delight as Riley burst into another round of curses and dire threats of what she was going to do to him the moment she got free.

"Stop that!" she squeaked in outrage even as her body heated up as he slid his hand over the cheek of her ass.

Vox breathed in deeply, sighing in pleasure as he picked up her reaction to his touch. She still wanted him even if she refused to admit it. He was not going to let her remain under the misconception that she would be returning to Earth. Creon had told him what Carmen had shared about her conversation with Riley. He needed to get her onto the *Shifter* and back to Sarafin as soon as they met up with Creon's brother, Mandra, and took care of Raffvin. Once he had her back on his planet, he would seal her in his quarters and make love to her until she accepted her fate.

Riley sniffed in frustration, tears burning at the back of her eyes. She was so damn confused! She thought she had her emotions, and her body, back under some small amount of control, but the moment he touched her it was like she had grabbed the wrong end of an electric fence. Her whole body came alive, inside and out. Hell, right now it felt like whatever had been moving around under her skin was trying to brush up against Vox.

She drew in a deep, calming breath. The scent that exploded through her had her practically writhing with need, which really pissed her off. Since when could she smell everything so much better? The warm, musky masculine fragrance made her think of cool forests, soft grass, and hot bodies tangled around each other. Just the thought of it turned the burning need in her up another couple of notches. She was so going to kill his ass for making her feel this way!

"Guall's balls, Riley. I need you," Vox's husky, deep voice muttered. "As soon as we are on my warship I am locking us in my living quarters," he promised as he moved with long strides down the corridors, ignoring the warriors who stopped to stare.

Riley trembled at the dark promise. "I can't go with you. Cal and Mel said Creon is taking them back to Earth. I have to go back!" she wailed, trying to fight her own desires.

"Never! I am never letting you go. My cat and I have claimed you. You are now my queen," Vox growled out in fury. "I will never let you return to your world."

Riley bit her bottom lip. She couldn't go with him! There were too many things she still needed to do. She had a family, damn it. It might be small and dysfunctional, but it was still her family. She and Grandma Pearl and Tina might fight like roosters in a cock fight, but they were still very loyal to each other. Then, there was her ex-boss and his insane father. She had a moral and ethical responsibility to stop them from hurting others, didn't she? Finally, there was the fact that she didn't want to turn into a hairball and eat people. She liked fur but turning into a walking coat complete with a tail was not on her bucket list of things to do before she died. Which was the added bonus to her reasons—she was bound to end up dead. It happened in every single movie she'd watched! No, she needed to stay where she was at and think with her head, not her heart.

Riley gasped when she was suddenly lifted off Vox's shoulder. He slid her down his long, hard length until her feet touched the floor. She used her one free hand—he refused to let her other one go—to push her heavy mane of hair out of her eyes. She looked around, disoriented, before she noticed they were in the same docking bay they had arrived in several days earlier. Now, though, there was a strange-looking shuttle with a long, narrow nose that gradually widened toward the back. A small group of men stood talking with Lodar and Tor.

One of the men turned to look at her through narrow, intense eyes. Riley stumbled back a few steps before Vox's grip on her wrist stopped her.

"That is my younger brother, Viper," Vox stated, looking down at her with a sharp-toothed smile. "I think he just found out about you."

"Great," Riley hissed. "You carry me in here like a damn rug over your shoulder, messing up my hair and putting your hands where they don't belong, then introduce me to family. That is so totally wrong on way too many levels."

Vox turned her around to face him. His face was cut in stone as he looked down at her defiant one. He could see the flash of fear in her eyes before she covered it up with that stubborn look she got. His heart melted a little when he realized that she was terrified but trying hard not to show it.

"You do not have to be afraid," he murmured quietly. "No one will hurt you. You will learn to adjust once you are on my world."

Riley's eyes flashed at the reminder that she wasn't being given a choice. *Well,* she thought savagely, *since when have I ever let that stop me?* All she needed to do was get back to her living quarters and lock herself in her room until they reached Earth. *And,* she thought savagely, *I won't be coming out until I see the big, blue marble for myself. No more trusting the two Cheshire cats!*

"I am not afraid because I am not going anywhere with you," she hissed out as she kicked her pointed-toe boot into his shin.

"Son of the gods," Vox yelped as he jumped back.

Riley used her free hand to yank down on the weakest spot of his grip breaking free from his hold. That was a clever move that she learned in a Crisis Prevention Intervention class that she took with a bunch of teachers. She drew her hand back as Vox reached for her and popped him as hard as she could on the tip of his nose just the way her Grandma Pearl showed her. She cried out when she realized she forgot to keep her thumb on the outside of her hand, but it still had the effect she was hoping for. Vox's head snapped back, and she knew he would have tears in his eyes.

Riley vaguely heard several of the men who were standing next to the shuttle yell out as she made a dash for the doorway. She could hear Vox snarling out loud curses. She was almost to the doorway leading out of the docking bay when Bob and Fred came through it, blocking her escape.

"Move! Move!" Riley screeched as she looked over her shoulder to see Vox turning to glare at her with murder in his eyes. "Oh shit! Move!"

"Riley, what did you do to him this time?" Fred asked looking back and forth in terror as Vox started stomping toward them with blood trickling from his nose. "He doesn't look like he is happy with you."

"You think I don't know that?" Riley growled out. "Bob, get out of the way."

"Riley, you are his mate..." Bob started to say before his voice died.

Riley glanced over her shoulder before she let out a loud groan. Turning, she raised her fists up and glared at Vox defiantly. He didn't look pissed, he looked like a volcano about to blow its frigging top!

"Vox, you just stay away from me," she bit out. "I don't want to have to hurt you but so help me I will if you don't leave me alone! I am not your queen, I'm not your mate, I'm going home!"

"I...am...going...to...whip...your...ass...for...this, Riley," Vox gritted out slowly between his clenched teeth.

Riley stumbled backward as she took in his dark face. Maybe the bop on the nose had been a little too much. She might have been able to get away with just the kick. Right now, she was cursing the fact that she didn't have her mini-Taser or pepper spray on her.

Note to self, she thought frantically. *Never go anywhere without it.*

"Just let me go," she responded softly, trying to get him to understand that this really wasn't a good idea. "I'm nothing but a pain in the ass, just ask my grandma and sister. They were forever telling me I was a headache waiting to happen. I don't belong on your world. I'm not queen material. Hell, I'm not even girlfriend material!" she added with a self-deprecating smile. "Just ask any of the guys who thought I was. Not a single one lasted more than a week."

Vox slowed as he came to tower over her. He shook his head as he took in her delicately raised fists. He could see the redness on her knuckles where she had hit him. His eyes roamed over her face as she stared up at him with wide blue eyes. The fierce determination on her face showed she really believed what she was saying. His eyes paused on where she was biting her lower lip. His body jerked in response as he remembered her soft kisses on his face, neck, and chest while he made love to her. He could see the pulse beating rapidly in her neck, begging him to taste her sweet blood again. As he stared at the rapidly beating vein, it dawned on him that she was terrified.

Take mate, his cat hissed at him. *Mate fight, but I want my mate.*

She's scared, Vox murmured. *She acts tough, but she is really very scared.*

We protect. We teach her to love us, his cat snarled back, pacing. *I feel my mate. She is close.*

I know, Vox replied carefully. *I think that is one of the things scaring her. I will not let her go.*

Good, his cat purred. *I need her.*

So do I, my friend. So do I, Vox replied.

"Riley, I won't let you go," he responded quietly.

He reached for her in a move so fast it startled her. She reacted without thinking, swinging her arm around. Poor Fred was standing off to the side so when Vox grabbed her one wrist, she turned, knocking him upside his right head which knocked it into his left one. He howled in pain as Riley turned again to hit Vox in the stomach. Vox pulled her arm around behind her back, twirling her and her fist became stuck in Bob's rounded belly instead.

"Now look what you've made me do!" she cried out, struggling to break the hold Vox had on her arm which was behind her back. "I'm stuck. Let me go!"

"Let her go!" Carmen's voice rang out from the doorway behind Bob, who was trying to pull Riley's hand out of his stomach.

"Carmen," Creon warned as he grabbed his mate who was moving into a defensive stance. "Let him take care of her."

"She told him to let her go. This is her decision," Carmen snapped back at Creon before turning back toward Vox. "She doesn't want to go with you. She wants to return to her family back on Earth."

Vox glared at Carmen over his mate's head. "She is mine!" he snarled back. "She goes with me."

"For the last time, I am not yours! I am Riley St. Claire from Denver, Colorado, and I am going home—alive, in one piece, without things bursting out of me or changing me into a zombie, or making me want to eat dead people," Riley cried out in frustration as Bob finally freed her hand from his stomach. "Oh, Fred, baby, I'm so sorry I hit you. Vox shouldn't have moved."

"That's okay, Riley," Fred said shuffling backward away from where she was still trying to break free from Vox. "It doesn't hurt that much."

"Riley, if you want to stay, I'll help you get home," Carmen said, taking a step closer.

"Yes, I want—" Riley started to say before she found herself lifted into a pair of arms that closed around her like steel bands.

Carmen's outraged cry echoed with Riley's as Creon lifted her into his arms as well. "Get her to your shuttle now, Vox," Creon growled out as his own mate began to struggle.

"Creon, so help me I am going to put your ass down for this," Carmen snapped out as she tried to break free of her mate's hold.

"I am not going with him, damn it!" Riley yelled, getting one of her hands free and pulling on Vox's short hair as hard as she could.

"That's it! Viper, get me some restraining cuffs," Vox yelled out over his shoulder at his brother, who had been watching the whole scene with disbelief.

"Here you go, brother," Viper said, looking on as his brother lowered the voluptuous alien female down to the floor of the docking bay. "Are you sure you want to bring her?" he asked as he handed his brother the restraining cuffs.

Vox growled as he straddled his mate, holding her face down with one hand between her shoulder blades while he used his other hand to grab at her flailing wrist. He pulled first one, then the other around and cuffed them. The thought of taking her like this burned through him with such ferocity that he had to close his eyes and recite another training script before he could rise up off her.

"Bob! Fred! Do something!" Riley wailed as she was rolled over and picked up again. "You have to help me!"

Bob put a hand out to stop Fred when he took a step toward Riley. "He will be a good mate for you, Riley St. Claire from Denver, Colorado. I will always be there should you need me."

"I need you now, you big bowl of Jell-O." Riley sniffed. "You have to help me get back home."

Bob smiled gently and moved closer to where Vox was tenderly holding her now quiet form. He reached out and touched her cheek with a plump, green finger before stepping back again. He looked fiercely at Vox who fought back a grin that the huge, gentle Gelatian would think to threaten him.

"I *am* sending you home, Riley," Bob said, still looking at Vox. "I am sending you where you should be."

Riley's face turned mutinous as she glared at the huge green creature who she thought had been her friend. He was just like the rest of the male species. They took what they wanted and didn't give a damn about the consequences. A fat tear rolled down her flushed cheek as she glared at Bob with a look of betrayal.

"I thought you were my friend," she sniffed. "I should have known better."

Bob looked down sadly at Riley. "I am your friend, Lady Riley. That is exactly why I am doing what I am."

"But…" Fred's right head started to say before his left head turned and hushed him.

"Bob's right. Riley is Vox's mate. We cannot interfere," Fred's left head said sternly.

"I don't need either one of you!" Riley said hoarsely. "I can get away on my own. You just wait. The first trader I find I'm going to kidnap his ass and make him take me home. You just wait and see! I'll be home before you know it!"

"I hate to break up this little party, but we've got to go! I just received a message from Adalard that they need help. Mandra has gone in after Raffvin," Ha'ven said grimly, coming up behind everyone.

"Vox," Viper said, drawing his older brother's attention back to the situation at hand. "We must go."

Vox nodded grimly, cursing Creon's brother for confronting their uncle on his own. He had read the reports sent to Creon about the destructive weapon Raffvin had that could destroy their symbiot. If Mandra was killed, it would mean the death of Carmen's sister, Ariel, as well. It was foolish for him to take such a chance, but Vox knew he would have done the same thing if given half a chance. The *Shifter* would travel beside the *Horizon* to Raffvin's hidden base. He was determined to make the traitorous Valdier royal pay for what he had done not only to him, but to his friends.

Chapter 16

Riley twisted around until she was in a sitting position on the bed. Vox had continued to ignore her protests as he and the other men boarded the shuttle that took them to the other warship. Riley had been quiet when they had exited the shuttle simply because she was too scared to say anything. There were hundreds of tall, deadly looking men working on the huge ship. Well, they were working until they saw Vox carrying her possessively in his arms. If she thought Viper and some of the other warriors were intimidating, it was nothing compared to a ship load of dark, suspicious, and intense stares. Only Lodar and Tor were at ease, joking as one carried her huge handbag and the other rolled her bright pink suitcase behind Vox as he carried her down corridor after corridor. She had gotten so confused she knew it would take her a month to figure out how to get back to the docking bay.

He had quickly deposited her on the bed. His fierce look and the grim tightening of his lips should have warned her he wasn't going to undo the restraining cuffs he had put on her. Instead, he had attached them to a metal bar at the head of the bed. She had called him every single name she could think of from a hairy-ass horny toad to a grub-eating parasite. Tor and Lodar had chuckled until she started in on them.

Vox growled out under his breath at them, and the two laughing hyenas disappeared, leaving them alone.

"I have to check on the ship, meet with my brother, and go over a few other things before I return," Vox said, brushing her wavy hair back from her face. "I cannot take a chance of you getting into anything."

"The least you can do is let me go!" Riley snorted angrily. "You can lock me in the room. You don't have to leave me hooked to the frigging bed!"

"I am not willing to take the chance of you figuring out how to get out," Vox replied. "I will not be long," he added brushing the back of his knuckles along her flushed cheek.

"I don't care how long you take! You can just forget I'm even here. I hope you get lost. I hope you—"

Vox cut off her words the only way he knew how, with his lips. He held her head still between the palms of his huge hands while he devoured her. His need for her threatening to override his sense of responsibility to his men. He drove his tongue deep into her mouth, dueling with her tongue as she fought back with a ferocity that ignited his blood to boiling.

He reluctantly pulled back and pressed his lips to her forehead. "You fire my blood, Riley. I have never felt this way before about another female in my life," he whispered.

Riley pulled back and gazed up into his eyes to see if he was just saying that to make fun of her or if he really meant it. The look in his eyes was so intense she drew in a shocked breath. He looked like…like…like he loved her! It was the same look some of the male leads had for the heroines in the movies.

"I will return soon," he repeated, brushing a hard kiss over her lips and leaving her lying on the bed, stunned.

That had been one nap and several hours ago. Riley now believed that she had been totally mistaken about the look in his eyes. It had not been love; it had been lust. Just like every other guy she had ever met. She worked herself into a fine temper as she lay there. She also needed to pee! Since it didn't look like Vox was going to be returning anytime soon she figured it was time to get herself out of the pickle she was currently in. It wasn't like this was the first time she had been in this situation. Well, not exactly this situation but not the first time she found herself handcuffed. No, that privilege was for the idiot cop who thought he could offer her a deal in exchange for a speeding ticket when any fool could have told him that speeding was an impossible task for her little Ford. She had kneed the guy in the balls when he did a pat down on her.

"I am so going to kidnap me a trader," Riley muttered. "I don't care who it is. I'm going to head home. If I need counseling when I get there, who cares! Everyone has a counselor now a days. It is considered the 'in' thing."

Riley worked one of her earrings off and gave a regretful sigh that she was about to destroy it. Straightening the long metal loop, she worked at the lock until she heard the slight click. The cuffs fell off. Riley breathed a sigh of relief. Thank God, Tina had shown her how to pick locks. Her little sister might have a metal bar up her ass most of the time, but she was a very avid reader. Tina had checked out a book on how to pick locks from the library one summer. She and her little sister had spent the rest of the summer picking every lock they could just to see if it really worked.

Riley slid off the bed and hurried into the bathroom. A loud sigh of relief escaped her as she relieved her overfull bladder. *Hell hath no fury like a woman denied a bathroom when she needs it,* she thought savagely. She would love to tie his ornery ass up and see how he liked it!

As soon as she was finished, she marched over to her large handbag and began rifling through it. She laid her mini Taser and pepper spray on the bed before she unzipped her suitcase to find something suitable to wear for her great escape. She pulled out her black leather pants and a black T-shirt from the bar with the slogan "Bike, Boobs and Beer—I have it all at The White Pearl." She quickly dressed in her weekend-at-the-bar outfit. She even attached the spiked dog collar she had picked up for Halloween last year. She pulled her black, stiletto ankle boots out and pulled them on. She knew she looked hot in this outfit. Craig, her grandma's three-hundred-pound bouncer, always groaned when he saw her dressed like this. He knew he would be ultrabusy when she did. Last, she pulled out the jacket her sister had gotten her for her birthday a few months ago. It was a fake, black mink jacket complete with a fake mink head draped over the left shoulder. The beady little glass eyes dared anyone to mess with her for fear of taking its place around her neck. She slid the jacket on, figuring she would need it. It was the only one that really went with the leather pants besides the one jacket Vox had already destroyed.

"And if I had more time, I would make him pay for a replacement," Riley growled out.

Determined to leave in style, she pulled her makeup bag out and added a dramatic touch of varying shades of blue around her eyes to make them pop before doing a heavy outline of black liner and mascara. Bright, glossy red lips and a swipe of blush and she looked like one very bad bitch. Grabbing her hair gel, she poured a generous amount into the palm of her hand and ran it though her wavy strands. Pulling her brush out, she quickly pulled her hair into a tight, slick bun. She pulled out the crystal hair clip and fastened it to hold it in place. She studied her reflection for a moment before adding a pair of huge silver hoops. Damn, she made the "bad girl" look good even if she was an Amazon!

She would like to see any of those guys give her the "look" like they did when Vox brought her aboard. Turning, she snatched up the mini Taser and slid it into the back of her waistband under her jacket before pocketing the pepper spray. Finally, she slung her large handbag over her shoulder. She was so totally ready to go kidnap someone and get the hell out of here!

Riley ran one hand over her slicked-back hair one more time before heading for the door. It opened as soon as she brushed her hand over the panel. With a self-satisfied smile on her bloodred lips, she strode out of the room like she own the place. Two men walking toward her stopped in shock as she approached them. She ignored their stares and added a little more sway to her hips as she approached. Just as she reached them, she thrust her hands out, palms flat against their chests, and shoved them to the side.

"Out of the way, boys," Riley snarled in a husky voice. "Momma is looking for an exit, and she is ready to bust any balls that get in her way."

The two men stumbled back in shock and watched as Riley walked away, their eyes glued to the tight black leather covering her lush rounded ass. Both men growled low with desire as they watched the seductive sway of her wide hips.

They turned, looking at each other before a huge grin creased each face. "Mine!" they both growled out at the same time.

* * *

Vox ran his hands through his hair again as he listened to Viper cover the events that had happened since he, Tor, and Lodar had been kidnapped. Gods, he could barely keep his mind on the tasks at hand. His mind kept drifting back Riley. He couldn't forget the passion in her kiss, the way she looked spread out on his bed with her hands bound, and the thrust of her beautiful breasts. He remembered how they overflowed his hands as he sucked at the taut peaks when he claimed her. It had been too long since he had even a moment alone with her. He needed her.

"Vox!" Viper snapped. "What is wrong with you? You have been groaning for the past several minutes. Do you need a healer?"

Vox jerked and looked at his brother in irritation. "No, I don't need a healer. I need Riley!" he retorted in frustration. "I need to mate with her. I haven't been able to think straight since I first saw her," he admitted reluctantly.

Viper frowned darkly. "Does she have some type of control over you?" he demanded, looking hard at his older brother.

Vox shook his head. "I don't know. She is my mate. I've heard talk of when we found our mate we would need them with a need unlike anything we have ever felt before, but I never really believed it. I know how father is with mother, but I just thought it was him and her. Now I am not so sure. All I can think about is being with her," he said, rubbing his hand over the back of his neck before clenching his fist and laying it on the conference table in front of him.

"How did you meet her?" Viper asked with a deceptive calm.

Viper was really worried about Vox. Never before had he ever seen his older brother act like this, especially around a female. He had never seen a species like her until he caught sight of Creon and Mandra's mates. They looked different from the one Vox had, but their features were close enough he was sure they were the same species. He wondered if this was an unknown alien species' way of infiltrating their worlds and taking them over. He would need to contact their parents and brothers and warn them of Vox's unusual behavior. It might be necessary to eliminate the female if she posed a danger.

Vox leaned back and looked at his younger brother with a small grin. "She was giving the Antrox running the mining asteroid a piece of her mind. She was the most beautiful thing I had ever seen. Her eyes were flashing fire, her body was made for loving, and her voice was like…" Vox shook his head at his brother's open mouth look of disbelief. "I knew she was my mate immediately. There were five of us in the Choosing Room. She chose us all. When the Antrox tried to tell her she couldn't, she gave him one look, and the next thing I know we were all escorted to her living quarters."

"She chose five mates?" Viper asked in disbelief. "How could she choose five?"

"She is Riley St. Claire from Denver, Colorado, and she can do whatever she wants." Vox grinned as he repeated his mate's words. "When I tried to claim her, she knocked me on my ass—twice! She was magnificent."

"So, how did you escape? You said you would tell me when you got on board," Viper asked in confusion.

"Riley," Vox said with another shake of his head.

Viper listened in disbelief as Vox explained about the tools, Riley getting hurt and having to go to medical, and what happened the next morning. He found it impossible to believe that a female could do the things that Vox was saying. Sure, he knew of the females who had betrayed them. He currently had two of his brother's females locked up. Still, they used their bodies and wiles to fight. They didn't go shooting, blowing up, or fighting against males. His suspicions that this species might be a deadly opponent that needed to be eliminated was growing. They could be extremely dangerous if they were allowed to run free or even mate with the most powerful members of their species. His thoughts turned to the fact that all five of the Valdier royals were mated to such creatures. Their takeover had already begun.

"You cannot mate with her," Viper said coldly, looking at his older brother with determination. "She needs to be either contained or eliminated."

Vox surged out of his seat, reaching out and grabbing his brother around the throat in a deadly hold. "She is my mate. No one will touch her. No one will harm her. She is your queen, and you will not forget that," he snarled, his teeth growing longer as his cat rebelled against the other male.

"You are not thinking clearly," Viper growled hoarsely, ignoring the tightening on his throat. "I swore to protect our King and our people. I will not let an unknown species threaten either of them."

Vox stared into Viper's dark green and yellow eyes and swore. "She is no threat."

The door opened just as Vox let Viper go. "My lord, the female has kidnapped Nahuel. She is demanding he take her to an unknown planet."

Viper rubbed his neck and threw his brother a disgusted look. "No threat?"

"Shut up, Viper," Vox grunted out as he headed out the door. "She is always doing things like this."

..*

Riley wasn't sure her bad-ass-girl outfit was working. Instead of scaring the men away, they seemed to be multiplying—exponentially. The two she had encountered originally were still following right behind her, and if she wasn't mistaken, they were purring.

"Will you two go take a hike off a short bridge?" Riley snapped out as she turned and walked backward. "Go on, shoo, get out of here, go fetch a stick or something."

Tadzio grinned as his eyes dropped to the deep V on Riley's shirt. His eyes were glued to the abundant cleavage showing. His eyes rose to look at her glistening lips.

"The only thing I want to fetch is you," he growled out. "Do you have milk in those?"

Riley was so stunned that she stopped walking backward in shock. Her mouth dropped open as she stared at him in disbelief. What was it with men and boobs? She totally could not understand their fascination. They had them too, but that didn't mean women went around staring at them.

"I know you did not just ask me something so rude!" she snapped out indignantly.

"Yes, he did," Nahuel replied with a grin.

Riley's mouth snapped shut at the same time as her eyes narrowed dangerously. She rolled her shoulders as her hand slipped to the waistband of her pants. It looked like the mini Taser was going to be used sooner than she thought. She took a seductive step toward them as a small crowd of men gathered around her.

Biting her lower lip, she pushed it out so it pouted as she looked both men over carefully. "Would either one of you two gorgeous hunks happen to know how to fly one of those shuttle thingies?" she asked in her best Marilyn Monroe voice.

Nahuel's eyes glazed as he watched the voluptuous female walk slowly toward them with a roll of her hips. "I am one of the best pilots on board," he answered in a hoarse voice.

Riley walked up to him and ran her fingernail down along his cheek over to his nose where she tapped it gently. Leaning into him, she let him feel her warm breath on his lips as she answered him. A smile curved her lips as her other hand moved to the belt loop on her pants where she had hidden the wrist cuffs Vox had used on her.

"Well, I guess today is your lucky day," Riley breathed out huskily. "Yes, they do produce milk but only on special occasions."

Nahuel's eyes rolled in delight just as Riley slapped the wrist cuff on one of his wrists before she ducked under his arm, twisting his arm behind him at the same time as she kicked the back of his knees, dropping him to the floor and slapping the other one on. When Tadzio took a step forward, she lifted her hand and touched his chest, squeezing the trigger on the newly recharged Taser. She would have to remember to thank Tor for the neat little recharger he had given her. It had come in handy.

Tadzio jerked and dropped as spasms went through his body. Riley jerked Nahuel up and pressed the Taser into his lower back in warning. It took a couple of seconds for the men surrounding her to realize what she had done. When they did, they jerked back defensively.

"Now, if you don't want to enjoy the same level of discomfort as your friend, you will do as you are told. You are now my prisoner. I want you to take me home," Riley said in her normal voice. She grinned at the huge alien she had captured with excitement as she hadn't really thought it would be that easy. "Come on, chop-chop. I'm not getting any younger."

Tadzio groaned as his body jerked again. "What did you do to him?" Nahuel asked, looking down at his friend with narrowed eyes.

"Oh, he'll be all right in a little while. I did the same thing to Vox. I think it took about an hour or so. He recovered from that much faster than he did the pepper spray. Poor Tor was miserable for hours afterward, even though he kept telling me he wasn't. Oh, can you remind me to thank Tor for the charger. My poor Taser would have been dead if not for him," Riley replied cheerfully. "Now, let's go. I need to get away before the big hairball finds out I've escaped from his living quarters."

"You are too late. The 'hairball' already knows," Vox growled out loudly as he came down the corridor toward her.

"Great! Just great! I finally have everything going my way and what happens? Busted! That's what! I swear I hate being the supporting character," Riley grumbled as she tried to shuffle Nahuel so he was between her and Vox. "If I had been the heroine I would have not only been on a supercharged shuttle heading home, I'd have a ton of gold and been eating caviar on little toasted crackers."

Several of the men standing around choked back a chuckle as they listened to Riley talking to herself. They had her surrounded so they knew there was no way she would escape, but they could tell that she really believed she had the upper hand. Now, they watched as the fiercest warrior on their planet faced off with the unusual female.

"Riley, let him go," Vox growled out.

"No! I caught him fair and square. He's mine!" Riley snapped back.

"If she really has milk, I am totally willing to remain in her captivity," Nahuel offered with a grin.

Vox snarled at Nahuel. "Her milk is mine!"

"Hello! Do you two have any idea how embarrassing it is to be talked about like I am some kind of a milk cow? No one is going to be drinking any milk from me. Now get your minds out of the gutter and shut up already!" Riley's voice rose at the same time as her temper and the burning inside her rose as the damn thing hiding under her skin threatened to break free again. She looked furiously at Vox. "I want to go home! I captured me a pilot so I should be able to just go."

"I already told you no," Vox snapped back as he took a step closer to her. "What have you done to your hair?" he demanded studying her face and realizing she looked—sexy as hell!

"Why?" Riley asked forgetting that she was supposed to be holding onto Nahuel for a moment and running her hand over the slicked-down strands. "I call this my bad-girl hair. I wear it like this when I go to the bar sometimes. Don't you like it?"

The moment she released him, Nahuel jerked forward and turned away from her. He grinned as he snapped the restraint on his wrists. He had learned that trick when he was in basic training.

Vox's deep snarl ripped through the corridor as his cat reacted to the creature wrapped around his mate's neck. Vox shifted between one jerky step and the next as his cat took over. He vaguely heard Riley's scream followed by his brother Viper's roar to stop, but none of it mattered. The beady-eyed creature stared in challenge, as if daring him to take Riley from him. Vox's teeth sank into the neck of the creature just as his massive paws knocked Riley over Tadzio's inert figure. He pulled, listening with satisfaction as the creature came apart in his mouth. The creature tasted foul, but he didn't stop until he had torn it to tattered pieces. Only then did he realize that Riley wasn't yelling anymore. It was her heartbreaking sobs that finally broke through the haze of rage coursing through him.

He shifted back to his two-legged form, straddling her as she looked up at him with a quivering lip and quiet sobs choking her. He looked down at her bright blue eyes in confusion. He had done it again. He had destroyed another one of her jackets, only this time she wasn't laughing.

"What?" he asked as he reached out to touch her lower lip. "I did it again, didn't I? I messed up."

Riley just looked at him as tears escaped from the corners of her eyes. "I hate you! It was the last thing she gave me, and you ruined it," she whispered as her lower lip quivered uncontrollably. "I knew she loved me when she gave me this jacket for my birthday, and you ruined it."

"Who?" Vox asked quietly, ignoring the men who were silently helping Tadzio to his feet.

"My little sister, Tina," Riley answered as she turned her face away from him and closed her eyes, shutting him out. "I miss my family," she said quietly.

Viper stared down at the female who had seemed so different and realized that maybe he had been a little harsh in his judgment of her. Right now, he wanted to promise her whatever in the gods she wanted. He wondered if this was what his brother felt whenever he was near her. There was something about her that pulled at something deep inside him. He shook his head.

It had to be a trick. Surely this was part of their power. He watched as Vox gently pulled his mate into his arms, muttering words of apology and promises he would make it up to her as soon as he could.

Chapter 17

Two days later, Vox was ready to start another war. He wanted—needed—to kill something or someone. Once Riley had gotten over being so upset, she had become very, very angry. She swore she would drive him to the brink of insanity if he didn't return her home. She had started singing a song that was about to drive him to that point. Out of desperation, he had contacted Creon and demanded he tell him the location of Earth. A rueful smile curved his lips as he thought of his mate's tenacity. It was one of the things he loved about her. She had finally worn herself out that first night and fallen asleep. The problem was she started again the moment she woke up and had been working on him for two solid days. That was when he made up his mind he would compromise with her. He would not take her back to her world, but he would bring a bit of her world to her.

"I will be going to Earth after we have taken care of Raffvin," Creon responded quietly. "My mate needs closure on the life she had before. I owe this to her and to us so that we can move forward."

"I want you to take Viper with you," Vox stated. "I want him to bring Riley's sister and Grandma Pearl back to her. She misses them. I cannot return with her to her world. There are still traitors among my people I need to take care of. He will go in our place to her world for them."

Creon's eyebrows rose. He remembered the young Sarafin royal as being a bit of a hot head, not unlike himself. He wondered how Viper would handle being around females who were so different from what he was used to. His lips curved as he thought of what his own mate's reaction would be to the news he planned to return with her to her world to say good-bye.

"I will talk to Kelan. He has returned with his mate Trisha to retrieve her father," Creon shared. "I will let him know that Viper will be joining us. From what Mandra said the last time I talked with him, there might be a few more. Adalard, Bahadur, and Zebulon wanted to go as well. So far the only one resisting is Ha'ven. He states he has enough females to choose from and doesn't need any more."

"Viper is only going to retrieve the females, not mate with one of them," Vox stated firmly. "I will brief him. He will need to spend time with Riley so he knows where to begin his search."

"So, how is it going with your mate? You look a bit—tired," Creon said with a grin.

"She has most of the crew ready to throw me in one of the detention cells," Vox replied just as the door opened and Viper walked in with a dark scowl on his face. "I have to go. I will contact you again in a few hours."

"Good luck, my friend," Creon said with a laugh as he signed off.

"We should be within range of Raffvin's hidden base by tomorrow," Viper said, walking over to the wall replicator and ordering a drink.

"Good, I am ready to be done with this," Vox said turning to study his brother. "I have a mission for you."

Viper turned with his drink in his hand and raised his eyebrow at the edge of authority in his brother's voice. He only used that tone when he was giving him an order that he knew Viper wasn't going to like. Viper took a slow drink before he responded.

"What is it?" Viper asked, moving over to the conference table and sitting down across from Vox.

"I need you to return to my mate's planet and retrieve her Grandma Pearl and her younger sister, Tina," Vox said forcefully.

Viper sat back and gazed at his brother with a frigid look. "Why send me? You could send another warrior. I am not an escort. I'm an assassin if you need one or a spy should the need arise," he replied in an emotionless voice.

"I want someone I can trust," Vox replied softly. "I am not asking, Viper. I am ordering you to go. Creon will be returning to his mate's planet. Kelan is already there. I will have Riley share everything she can with you to help you."

"Do you trust her? What if it is a trap?" Viper asked, slamming his hand down angrily on the table. "Have these females taken all your wits from you and the Valdier?"

Vox growled low, the sound rumbling in warning that Viper was treading on thin ice. "Do not question my sanity unless you are willing to challenge me for my position. You may be my brother, but I will not let you or anyone else question my leadership or my mate's loyalty to me."

Viper's lips tightened. "Loyal to you—but what of your people?" he snarled back.

Vox stood up, towering over his brother who was still sitting. "She chose five mates when she should have chosen just one. She did it to protect the males who were left from being used as food. She was prepared to die even as she freed all the prisoners on that mining asteroid. She would have if I hadn't stopped her. She is my mate, Viper. Accept it. She is your queen, and you will not disrespect her—ever. It is your duty to protect her at all cost, even if it means with your life."

Viper set his barely touched drink down and stood up stiffly. "As you wish, my lord," he said formally, bowing his head in stiff respect. "I will get the necessary information from my queen and prepare to leave as soon as our strike on Raffvin is complete."

Vox watched as his younger brother turned and strode out of the room, leaving him alone. He rolled his shoulders in an effort to ease the tight muscles in them. If he had known having a mate was going to be so much work, he might have thought twice about it. That was until images of Riley's flashing eyes, the twinkle in them when she got into things she shouldn't, her wild mass of hair twirling as she laughed or walked, and her gazing up at him with burning eyes flared through his mind. He wondered how he was going to survive until she forgave him. His eyes lit up as he thought of how he had left her sleeping just a short time again. Maybe it was time to wake her up. If he kept her too tired to argue and too satisfied to be mad, maybe he could win her love.

Finally! His cat hissed.

Oh, shut up, he grunted as he felt his body react to his thoughts. He was going to go claim his mate over and over again until she couldn't think to be upset anymore. Then, he would tell her about Viper going for her family. That should make her forgive him once and for all. With the hope that this plan worked, he stood up and strode determinedly out the door heading for his living quarters and Riley.

* * *

Riley groaned as waves of heat flared inside her. Her skin tingled where it touched the hot flesh rubbing against it. She was having the most delicious dream. A hiss escaped her as sharp teeth nipped at first one nipple, then the other until both throbbed and ached for more. Her legs fell apart at the first tug on her neatly trimmed silk curls. A loud cry burst from her as thick fingers rubbed her clit, making her slick and swollen with their determined search.

"Vox," she whispered sleepily.

"Yes, my fiery little mate," Vox replied as he ran his lips down over her softly rounded belly. "You were made for loving, Riley" he groaned as he tugged on the silken curls. "I love touching you and how responsive you are to me."

"That feels so good," she moaned as she bit her lip as sharp waves of heat flooded her. "You better not stop if you want to live."

Vox chuckled as he gently opened her to his lips, nipping at her engorged clitoris and purring as her body reacted to his with undeniable passion.

"I wouldn't even think of it," he responded huskily as her scent overwhelmed him and his cat.

He was going to have to tell her before too much longer about the changes occurring within her body. His cat could not wait much longer. He buried his tongue inside her, lapping at the delicious moisture as it flowed over it. A loud purr escaped him as his cat responded to his mate being close. He moaned when Riley lifted her legs and draped them over his shoulders, pulling him closer. Her body moved in increasing agitation as she came closer to her climax, and he increased the pressure, wanting to taste her release.

He slid his hands under the soft flesh of her ass and lifted her so he could drink deeper from her flowing well. Her loud cries told him she was enjoying what he was doing. He spread his fingers out, squeezing her ass as he nipped her swollen nub with his sharp teeth and was rewarded when her body exploded over his tongue.

"Yes!" she hissed out, bunching the covers of the bed in her fisted hands. "Oh, yes!" she moaned, shuddering and letting her legs fall weakly to the mattress.

He chuckled as he released her, moving quickly to sit back and sliding his hands under her. "My turn," he growled out in excitement.

He flipped her over so fast she didn't have time to protest. Gripping her around the waist, he lifted her at the same time as he aligned his thick, hard cock with her dripping channel. He pulled her back toward him and watched as his cock disappeared slowly inside her, his thumbs caressing the sweet globes of her ass. He drew in a shuddering breath at the beauty of the sight, his hands tightening on her hips to hold her still so he could control the pace.

"Oh, God!" Riley breathed out, throwing her head back at the feeling of fullness invading her body.

"Oh, Vox!" he growled in response, watching her beautiful curls flow along the delicate curve of her back.

Streaks of swirling black suddenly appeared, teasing him and his cat with what she would look like in her cat form. He held his breath, pushing in and out of her body slowly, trying to draw more of her cat to the surface without having her shift. He groaned as the swirls danced to the rhythm of his thrusts. Never in his life had he ever seen anything more breathtaking. His eyes jerked up to Riley's when she glanced over her shoulder at him as he mounted her with strong, swift strokes. Her eyes had changed slightly, becoming more tilted at the corners and the blue was swirled with darker blues and golden yellows. Her pupils were more elongated, as well. He felt the pull of her gaze as he increased the speed of his claiming. He was drowning in the beauty of them as much as in the feel of her body wrapped around his. The combination was too much for the fragile hold he had on his control.

"Riley!" he roared as his body jerked suddenly, exploding inside her with such force he fell forward over her back in gasping pants. "Oh gods, Riley, I need you."

Riley's body clenched around his as she felt his cock swell and lock deep inside her. She didn't think she would ever get used to the erotic feeling of being locked as one with him. Her vaginal channel rippled with shockwaves as her orgasm wrapped around his cock, pulling him deeper into her in response to his own powerful one. Her head fell to the bed as she struggled to catch her breath and not collapse under him. She wouldn't have been able to anyway with the way he was gripping on her hips as if he was grasping a lifeline.

..*

The next morning she realized one thing, if she thought he would make love to her and leave, she had been sadly mistaken. They had both fallen into a deep sleep after the third time he took her, this time with her sitting on his lap while he pounded into her and sucked on her breasts until she was totally mindless. Even then, he had only slept for a few hours before he woke her again loving her over and over in positions she turned hot just thinking about. He continued his systematic attack throughout the night, barely letting her fall asleep before he woke her to start all over again. She had no idea how he could function since she was a melted puddle against the sheets, but once he started touching her, she didn't care how he did it, just that he didn't stop.

"You are going to be the death of me," she moaned as she felt his hand moving over her hip again. "If I could bottle whatever you have inside you and sell it back home I'd be a billionaire within a week!"

Vox's hand tightened on her hip at her mention of her home world. "I need you to talk to Viper. He will be going to your world."

Riley jerked in surprise and rose up to look at Vox with her mouth hanging open. "When do we leave? How long will it take? Oh my God, I didn't think I would ever make it home again! I'll have to go see my Grandma Pearl and Tina. I won't make the mistake this time of not telling them how much I love them and that I wouldn't trade them for anything in the world, no matter what I normally tell them. Oh!" She released her pent-up breath and sat up, uncaring of the sheets that dropped to her lap showing all the love bites that Vox had left against their creamy flesh. "I have to get the paperwork to the proper authorities about my ex-boss and his dad too! How long did you say it would take for us to get there?" she asked, impatiently pushing her wild curls out of her face.

Vox's mouth pulled into a straight line as he realized Riley misunderstood his explanation. "Riley, I said Viper is going, not you. You will be returning to Sarafin with me. Viper will transfer to the *Horizon* and travel with Creon and his mate back to your world."

"What the hell are you talking about?" she demanded, glaring down at him where he lay watching her with a deep frown. "If he is going there is no reason I can't tag along. I never unpacked, and I can be in and out of the shower in minutes and ready to go."

Vox's hands whipped up to grip Riley's upper arms in a fierce hold. "You think to leave me after the last few hours?" he asked in disbelief. "I have chosen you as my queen! You are my mate!"

Riley frowned, pressing her hands against his chest in confusion. "I thought you were going too. Besides, I never said I wanted to be a queen! Hell, I couldn't even get a date to the prom, what in the hell makes you think I'm queen material? Why are you sending Viper to Earth if not to take me back?"

Vox fought the urge to wrap his hands around Riley's neck instead of her arms. "To get your Grandma Pearl and Tina, of course. You said you missed them. I will bring them to you so you won't. I need you to explain to Viper what he needs to know so he can return with them," he said with a frustrated release of his breath.

Riley's mouth dropped open again, but this time instead of excitement in her eyes, there was horror in them. "Are you nuts?!" she screeched.

Chapter 18

Vox ground his teeth in frustration as Riley trailed behind him. She had not reacted anything like he expected after he informed her that he was sending Viper to her world to retrieve her family. In fact, the look of horror when he told her made him question his own sanity. He needed to make sure he told Viper to handle Grandma Pearl with extreme caution or he might end up with his head mounted to the wall of her "bar," whatever that was. It wouldn't make a difference, if Riley missed her family it was the only way to solve the situation.

"Grandma will eat Viper alive! Forget the barbecue sauce—think sushi!" Riley insisted as she hurried to keep up with Vox as he headed for the bridge.

"I will warn him that your Grandma can be difficult—and dangerous," Vox insisted. "I will not return you to your world, Riley. You belong by my side. If the only way for you to be with your family is to bring them to Sarafin, then that is what will happen."

"But what if they don't want to come," she demanded. "You have no idea what they are like! They are nothing like me," she added. "I am the mild one of the three of us."

"Gods!" Vox muttered under his breath. "I find that hard to believe."

"What is that supposed to mean?" Riley asked indignantly.

"I can't believe they can be worse than you," Vox admitted as he strode onto the bridge.

Riley stopped with her mouth hanging open before her eyes flashed. "I am *not* that bad!" she protested.

Vox turned as he was about to enter the commander's room and raised his eyebrow. "Would they have spent the last two days singing that Gods awful song?"

Riley flushed and her mouth tightened. "It's driving you nuts, is it? No, they wouldn't have spent two days singing. Grandma Pearl would have whipped your ass into the ground or filled it full of rock salt! Tina would be too dignified to sing; she would have frozen you out to the point your dick would have been a popsicle," she snapped defensively. "The whole purpose of driving you nuts was so you would take me back! I have to take care of my old boss and his dad, and I don't want to die!"

Vox realized that every warrior on the bridge had stopped what they were doing and were listening in fascination to their conversation. He stepped closer to Riley and gripped her arm, tugging her into the conference room, making sure the door was closed before he said anything else. He saw the genuine fear in her eyes, as well as the determination.

"I would never let anything happen to you," Vox said as he ran his thumbs back and forth over her arm where he was holding her. He hid the grin as he felt her body react immediately to his touch.

"You can't know for sure. Look what you did to the jacket Tina gave me! That could have been me instead," she insisted, looking up into his brilliant tawny eyes. "In every movie I've ever seen something bad always happens to everyone but the lead characters. Hell, even some of the romance books I read do the same thing! If you can rip up not one but two of my jackets by mistake, how do I know you won't accidently do the same thing to me one day?"

Vox let out an exasperated sigh. "Nothing is going to happen to you! This is not some entertainment holovid, Riley. Accept that Viper is going to bring your family here, and I promise to never kill another one of your jackets ever again," he growled out in frustration before he turned around to patch into the conference call with Creon, Ha'ven, and Adalard.

Damn it! Riley thought crossly. *How am I supposed to convince him that bringing Pearl and Tina here isn't a good idea if he refuses to listen to me! God, I can't even imagine what they would do. Tina...* Riley knew her little sister would not handle being around so many guys very well. A bad incident when Tina was in her last year of high school had made her sister skittish about any of the male species, regardless of whether they were aliens or not. That was what motivated Pearl to move them to San Diego from Los Angeles. Things had changed when Pearl inherited a bar from an old boyfriend who died from liver disease. Tina became the manager, handling all the bookkeeping after she got her online accounting degree. Unfortunately, she became even more reclusive. She refused to leave the office during open hours and never went anywhere without an armed escort, namely Pearl, when they left at night.

Well, if singing is getting through to him, then singing it will be! she decided with a reluctant sigh and broke into her off-key rendition of "Ninety-nine Bottles of Beer on the Wall." *A girl has to do what a girl has to do.*

Vox's loud groan filled the room as he clenched his fists in a desperate attempt to not wrap them around Riley's neck. Instead, he opened communications with the *Horizon*. He was sure if he could kill Raffvin and some of his men, he would feel much better.

He saw Ha'ven and Creon on the *Horizon* and Adalard and Zebulon from the *D'stroyer* on the display screen. He listened as Adalard explained Mandra had been gravely injured during the attack on his uncle's base. Bahadur, one of Ha'ven's generals who had infiltrated Raffvin's inter-group, explained Raffvin had decided to abandon the base. He ordered it and all the inhabitants he had enslaved to be destroyed. Mandra had made the decision to attack.

"What of Raffvin?" Ha'ven asked his younger brother, Adalard. "Were you able to kill him?"

Vox listened as Zebulon filled him in on the current status of the situation. He was furious Raffvin had slipped through their grasp again and worried about Mandra. He knew how fierce a warrior the huge Valdier was during battle. He was glad his friend would survive. He grimaced when Riley hit a particularly bad note. He suspected it was on purpose. He knew exactly what she was trying to do, and it was time he finally let her know one of the reasons why he could not return her. He had a feeling she was not going to be very happy about it considering it was one of the things she kept insisting she was terrified might happen. He ended up cutting the meeting short since there was nothing else that could be done until Raffvin was found. In the meantime, he had a brother to send on a mission, traitors at home to take care of, and a mate who was about to find out she was no longer completely human. Out of the three, the first two were going to be much easier than the last, he suspected.

* * *

Lodar knelt down next to Vox with a fierce frown on his face. Tor stood over to the side with an equally accusing look on his. Vox sat on the floor of the training room where he had brought Riley, looking up at two of his most trusted warriors and closest friends with a pleading expression on his normally impassive face.

"What did you expect!" Lodar growled out in accusation. "She told you she was terrified of something bursting out of her."

"That she did," Tor agreed, ignoring Vox's heated look.

"She said she didn't want to turn into anything," Lodar continued. "What part of your plan made you think blurting it out to her and then calling her cat forth was a good idea?"

"I don't know!" Vox admitted as he ran his hand down protectively over Riley's still, white face. "I thought if she understood why she couldn't return to her world she would finally be more—submissive," he finished a little weakly.

"How can you even think to use the words submissive and Riley in the same sentence?" Tor asked in disbelief.

Vox growled at his chief engineer's tone. "She would never have believed me otherwise," he insisted, brushing her hair back from her face. He turned to Lodar. "Can't you do something?"

"She fainted," Lodar replied drily. "The best thing is to wait for her to come around. I am not sure if you want to be here or not. She might just succeed in killing you this time."

Vox ran his hand over his face and lowered his head in despair. "You are probably right. Are you sure she is going to be all right?" he asked huskily.

Lodar laid his hand on Vox's shoulder and gave it a sympathetic squeeze. "It was just a shock to her system. All the scans came back normal. She'll be fine."

Vox nodded in relief. "Leave us, then. I think it best no one else is here when she wakes." He looked up at Tor who straightened from where he was leaning against the wall. "Has Viper left yet?"

Tor nodded. "Yes. He was not happy, but he is aboard the *Horizon* on its way to Earth."

"Good," Vox replied with a sigh. "Keep me posted on what is going on. I will join you in a few hours. Set our destination for Sarafin. I have some traitors that need to be dealt with," he said with a hard, cold edge in his voice.

"Good luck, my friend," Tor said as he smiled gently down at Riley's face that had a bit more color in it than a few minutes ago. "I have a feeling you are going to need it."

Lodar laughed as he stood up. "Just make sure she doesn't have anything hidden on her."

Vox shuddered when he thought of the two small devices that she was so fond of. He had found them and hidden them in a locked cupboard in their living quarters. He had also gone through the large pink case she had, but he couldn't find any other harmful devices in it. He hadn't had a chance to check the large bag she was so fond of as she always had it with her.

He looked around the large training room. There were weapons lining the walls on three of the four sides. Perhaps this wasn't the best place to bring her for her first shift. He knew she was ready for it. His cat was more than ready for his mate, and he could sense hers was close to the surface. The last time he made love to her he could see the swirling lines of her cat running along her skin. He could also feel the increased heat of her body against his.

Just the thought was enough to make him hard. His cock swelled as he remembered the brief glimpse he had gotten of Riley in her cat form. She was magnificent! She wasn't all lean muscle and sleek lines like the females of his world. She was nice and plump, with a rounded stomach that made his cat want to flip her onto her back so he could rub against it. She had been solid white with dark swirling lines of black through her coat and the beautiful blue eyes that made him feel like he was drowning every time he looked into them. Her face was framed by longer white hair that showcased the delicate lines of her face. His cat had gone wild. Unfortunately, Riley had taken one look at her front paw and fell over unconscious before he or his cat could do anything. Maybe he should have warned her what was about to happen instead of shifting and calling forth her cat before the door even finished closing all the way.

He glanced down and was surprised to see steady blue eyes gazing up at him in wonder and fear. He gently touched her cheek with a finger, stroking the silky skin. Neither one of them said anything as he sat holding her possessively against his body. He saw the confusion, the questions, and the wonder fighting each other as the magnitude of what happened flickered through her mind.

"Ever since I met you I have made one mistake after another," Vox admitted in a quiet voice. "I have never felt the emotions that you bring out in me. I have always been in control but with you that control disappears. My body burns for you all the time, Riley. I love listening to you, even when you are singing that gods-awful song. I love watching your eyes flash with fire or laughter. I love how protective and fierce you are for those you care about. I love how you are soft to the touch and the passion in you when I make love to you. Most of all, I love you more than life itself," Vox finished softly.

Riley blinked up at the most handsome, confusing, and unusual man she had ever met. He had totally turned her life upside down. He confused her with all the emotions he woke inside her when he was near and scared the hell out of her more than she had ever been before because she knew he had the power to break her heart. That was something she had protected ever since her mom took off all those years ago.

"Can you ever forgive me?" Vox whispered with regret. "Can you find it in your heart to at least give me another chance to not mess up?"

A smile tugged at the corner of her mouth as warmth filled her. "You love me?" she asked with a sparkle of hope in her eyes.

Vox closed his eyes for a moment before he opened them and sighed heavily. "With every fiber of me and my cat's being."

Riley reached up and tugged his mouth down to hers. She kissed him with everything she had inside her. She let all her fear, hope, and love flow into it, showing him everything that she didn't know how to express. Her lips caressed his, her tongue running along them until he opened to her. Her arms wrapped around his neck, pulling him off balance until he was lying over her.

He pulled back far enough to look down at her. Her eyes were shining brightly and a small smile curved her swollen lips. His eyes searched her face for anger, rejection, horror, but he saw none of that. Instead, he saw wonder, acceptance, and—love.

"You love us," he breathed out.

"I have from the first. I just couldn't believe I could be the heroine in the story. How could a guy like you want a smart-mouthed, maturely figured girl like me? You are one sexy alien, Vox d'Rojah," Riley admitted. "You could have any girl you wanted. Why would you want me?"

Vox threw back his head and laughed before he looked down at Riley with a huge grin on his face. "I love your smart mouth. I am never bored. Your mature figure is…" A deep purr rumbled from him as he glanced down at her overflowing breasts trying desperately to escape from the top she was wearing, and then down to her hips. He rubbed his swollen cock against her and chuckled when she gasped. "You are perfect. You are the only woman I want, Riley St. Claire from Denver, Colorado. You are the only one who can bring my blood to a boil. I would choose you over any other female," he vowed with a soft, rumbling growl.

Riley licked her bottom lip, moaning with need when her tongue was not the only one licking it. She was startled by the purr that escaped her as Vox's tongue touched hers, stroking it and her lip at the same time. She drew in a sharp breath as she felt his sharp teeth nip at it, her body arching in response.

"Vox?" she breathed out.

"Yes, my mate?" Vox purred deeply, rubbing his hips back and forth against her.

"Can I… Did I…turn into a cat?" Riley asked hesitantly.

Vox pulled back with a wicked smile on his lips. "Yes, you can and you did. You are a beautiful cat, Riley."

Riley's eyes widened in shock before she bit her bottom lip. "Can I do it again?" she asked anxiously.

"Would you like to?" Vox asked cautiously.

Riley thought for a minute before nodding shyly. "Yes. Yes, I think I would like to try it again very much," she said determinedly.

"Then come to me, my mate," Vox growled out in a low, gravelly voice that pulled at something deep inside her.

Vox rolled away from Riley, shifting as he did until his massive cat lay watching her intently. Riley felt her body tingling all over before she rolled over as a shimmering light engulfed her. She felt the shift as it flooded her. This time she embraced it. A sense of relief poured through her as she let her cat out.

Yes! Her cat purred. *At last!*

What the fuck? Riley gasped, startled.

Oh, I plan to do that too, her cat responded with a deep purr.

Riley gaped at her cat. *You shameless little hussy.*

Not hussy—pussy! Her cat purred, turning her back to Vox and flicking her tail back and forth seductively.

Holy shit, Riley breathed as the heat she had experienced burst into a raging inferno.

Her cat stood up and stretched, putting her front paws out in front of her and lowering her head at the same time she rose up on her back legs flicking her tail. A loud rumble filled the training room as Vox watched his mate. The scent of her heat slammed into him like a wave crashing onto the cliffs. A loud snarl burst from him as he crouched and moved into position to pin her. Riley rose up and shook her larger body. White hair shimmered as it rippled back and forth with the movement. Her beautifully sculpted head turned, and her lip pulled back just enough for her to flash her teeth in warning. Vox advanced on her slowly, his larger body throbbing with need and desire as his cat watched his mate tease him. She was playing a very dangerous game. He knew she didn't have a clue as to what she was doing, but her cat probably did. That damn tail of hers was practically begging him to snatch her and mount her. A low growl of warning escaped him as she flashed her teeth at him again. Her cat wanted to play hard to get. That was not going to happen. He had caged his own leopard too long to deny it any longer.

Riley turned as Vox charged at her. She swatted at him with her paw, but the blow didn't even faze him as he knocked her over onto her side, pinning her by the neck. She tried to get her back legs up under his belly to throw him off, but he growled in a low, dangerous tone that froze her. He kept his grip on her neck as he straddled her body with his bigger one. Riley shivered as she felt his thick, heavy cock brush along her belly.

Vox? she breathed nervously.

I won't hurt you, Riley. Let my cat take his mate. He needs her like I need you, Vox's low rumble whispered across her mind.

I can speak and understand cat? she asked as she let her head fall back against the padded mat.

Vox coughed out in a deep, gruff sound that tickled the fur near her ear. Riley hissed as he loosened his grip enough for her to roll over. She thought he was going to let her get up but instead the moment she was on her belly, he bit down on her again, placing his two front paws on either side of her shoulders while he pushed her head down closer to the mat. She snarled when his thick cock slid deep into her. He began rocking back and forth, taking her hard. Riley ignored the tearing of the mat as she dug her claws into the padded material. She hissed, arching her back so that he could drive into her even deeper as pleasure and warmth flooded her.

Her body jerked as spasms rocked her world. She let out a loud, wild cry that would have scared her if not for the pleasure sweeping through her in endless waves of ecstasy. A few more strokes and Vox's loud roar shook the weapons on the wall. The huge male was locked to the smaller female caged under him as his body felt the ultimate release.

Mine! his cat roared. *My mate, my mate,* he snarled over and over.

I love you, Riley purred out as her body melted down onto the matting. *Please, don't ever let me go.*

Vox licked the fur around her muzzle gently, cleaning her with his rough tongue. *Never, my fierce kitten. Never will I let you go.*

Riley closed her eyes as Vox continued to clean her. She barely moved when he wrapped his larger form around her. A sigh escaped her as she settled into a deeper sleep, exhausted after everything that had happened over the past couple of hours. Vox laid his head down gently over her neck. His mind drifted as he thought of how much his life had changed since he first saw his beautiful, buxom mate standing up on the choosing platform giving the Antrox a piece of her mind. He rubbed his head along the still damp fur of her neck where he had held her down and couldn't help but think he might just have to thank Raffvin before he killed the bastard.

Chapter 19

"Guall's balls, not again!" Vox cursed as he stormed out of the commander's conference room and hurried off the bridge after he received a report from Lodar that Riley was loose again. "I am going to chain her ass to my bed as soon as I catch her—again."

The *Shifter* was scheduled to dock with the Transfer station in orbit around the planet in a little over an hour and his mate was sashaying her furry little ass up and down the ship. All the males were already about to revolt against him because of her and that was before she learned how to shift into her cat. They were determined to protect her even if it meant from him after he destroyed another one of her jackets by mistake. News had swept through the ship of how he had made her cry. Now, the news was spreading about how gorgeous she was in her cat form and every warrior was doing their damn best to catch a glimpse of her. The last three days had been a nightmare for him. Riley in her two-legged form was enough to drool over. Riley in her four-legged form was enough to cause every hot-blooded male in his prime to become filled with razor-edge sexual frustration. She had no idea just how damn sexy her wider hips, soft plump belly, and flashing tufts of white fur were to a bunch of cat-shifting warriors who had been in space for far too long. Not to mention she didn't know how to walk like a damn cat! She pranced everywhere she went, her tail flicking this way and that in innocent invitation to every male she came across.

"Riley!" Vox roared as he watched his mate's sassy hips swaying seductively to and fro. Hell, he would be lucky if he didn't shift and take her right there in the corridor. "Guall's balls, female, you are about to cause every male on this warship to have to seek privacy to relieve themselves if you don't get to our living quarters right now!"

Riley turned her head and snorted in disbelief at Vox, her big, blue eyes staring at him like he was crazy. She sat down in the middle of the corridor, shook her head, and lifted a paw up as if inspecting her pink claws while she waited for him to reach her.

Pink claws? Vox shook his head. *Who ever heard of painted claws?*

He didn't even want to know how she was able to paint the claws of her cat pink. He had never seen anything like it. From the looks of all the males standing in the corridor watching her with lust-filled eyes, neither had anyone else. Vox snarled out in a low dangerous tone to the warriors to get back to work.

He slowed and shook his head at his wayward mate. Ever since she woke up in the training room, it had been a challenge to get anything done. Between wanting to fuck her in both her two-legged and four-legged forms and trying to keep her isolated as he sensed her going into heat, he had been trying to finalize preparations for their return to the planet. On top of that, Riley had taken to shifting back and forth at random and unexpected moments. It was driving both him and his cat crazy as they were both in a highly sexually charged state.

He also needed to inform his parents and other siblings that he had mated. He could only imagine how his father and mother were going to react to that. He might be the King of Sarafin since his father stepped down to spend more time as a diplomat for their world, but he still respected his father's knowledge, skills, and power. He knew his father expected him to fulfill the terms of the treaty even though there was no way he could do it now.

Vox stopped and looked down at Riley for a few seconds before he knelt down on one knee in front of her. He chuckled and shook his head when she ran her long, slender tongue along his neck as he bent closer to her. He threaded his fingers through the hair along her jaw and ran them up until he could pull gently on her right ear.

"You have no idea the mayhem you are causing, do you?" Vox asked quietly as he stroked her.

Within the blink of an eye, Riley was sitting in front of him in her two-legged form. "Oh!" she huffed out, blinking up at Vox with wide, startled eyes. "I'm still working on the shifting thing."

Vox's eyes widened before they closed half way. "You have to remember what you are wearing when you shift as well, my beautiful little mate," he groaned huskily. "I am going to have to kill every male on board the warship if they see you like this."

"What?" Riley asked, confused before looking down and realizing she was wearing just her camisole and a pair of dainty matching boxers. "Oh shit!"

Vox groaned as he saw her pebble-sized nipples harden into tight buds. His eyes quickly scanned the area, freezing on a supply room door. He rose up, pulling Riley behind him. Opening the door, he pulled her inside and shut the door quickly behind them. He didn't give Riley a chance to protest. Gods, his body was hard as a rock for her again. He would never get enough of her. Turning her so she was trapped against the wall in the tiny room, he gripped the silky material covering her ass and pushed it down desperately.

"Release me," he demanded harshly. "Now, Riley, or neither one of us will have any clothing left to wear."

Riley chuckled as her hands quickly moved to the front of his pants. "You can be so bossy sometimes," she teased as her hand slipped between the loosened material of his pants and his skin. "I love the way you feel," she admitted with a shy smile as she wrapped her hand tightly around his swollen cock as his pants fell down around his ankles.

"Gods, Riley," Vox croaked out as his eyes rolled back when she began sliding her hand back and forth from the base of his cock to the tip and back again.

He braced his hands against the wall on each side of her head, groaning in pleasure. He didn't trust himself to not hurt her as sharp waves of need and desire rushed through him to settle heavily in his balls. He leaned his head back, closed his eyes, and breathed deeply, hoping to get some type of control over his body. He was trying to recite the training lectures from his youth when all thought disappeared as his mind became a haze of ecstasy.

A shudder shook his body, and his head fell forward as he watched in disbelief as his mate replaced her hand with her mouth. Never in his existence would he have allowed a female of his species to do what his mate was doing. Gods, he had never even dreamed of it! A Sarafin female had sharp teeth like the male. They were not known for being very gentle during sex either. A male chanced losing his manhood should the female become too rough or enraged during sex. He had never heard of a male risking such an injury. Now, he panted as he watched the most erotic sight he had ever seen in his life being performed by his mate.

"You taste so good," Riley purred out as she ran her smooth teeth up his length. "I've wanted to do this to you ever since you made love to me the first time."

Vox's hands curled into tight fists as he watched her tongue flick out over the tip of his cock, licking the dewy drops of pre-cum before she sucked almost the whole length of him into her hot mouth. His gasps filled the small room, and his body shook with the effort it took not to collapse in a puddle as she sucked harder and harder, her lips wrapped tightly around his thick cock. He knew it must be difficult for her, but she breathed through her nose and continued sliding her head up and down, twisting and turning before pulling all the way out until he heard the slight pop as the tip of his cock slid out between her rosy lips. He sucked in a deep breath only to lose it in a loud swooshing sound as she repeated her assault again and again until his balls were so tight from holding back that he thought they were going to explode.

"Now," he hissed out hoarsely. "I need you now!"

Riley was totally oblivious to the effect she was having on Vox. She was focused on the pleasure she was receiving from exploring him in a way she had only read about and from the X-rated videos Grandma Pearl sent her for her last birthday. She, out of respect for her Grandmother of course, had to watch all of them—multiple times—so she wouldn't hurt Pearl's feelings. She was finding out that watching something like this and doing it were two totally different things. She had sat in awed shock and a little bit of skepticism when she had watched the videos. While they had been interesting, this was pure unadulterated pleasure.

"What?" she asked breathlessly when she found herself being lifted roughly.

"This is what," Vox growled out between gritted teeth as he stepped forward and lifted her so she was forced to lift her legs and wrap them around his waist.

Riley leaned forward, wrapping her arms around his neck as he pushed into her with one powerful thrust, impaling her. Her screams were muffled by his neck as he pulled back, gripping her thighs in his huge hands before he thrust up into her again and again, moving faster and faster until both of them were shaking. Riley felt her vagina clench and begin to spasm in rippling waves as the heat of his cock rubbing back and forth against her slick channel pulled on oversensitive nerves until she was having one pulsing orgasm after another. Afraid someone would hear the scream trying to burst from her lips, she leaned forward and bit down hard on the curve between Vox's shoulder and neck instead. His loud roar hurt her ears as he exploded deep inside her. She quaked as the hot streams of his seed poured deep inside her. She felt him swell to the point she moaned at the discomfort of it.

It feels like he is trying to lock himself to me and never let go, Riley thought in a daze.

"If it was possible, I would do it," Vox groaned out as his body jerked over and over, uncontrollably. "I swear if it was possible I would lock myself to you and never, ever let you go."

Riley had no idea she had muttered her thoughts aloud until he responded to her. "I can feel you moving deep inside me," she whispered as a light but consistent tugging pulled at her womb.

"I am giving you my cub, Riley," he admitted hoarsely. "You carry our young now."

Riley's head dropped to his shoulder as shock washed through her. The tugging continued, as if he was trying to bury himself inside her. She shivered as she replayed his words in her mind. Cubs, he was giving her his cubs. In her mind, she had a mental image of her giving birth and looking at a bunch of hairy kittens. She shook her head in disbelief. That was impossible. They were two different species. There was no way they could have babies!

Our baby, her cat purred in contentment as the tugging slowly faded.

Riley's head jerked up so fast she bumped Vox in the jaw. She stared at him with wide, frightened eyes. "Baby?"

Vox released her left thigh so he could brush her hair back as he continued to press her body against the wall. "I was very excited. I could not resist," he said with a mischievous grin.

Riley's eyes narrowed as she saw the smug grin on his face. "I hope you are joking!" she growled out as she wriggled against him when the full meaning of what he and her cat were saying sunk in.

His eyes closed as he felt her squeezing his cock as he pulled out of her slowly. "No," he groaned as his cock slid free from her warmth. "I can't wait to see you rounder than you already are," he murmured squeezing her ass as she slid her legs down.

"Rounder than I already am? What the hell is that supposed to mean?" Riley bit out, shoving him until his back hit the door of the closet they were in. "I can't believe we just got it on like a couple of teenagers in a..." She looked around the tiny room. "You fucked me in the cleaning closet?" she asked in disbelief. "And what the hell do you mean by rounder? Are you calling me fat? I want you to know I am *not* fat! I have a mature, womanly figure is all," she said as she reached down, grabbing her lacy boxers and sliding them up her legs with a wiggle. "There is no way I can have a cub, by the way. It is physically impossible. You are an alien, and I am human. Our DNA is totally incompatible, making having babies out of the question," she added as she pulled her top down.

Vox watched as Riley jerked her clothes on. His eyes followed her every movement as she elbowed him in the gut while pulling her cute little bottoms on. He had to duck as she lifted her arms to pull her top down and grab a handful of her hair. She was breathing with quick, little puffs like she was fighting for air.

"Pull your pants up!" she snapped out as she twisted her hair up into a messy ponytail. "Everyone is going to know exactly what we were doing in here!" she practically wailed as she felt the dampness between her thighs from his seed.

He wasn't about to tell her most of the crew would already know, if not from his roar, then from him dragging her into... Vox grimaced when he realized he had taken his mate in the small room reserved for cleaning materials. She was also in the beginning stages of heat, making it virtually impossible for him to ignore her even if he wanted to, which he didn't. Every male on board could smell her. That was why he had been trying to keep her contained. A female in heat could easily cause a riot on board. Breathing in deeply, he could sympathize with the other males. She smelled absolutely delicious, which was why he had either Lodar or Tor guarding her when he couldn't be with her. They were the only two he felt confident he could trust around her. Now that she was with his cub, her scent would change, warning other males she was no longer ready for breeding.

"If that wasn't enough, our combined scent would be enough to let them know," he muttered under his breath, thinking about how no one could mistake his claim now.

"What scent? Let them know what?" Riley demanded as she stared in horror as he refastened his pants.

"Riley, the Sarafin are cat-shifters. We have a very good sense of smell. It is not unusual for males to be able to smell when other males have had sex with a female," he explained.

"Are you telling me they can smell us? Together? What we just did?" she asked, feeling sick to her stomach.

"Of course," Vox replied, not understanding why she was so upset.

This would be worse than Todd Patterson at a high school dance. Then, he and his friends had only thought about what they would do with her. If what Vox said was true, all the warriors on board would know exactly what they had been doing in the cleaning closet! Riley's face flamed at the thought of all the men staring at her like she was some kind of two-bit tramp. After all, it wasn't like she and Vox were married. That was one of the things she had always sworn would happen before she gave in to a guy. She looked at her bare finger, and tears formed in her eyes. She had done it again. She had forgotten about her cardinal rule to remain firm on a ring and marriage. It was true Vox had promised her forever, but he hadn't followed it up with even a suggestion of either. Now, he was talking about her having babies! It was her worst nightmare coming to life. She was about to become a single mom just like her mom and her grandma.

Vox frowned when he saw Riley's mouth tighten in hurt and determination. "What is wrong? Do you not want my cub?" he asked, offended by her denial of their compatibility and being upset that other males would recognize his scent on her.

Riley pushed her hair out of her eyes where it had fallen and tried to push the loose strands up into her ponytail. "I want a ring—and marriage as soon as possible! I won't have any baby unless we are married."

Vox was not sure what this "marriage" was, but he knew one thing—she would be having his cub with or without it. He took a menacing step closer and growled down at her in warning. He would not tolerate her thinking she would not carry his cub.

"You will carry my cub without 'marriage.' You have no choice in the matter; it is already done," he snapped, waving his hand curtly in front of her face. "If you try to deny it, I will lock you up."

Riley's eyes flashed in fury. "Well, if you want a kid you have to marry me first. If you don't, you can forget it! I'll be the only one claiming her."

"You would try to deny me my heir?" he hissed out in disbelief. "I am Vox d'Rojah, King of the Sarafin Warriors and leader of my people," he snarled. "You will not tell me what to do! I tell you! It is time for you to learn how to be submissive to me when I give a command!"

"I don't care if you are the President of the Universe!" Riley growled back. "I am no one's submissive. If you want submissive, go practice bending over and kissing your own ass in the mirror, because it won't be me doing it."

"Guall's balls, Riley," Vox swore. "I have never allowed anyone to talk to me that way."

"Well, maybe if they did you wouldn't be such a horse's ass!" she snapped back.

"You will obey me in this, or I will make you," he vowed.

"You and whose army?" she snorted back. "I want a ring and marriage or I am totally out of here!"

Vox swore under his breath. He did not know what this "marriage" was or why she suddenly wanted jewelry, but he would be damned by the Gods before he gave it to her before she agreed to have his cub! How dare she say she wouldn't have his son unless he gave her marriage! He could understand the ring. Even the females of his world liked jewelry, but if this "marriage" thing was something from her world, then she would just have to wait. He would ask Viper to bring it back with him the next time he talked to him. He would keep it safe, but he wouldn't tell Riley about it until he had it in his hand and could force her to agree to his terms. He wouldn't hand it over to her until he had her promise to obey him. It was about time she learned he was the male and she was the female. It was her place to do as he said!

Vox smiled sharply down at her furious face. "I have no need for an army. You do not go anywhere unless I say," he stated coldly.

"We'll just see about that!" she replied quickly reaching beside him and slapping her hand on the panel to open the door.

Vox grunted as he fell backward out of the door as it gave way behind him. He landed on his back with a very furious, very determined white female tiger with blazing blue eyes staring down at him. She showed her teeth and snarled before she placed her left back paw squarely on his crotch and pushed down. Vox sucked in a breath hoping she wouldn't extend her claws to match the weight of the pressure she was applying. He understood the warning. He was in a very nerve-wracking position at the moment, and she was in no mood to negotiate who should be submissive; it wasn't going to be her.

"Riley," he bit out with a grimace of discomfort as he looked up into her snarling face. "Don't you dare."

The huge white tiger snorted before leaping off him and running down the corridor. Vox let his head drop back to the floor where he stared up at the ceiling until another face came into his view. He looked up into the sympathetic eyes of his chief engineer.

"What did you do this time?" Tor asked as he held out his hand to his friend and leader. "She looked as pissed as a traline slug," he added, referring to a nasty little creature on their planet that oozed pus when threatened.

Vox reached up and grabbed Tor's hand. "She insisted I give her something called 'marriage' and jewelry when I told her I had given her my cub. She refuses to have my son without the items."

"So, give them to her," Tor said as he watched Vox straighten his shirt and run his hand over the back of his neck.

"I will once she agrees to having my cub and submitting to me," Vox replied with determination. "She is the most stubborn, hard-headed, demanding—"

Tor drew in a deep breath and sighed in envy. "Sexy, beautiful, unusual—"

Vox's lips curved into a humorous smile. "—and passionate female I have ever met."

"Then explain to me why you want to change her?" Tor asked, looking with confusion at his friend.

"Because she will end up getting herself in trouble, and I might not always be there or have someone there to protect her," he admitted reluctantly. "I will ask Viper to bring this marriage thing back to her, and I can give her jewelry once we are down on the planet. That should calm her for a little while—hopefully."

"What did your father say about your mating to an unknown species?" Tor asked as they walked back to the bridge. He had already contacted Lodar who made sure Riley was safely back in her living quarters.

"I haven't told them yet," Vox admitted. "There is nothing he can do now anyway. I have given Riley my cub. I could feel the moment her body took my son into her womb. She is my queen, and there can be no denying it now."

Tor whistled under his breath. "You know he was determined for you to fulfill the treaty. He wanted to make sure there was an alliance with the Valdier that could not be broken."

"There already is," Vox said with an impatient wave of his hand, dismissing the reason. "A mating between Zoran's youngling and mine will ensure that. It is not necessary for me to also marry a Valdier princess to keep the peace between our people. Besides, we know most of those involved in starting the war and have dealt with them. Ha'ven, Creon, and I are continuing our joint effort to eliminate the rest. There is no possibility of it occurring again. I trust Creon and his brothers as they trust me and mine."

"Yes well, your father remembers. He does not forgive or forget as easily what happened to his sister and her mate," Tor reminded him softly. "He wants to ensure there is never a chance of it happening again."

Vox scowled as he walked onto the bridge. "I have said it will not and it will not. I will not discuss it further."

He watched as Tor nodded before moving away to finish directing the docking of the huge warship to the Transfer Station. His mind drifting back to the murder of his father's sister and her Valdier mate. He remembered his aunt's soft smile when she looked at the huge Valdier warrior the one time he saw him. The warrior had found his aunt injured after a particularly nasty battle near their family's village toward the end of the war. She had escaped into the lower mountains after the attack on his family's old mountain village. He and his father later learned the attack was designed to look like the Valdier had done it. In reality, it had been done by a group of traitors using the nearby battle as a cover as they tried to eliminate his family.

His aunt had fallen in love with the warrior named Trevon as he cared for her. Trevon had hidden her in a mountain cave high in the meadows away from the village. Vox remembered his aunt being beautiful and innocent to the vicious ways of war. Vox had no doubt that the warrior loved his aunt just as much. They had been murdered while he had been away trying to discover who was behind instigating the war between his people, the Curizan and the Valdier. Witnesses who were brought before his father to answer for the murders swore the warrior begged them with his dying breath to spare his aunt. They swore the warrior had never harmed any of the villagers. The blame lay with the small group of men who fed rumors and prejudices by the traitors in the village. A small group of villagers were horrified by his aunt's behavior in accepting a Valdier as her mate. They had tied her to a stake and slit her throat in front of his great parents, telling them their daughter's death was the penalty for her accepting a Valdier as her mate. The warrior, unable to save his mate, had been beside himself with grief. The villagers had struck out at the warrior. Wounded, the warrior had disappeared into the mountains. It was said on some nights it was still possible to hear his dragon's roar of grief and see the shadow of the dragon warrior searching for his mate.

His great parents were forced to watch helplessly as their daughter and her mate were taken from them. When his father returned from the village after the investigation, he had sworn that never again would this happen. He had forged a treaty with the Valdier king, binding their two species together in peace by promising his first male great child to the Valdier's first female great child. Vox was to mate with a Valdier princess as well. His father had chosen this path to seal their commitment to the Royal House of Valdier. Now, Vox had broken the treaty by mating with Riley.

Chapter 20

All Riley could think about was getting back to their living quarters and hiding. How dare he think it okay that every male on board the ship knew what they were doing? It was none of their damn business. The only consolation she had was that hopefully he hadn't made a bet with his friends as to who could bed the fat girl. A low mewing of pain sounded from her throat as she neared their living quarters.

Mate gives us baby, her cat hissed quietly to her. *Mates not give baby if they do not want us.*

He said he won't marry me, Riley cried out in fury. *Well, fine! If Grandma Pearl can raise me and Tina, then I know I can do it. Who needs the big jerk anyway? I don't! I am Riley St. Claire from Denver, and I'm going home and raising my baby! I know Tina will help me; she has always loved kids.*

You Riley St. Claire of Sarafin now, her cat hissed back in irritation. *That our home now.*

Oh no, it's not! Not if that big doofus doesn't marry me. And if you argue with me about it I'll cage your horny ass and drop it off at the pound as soon as I get home! Riley replied to her cat as she shifted back into her two-legged form.

She walked straight to the bathroom, tearing off her camisole and boxers as she went. Stepping into the shower, she gave the request for it to turn on as hot as she could stand it. She scrubbed at her skin until it glowed a soft peach. She would be double-damned if she was going to let this make a difference. Sure, she loved the big lummox, but he needed to treat her with respect! That meant he needed to get down on his gosh-damn knees and propose. Hell, he could even add in a nice romantic dinner with wine and roses. She was worth it. She would love his ass like no other girl could, and she would never two-time on him like some of the girls she knew back home. She would have worshipped his sorry, hairy ass if he'd treated her right, but there was no way in hell that she would ever be submissive! The name Riley and submissive just didn't go together.

Stepping out of the shower, she quickly dried herself and walked over to her huge pink suitcase. Lodar said they would be leaving for the planet soon. She needed to wear something that would make Vox regret not thinking she was good enough to marry. She wanted to go for that right look of *Mrs.* Prima Donna/Kiss-My-Royal-Ass/You-totally-fucked-up-this-time. She bit her lip as she pulled out one combination after another before settling on a bright, multicolored, flowing, flowered skirt that floated around her making her feel feminine and delicate, matched with a white off-the-shoulder peasant blouse. She finished it off with a pair of deadly, four-inch-high pink heels. In this bad-boy outfit she not only looked like a million bucks, but she was almost as tall as Vox! She quickly added a touch of makeup and dried her hair until it fell in silky, wild curls down her back. Stepping back, she looked at her reflection critically.

"Damn! I clean up pretty good, even if I say so myself," she murmured with a grin. "Let's see what that pissy-ass tomcat thinks of me now! Who needs him! I'll show him what he is missing and then some. He'll be crawling on his furry belly back to me before he knows what is happening," she added before blowing a mischievous kiss to her reflection.

She stepped out of the bathroom and quickly packed all of her things back into her suitcase before picking up her oversized purse and grabbing the handle of her suitcase. She walked over to the door and stepped out with a toss of her head at Lodar whose eyes widened in appreciation as he skimmed her lush figure.

"Gods, Riley," Lodar muttered under his breath. "You are going to cause Vox to have a stroke. You know you shouldn't pull his tail the way you do, don't you?"

Riley grinned, showing off the dimples in her cheeks which drew another groan from Lodar. "You like?" she asked as she twirled around on her heels and giggled as she heard additional groans from Cross who had come looking for Lodar.

"Riley, how about running away with me?" Cross asked with a lascivious smirk. "My world is just as beautiful as Sarafin, and dragons are known to be better lovers."

Riley's husky laugh drew more men down the corridor to see what was going on. She walked by Lodar, handing him the handle of her suitcase with a wink as she threaded her arm around Cross's thick forearm. She brushed her hair over her shoulder, revealing the pale peach shoulder that had been hidden by the mass of curls.

"Let's go, boys!" Riley called out as she pulled on Cross, directing him to the lift. "I have a planet to visit, a king to show what he is missing out on, and plans for escaping back to my world to make. Who wants to join me?"

Chuckles filled the corridor along with a loud purring of male appreciation for the sinful sway to Riley's hips as she walked in her impossible heels. Lodar looked at the back of the Valdier warrior who was grinning as he listened to some tale Riley was sharing with him. He shook his head and actually felt sorry for his friend and leader. He was going to have his hands full with his little alien mate. Riley on a mission was not only scary but a truly beautiful thing—as long as she didn't blow anything up.

* * *

Vox's fist clenched and unclenched as he fought the urge to kill the Valdier warrior who was casting him sympathetic looks as they stood next to the transporter platform. When Riley had shown up at the departure tube with at least twenty warriors following behind her, he had been furious. He wasn't furious by the sight of twenty of his best warriors glued to her every word. He wasn't even furious with the way she clung to Cross, though he figured that would come later. No, he was furious at the ease with which she looked through him as if he didn't even exist.

He calmed a little when he realized it was a ruse. He could smell her hurt and see the slight tremor in her hand when she reached up to tuck a strand of hair behind her ear. He knew the other males could smell her hurt as well and were being very protective of her. When she raised her eyebrow at him, as if daring him to say or do anything about her white-knuckled grip on Cross's arm, he had to force himself to take a deep breath. He needed to be very careful in how he handled her. She was just stubborn enough to do something crazy—like try to kidnap another warrior to take her home. A smile tugged at the corner of his mouth as he remembered her standing in the corridor not too long ago. She had been so proud of herself when she thought she had Nahuel captured.

"My lord, we are ready," the warrior at the controls to the transporter platform called out.

Vox nodded and stepped up onto the platform. Cross lead Riley up onto the platform and gently peeled her fingers off his arm. He murmured something quietly to her before he stepped over to the other square marking the platform positions. Lodar handed the handle to Riley's suitcase to another warrior who would make sure it was transported down on one of the supply shuttles and delivered to the palace later.

"My suitcase," Riley said, taking a step forward with a worried bite to her lower lip as her eyes remained glued to the huge pink case. "It has all my worldly possessions in it."

Vox turned and looked into Riley's huge blue eyes and felt the familiar sense of falling into them. "It will be delivered safely to our rooms at the palace. I promise nothing will happen to it," he reassured her quietly.

"But…" Riley dragged her eyes away from Vox's dark, tawny eyes for a moment to glance at her suitcase before she looked back at him.

"I promise nothing will happen to it. We must go," he replied. "We are expected, and others need to depart as well."

"Will this thing put all my parts back in the right place?" Riley whispered under her breath, forgetting for a moment that a Sarafin warrior's hearing could easily pick up what she was saying.

Chuckles were covered as coughs as the warriors heard her fearful question. "Yes, my little warrior," Vox replied with an amused look in his eyes before they turned dark with desire as his eyes ran over her form again. "Everything will be exactly where it should be."

"Including—" Riley's throat worked up and down even as her hand went protectively to her stomach. "Including our baby?" she whispered.

Vox's eyes softened as he reached out and touched her cheek. "I would never allow anything to hurt either one of you, my mate. We will talk later about this 'marriage' you feel you must have and the jewelry that you want," he promised huskily.

Riley's eyes brightened until they were shining like the blessed crystals that sometimes washed up on the shores from their oceans. Vox cursed that he had been so stubborn earlier for not trying to understand how important these items were to his mate. He would definitely notify Viper this afternoon about returning with a "marriage" for his mate. If something so small put such a wondrous look in her eyes, he would never deny her anything she requested.

Lodar clearing his throat reminding Vox he was standing in the middle of the transporter room with dozens of warriors looking at him with goofy grins on their faces. He felt a heated flush rise up into his cheeks before he turned and nodded tersely to the warrior to begin transport.

* * *

Two hours later, Riley realized she didn't know what to expect when they left the *Shifter*. So far, the only things she had experienced were the trader's ship, the mining asteroid, the old freighter, and the warships. She definitely didn't expect to see a lush world of such incredible beauty that she could only imagine that this must be what heaven looked like.

Tall, dark rose-colored peaks rose above thick forests. The tops of the massive trees were covered with shimmering mists of white. Dozens of small flying vehicles rose and sank among the tops of the temples. In the distance she could see great cliffs rising out of an ocean of royal blue. Waterfalls tumbled down the ragged cliff rocks, falling in sheets of white down the edges until it disappeared into the rocks at the water's edge.

Riley stood on the balcony of the palace gazing out over the alien world. She giggled as she watched a group of children, some in the shape of miniature tigers, leopards, and other cat forms, running across an open garden far below her. She gasped as a pair of strong arms circled her around the waist and pulled her back against a hard, muscled body.

"I love the feel of you in my arms," Vox said quietly, rubbing his chin against her hair. A deep purring began vibrating his chest. "I love everything about you."

Riley turned in his arms with a disbelieving giggle. "Including my temper and smart mouth?"

Vox grinned down at her with warm eyes. He brushed his lips against her softer, plumper ones. "Especially your smart mouth," he whispered huskily. "You will make my men think I am turning into a kitten. I stop thinking when I am around you," he groaned as he rubbed against her letting her feel how aroused he was.

A shuddered rippled through her before she studied his face carefully. "Did you mean it earlier?" Riley asked serious, hushed tone. "That you would talk about us getting married?"

"I would give you anything you asked for," he admitted before capturing her lips with his.

He meant what he said. He did lose all sense of thought when he was around her. Everything about her drove him crazy, from her scent, to the touch of her skin, to the sound of her voice when she was muttering under her breath or giving him hell. He wanted it all. Every fiery, passionate part of her.

He broke away with a frustrated growl when he heard the pounding on the outer door to their living quarters. The insistent sound could only mean his family—namely his father—had discovered his mating. A wave of protectiveness washed through him as he stared down at his mate's flushed face.

Guall's balls! He snarled silently as he reluctantly pulled back when the pounding grew more persistent. *All I want is for everyone to leave me alone with my mate for a few months. Is that too much to ask for?* he wondered in frustration as Riley pulled away to go answer the door.

You and me both, his cat hissed back pacing. *I want to run and chase. I want to capture my mate.*

Shut up, Vox groaned in frustration. *This is difficult enough without you picturing how you want to mount her.*

Mates have sexy tails, his cat purred.

Vox's eyes focused on Riley's swaying hips as she walked across the room. Those damn shoes of hers were staying on when he fucked her! He wanted her to wear them and nothing else but the jewels he would drape on her. His eyes brightened as he thought of one particular set of blue crystals he wanted her to wear.

And they won't be around her neck or on her fingers, he thought as an image of her huge breasts cupped in his hands formed in his mind.

He was so lost in the images of Riley in nothing but jewels and heels it took a moment for him to realize there was an awful lot of yelling going on, and it wasn't all coming from his father. He shook his head and hurried over to where Riley and his father were standing practically face-to-face in challenge.

He stepped up behind Riley, wrapped his hands around her waist and tried to pull her back behind him. He grunted when she elbowed him in the stomach and barely missed driving a spiked heel into the toe of his boot. He danced to the side with a scowl and looked over Riley's shoulder at his father who was glaring at his mate with a red face.

"What is going on?" Vox snarled out darkly, furious with his father for upsetting his mate.

"You will send this piece of rubbish back to whatever world you found her! She is not your mate. You are already promised," his father snarled.

"I know you didn't just call me a piece of rubbish, you two-bit piece of cat shit," Riley snapped back, raising a finger and shoving it into Aryeh's chest. "I am his mate and he is mine! If you don't like it, tough shit! I chose him. Possession is nine-tenths of the law and, baby doll, he's all mine," she added with a menacing hiss of warning and a little shake of her head.

* * *

Aryeh stared in outrage and shock at the unusual female stabbing him in the chest with her sharp fingernail. He had never had anyone, even his own mate, treat him with such outright hostility before. His pleasure at finding out his oldest son had been rescued and returned was overshadowed by the threat of traitors within the palace walls and now his discovery Vox was mated to an alien female from an unknown species. As far as Aryeh was concerned, the female could join the other traitors in the dungeon.

Two of the traitorous females had been apprehended, but the male who had been working with them had not been captured yet. There was also the concern there might be others. One of his younger sons was working to discover who else might be involved. Aryeh wanted to talk with Vox about his two former bedmates to see if he could discover what type of information they might have obtained.

When he was informed that Vox had returned and taken his mate to his living quarters to settle in before he would be available, Aryeh had been shocked. He had not realized that Vox had stopped on Valdier to claim the Valdier princess Clarmisa who had been promised as his oldest son's mate. His shock changed to outrage when he discovered it was not the princess, not even a Valdier, but another whom Vox had claimed. He listened in growing fury as his advisor explained that his oldest son had mated with a delicate, unknown species that had been on the Antrox mining asteroid where Vox had been held during his captivity. Aryeh had stormed out of his office determined to find out for himself who this female was and eliminate her if necessary. He would not let the treaty be broken by a piece of female ass that had caught his oldest son's attention.

"You will return her or I will slit her throat," Aryeh said coldly, looking at Vox with determination. "You are promised to a Valdier princess. This…this thing is not even worthy of being a bedmate, much less your queen."

"You arrogant son-of-a-bitch," Riley snarled back. "I'll show you worthy."

"Riley," Vox bit out in exasperation. "Don't you dare!"

He struggled to hold her back from attacking his father. He knew it was an impossible battle when he felt the soft fur of her cat ripple over her arms where he held her. He growled deeply, trying to get her cat under control, but it was too late. Before he could stop her, she had shifted and knocked his father back through the door of their living quarters into the outside corridor, pinning him on his back as she snapped at him in warning.

Aryeh's eyes widened in disbelief as he stared up at the very pissed off white tiger sitting on his chest. The female was hissing and snarling in warning, but it was the look in her bright blue eyes that held his attention. She looked like she wanted to cry even as she snapped at him in warning.

"Aryeh, I believe our new daughter is not happy with you," his wife chuckled from behind him. "I like her. I don't believe I have ever seen anyone put you on your back before."

"She put me on the floor twice," Vox said with a grin to his mother. "She is very resourceful."

"*She* is listening to you talk about her," Riley said suddenly, sitting on Aryeh's chest with her arms folded. "And don't even think about growling at me again. I am in no mood to deal with your royal-assness!" she snapped at Aryeh with a frown. "Besides, you've totally made me mess up my hair! I swear, between you and Vox you both should have been neutered when you were babies."

Rosario chuckled as she moved forward and held out her hand to Riley. "Hello, daughter. Welcome to Sarafin."

Riley grinned, reached out her right hand and placed it in the slender palm that was offered. "Hi, I'm Riley St. Claire from Denver, Colorado. It's a pleasure to meet you," she replied with a dimpled grin.

A dry cough suddenly lifted Riley up a few inches. "Do you think you could get off me now?" Aryeh asked drily.

"Do you think you can be more polite?" Riley asked with a grin at Vox's dad. "You know, I think Vox takes after you more than his mom."

Aryeh grimaced and shook his head in disbelief. His gaze moved to his oldest son who was staring at the female sitting on him like he was a couch, as if she was the most precious thing in his world. His eyebrows rose when he realized that she *was* the most important thing when he caught her scent. He smelled—a cub!

"She is breeding!" Aryeh hissed out in surprise.

Vox reached down and quickly pulled Riley into the protective circle of his arms. "Yes, I have given her my cub. She is my mate and our new queen. You will treat her with respect and not threaten to harm her," he growled out to his father. "I don't want you scaring her."

Riley looked down at the huge bear of a man lying stunned on the floor. She gasped and moved closer to Vox when Aryeh flipped up, landing on his feet silently in front of her. Eyeing him warily, she watched as his nose flared again as he drew in a deep breath.

"Her species shifts like ours?" he asked curiously.

"No, my cat gave her part of our essences," Vox replied quietly. "We are one."

Rosario and Aryeh's shocked gasps filled the air. "Vox," his mother started to say, looking worriedly at her oldest son.

"It is done," Vox replied in a deep voice. "She is mine."

Riley looked back and forth between the shocked, pale faces of Vox's parents and the deep seriousness on Vox's face with growing alarm. "What? What is wrong?" she asked in a shaky voice. "What has he done that he shouldn't have?"

Rosario smiled gently at Riley before taking a step closer to their living quarters. "He did exactly what he should have done, daughter. Come, let us have some refreshments, and I will explain it to you since my son appears to have left out a great deal of your new world."

Riley bit her lip and looked back and forth between Vox and his mother. "Am I going to want to kick his butt after you are done?" she asked suspiciously.

"Oh, most assuredly," Rosario laughed as she stepped through the open door. "I have no doubt."

Chapter 21

Riley grinned as much as she could in her shifted form as she raced across the meadow with Vox in hot pursuit. She had been on Sarafin for over two months now, and she was loving it! Her first meeting with Vox's parents might have started out shaky, but now she could do no wrong and Vox couldn't seem to do anything right—at least as far as his family was concerned. They expected him to cater to her every whim whether she had a whim or not.

If she didn't know better, she would think his brothers were having fun making them up just so they could see their older brother running around like a chicken with its head cut off. Not a pleasant analogy but truthful all the same. He had come in yesterday morning soaked to the skin and covered in sand from scouring the beaches for little blue stones the color of her eyes. When she had asked why he had done it, he said Pallu, his youngest brother by several years, swore she had mentioned she wanted some.

His other three brothers had sent him on different scavenger hunts as well, laughing in delight when he returned, at times bruised and bloody from his journeys. He was about to leave on another hunt that morning when Riley begged him to take her instead to the ancient walled city where she heard Fred and Bob were visiting. They had come from the Curizan home world to visit and sell some of their wares.

He had guided her to a strange-looking device that looked like an oversized jet ski. After he helped her climb on, he told her to wrap her arms tightly around him before he powered it on, and they slowly rose up into the air. Her excited laugh drew chuckles from the surrounding guards who would follow them. Soon, they were gliding through the thick forests.

It had taken them a couple of hours to cover the distance between the two cities. Vox explained they could have made it sooner, but he wanted to show her a little of his world. Riley had grinned in delight as he glided through the thick forests, past thundering waterfalls, and over vast fields of flowers and farmland. Before she realized it, they were landing in a small meadow on the outskirts of the huge walled city.

"We will leave the gliders here. The city is often crowded with visitors from other worlds, and I thought you might like to stretch your legs after the long ride," Vox said quietly as he helped her off the sleek machine.

Riley groaned as she rubbed her palms down along the back of her thighs. "Thank you. I think my butt has fallen asleep," she replied with a grin.

"Shift and we can run for a bit," Vox chuckled.

Riley didn't need to be told twice. She called to her cat, teasing it that she thought she saw a mouse. Within seconds, her cat stood stretching in front of Vox. With a playful swish of her tail, she took off running in delight across through the high grass. Vox quickly shifted and followed her while the four guards with them secured the gliders.

A half hour later, the loud roar of Vox's leopard behind her called out to her to slow as they neared the outskirts of the city where Bob and Fred were currently visiting with Titus and Banu. Riley had learned that this 'zone' was under the protection of the two brothers. She was excited about seeing them as well but not as much as she was about seeing Bob and Fred. She owed Bob an apology for being mean to him the last time she saw him.

"Riley, shift," Vox called out from behind her.

Riley stumbled as she shifted in mid-stride. She was getting better at it but she was still a little clumsy. She turned and smiled brightly at Vox as he strode toward her. He still took her breath away just watching him. She had a feeling it would always be like that. She glanced down at the glimmering ring on her finger. After she had explained what a "marriage" was and the symbol of a ring, Vox had disappeared for a short period only to return with a bouquet of flowers—roots, dirt, and all—and a handful of rings. He had knelt down in front of her and asked her to "marriage" him. Her eyes softened when she remembered his intense stare as he waited for her reply. They had made love right there on the floor of the living room, rings, flowers, and dirt scattered around them unseen. Later, she had picked out a simple ring that had swirling bands of color that changed as it caught the light. It was set in platinum if she wasn't mistaken and took her breath away. It fit her perfectly, and she couldn't help but gaze at it every chance she got.

Vox had not been finished with her though. He said that Viper was on his way back with Tina and her Grandma Pearl. She had been so excited about the prospect of seeing them she missed the underlining sound of strain in his voice as he told her.

"He said he is still picking salt out of his ass," Vox had said in amusement. "You were not joking when you said your Grandma Pearl would fill his ass full of it. Viper discovered salt pellets will penetrate our fur. He also said your sister is excited about seeing you. They will be here for our marriage ceremony."

He did not tell Riley what Viper had really said about Tina. He was not sure Riley would appreciate some of the more colorful words, much less the threats, Viper had been shouting when he had talked to him last. Opinionated, stubborn, vicious, hard-headed were just a few of them, and those were the nicer ones. He also did not tell her how close she had come to losing her little sister. The information Riley had about her former boss and his father proved to be more dangerous than his mate realized. He had sent copies of the information to Viper so it could be turned over to the proper authorities on Earth. After listening to what happened when that information was shared, he shuddered to think about what would have happened to his mate if the trader had not kidnapped her. He had no doubt she would have perished. Viper had been in an uncontrollable rage as he related what had happened and how he had to take matters into his own hands, otherwise Riley would have lost both Tina and her Grandma Pearl.

"How much further? Are we almost there? Do you think Bob and Fred will be excited to see us? Oh, I hope they are doing well," Riley said as she bounced up and down.

Vox's gaze softened as he watched the excited bloom of color flush his mate's face. It was so much better than the paleness from this morning when she had been sick and threatening to castrate him again for getting her with cub. He had held her pale, shaky form as she lost what little she had in her stomach over and over, until she could barely lift her head. His gaze moved down to her belly. He could tell the slight changes in it already. Her waist was expanding ever so slightly and her huge breasts were even larger. His mouth watered at the thought of the milk they would produce. Hell, his balls drew up just at the thought, and he was ready to pounce on her again.

I can pounce, his cat purred softly. *I suckle from our mate.*

Guall's balls, this is difficult enough as it is! You know she will not be happy if we take her where the guards can see us again, Vox muttered in despair.

He knew because he had done it once already, and it had taken him hours to get her to come out of the bathroom where she had barricaded herself. She had sworn she would never come out again as long as she lived. He had to cover his mouth to keep the laughter in when she went on to explain how her petrified body would be enclosed in the magnificent bathroom for all to see in the future and historians would explain that she had died of mortification because her hairball soon-to-be-dead fiancé couldn't control his damn cock! He had totally agreed that he couldn't and didn't even want to try.

"Well?" she demanded thumping him on the chest to get his attention. "Do you?"

"Do I what?" Vox asked in confusion.

Riley rolled her eyes and groaned. "You were thinking about sex again, weren't you? You never hear what I say when you are thinking about it, which is like—always! I asked if you thought the guys would be excited to see us," she huffed out, turning back toward the walled city.

Vox reached out, spinning her around, and brushing her lips with his. "Yes, they will be excited to see you. Both have sent missives asking how you were doing. Fred even threatened to come steal you away if I didn't take good care of you."

"Why didn't you tell me?" Riley asked in shock that her two, dear friends had been checking up on her.

Vox flushed and looked away over her shoulder at the gates leading into the city. "I was afraid you would tell them you were unhappy, and they would figure out a way to steal you away from me," he admitted.

He turned back to face her when he felt her soft palm against his cheek. "I love you, Vox. I won't let anyone take me away from you."

"I love you too, Riley. So very, very much it scares me sometimes," Vox whispered. "I have never felt so vulnerable before or been afraid of anything—but the idea of something happening to you terrifies me."

Riley's eyes glittered with tears as she wrapped her arms around his neck, pulling his head down to her so she could kiss him. She ran her tongue along the seam of his lips, purring as they parted for her. Soon their tongues were dueling in a furious battle of passion and desire. She sighed when Vox reluctantly pulled back.

"If we do not stop, I will claim you right here and now. I don't think you will be happy with me if I do that again with the guards watching us," he grunted out tersely.

Riley chuckled as she pulled back with a deep breath. "I'm glad you have your head screwed on straight because mine is not working right, right now. Let's go before I forget we aren't alone," she said with a wink and a giggle at the responding growl.

* * *

They entered the city through the huge gates. Riley's eyes took in the neat, clean streets filled with merchants, residents, and traders of all shapes and forms. They walked along the beautiful cobbled roads littered with strange beasts pulling carts and wagons.

"Cybris is one of our oldest cities. It retains many of the same customs as it has for thousands of years. The residents voted to leave it as such, and it attracts many visitors from other star systems who wish to experience a true Sarafin city. The city was formed around the central palace where Titus, Banu, and my other cousins live. The walls were built to protect it from the creatures that live deep in the forests. They do not come near the city now as there is a security field that protects it, but in the days of old, that was not the case," Vox explained as he guided Riley along the walkway, ignoring those who bowed to him as they recognized him. "I have to meet with Titus and Banu about some issues. Will you be all right if I leave you with Fred and Bob? I will post a couple of guards as well."

"Of course," Riley assured him. "What could happen here?" she asked, spreading her hands wide at the crowd walking around. "This place is like paradise."

Vox chuckled as they turned down a side street and stopped at a gate. He pressed the button at the gate and stepped through when it opened. A moment later, the front door to the small cottage opened, and a short figure with two heads shot through the door in excitement.

"Riley!" Fred cried out in delight, rushing forward as fast as his little feet could carry him.

"Fred! You look fantastic!" Riley said, rushing forward and dropping down to her knees to hug her friend. She gave him a kiss on both of his cheeks, laughing as both turned a dark red. "You are just as cute as ever. How have you been?"

Both of Fred's faces beamed. "I have a mate, Riley. She is beautiful!" Fred's right head responded quietly as his left studied her carefully. "I want you to meet her," his left head added.

Riley's eyes widened with shock before she smiled and laid a palm on each of Fred's cheeks. "I would be honored to meet the lady who could capture your heart. You deserve it, and she better realize what a prize she has."

"I do," came the soft reply. "I am very fortunate."

Riley stood up and looked at the small figure that approached her hesitantly. The tiny figure curtsied when she stopped in front of Riley.

Riley smiled down and held out her hand in greeting.

"I'm Riley St. Claire, soon to be d'Rojah," Riley replied when she heard Vox growl out a warning when she said her last name. "The growly bear is Vox."

The tiny figure glanced in fright at Vox's huge figure. "I am Doral. It is an honor to finally meet you. Fred has told me how you saved his life," Doral replied.

The tiny female Tiliquan only had one head, but the rest of her figure was the same as Fred's. She wore a simple gown with a black apron tied around the waist. She had the same green, yellow, and red coloring, but her eyes were framed by long, thick lashes that swept down shyly under Riley's scrutiny.

"Do I not get a welcome?" a deep, melodious voice asked from the doorway of the small house near the gates of the city.

Riley's eyes softened on the huge gelatinous figure standing looking down at her. "Bob!" Riley cried out softly, stepping into the huge arms as they opened up for her. "I'm so sorry for what I said to you the last time I saw you," she murmured against his broad chest. "You were right, I do belong with him."

Bob's huge body shook as he chuckled. "That is good. I can rest knowing I made the right decision."

Riley leaned back and grinned up at her friend. "That doesn't mean I don't still have to put him in his place every once in a while."

Fred and Bob both broke out into laughter as they heard Vox snort. "Riley, I have to go. I won't be long," Vox said with a shake of his head. "Take care of her, my friends," he said, brushing a kiss across his mate's plump lips.

"We will! We will!" Fred assured him, coming up and taking Riley's hand in one of his while he clung to Doral. "You have to meet Bob's mate. Come, come, we have refreshments."

Vox watched as his mate was pulled into the small cottage. He nodded to the two guards with him. "Stay with her. Protect her with your life," he ordered.

"Yes, my lord," both men replied taking up position in front of the door to the cottage.

Chapter 22

Vox strode through the palace corridors to the conference room with a grim expression on his face. He had not shared with Riley the true nature of their visit. He had personally gone to interrogate his two former bedmates. He discovered that their betrayal was larger than he expected. He had managed to get the location of one of the rebel bases from Eldora before she died from a poisoned drink left for her. Pursia had hung herself the night before in her cell using the covers from her bed. Eldora had begged for forgiveness before she died, swearing she had been forced to betray him and his family. He discovered that Bragnar, one of the warriors assigned to the kitchens, was holding her younger sister hostage in return for her help. She told him with her last breath that Bragnar was responsible for the attempted poisoning of his mother several months before. If it had not been for his mother's lady's maid giving his mother the wrong bowl of soup, it would have been his mother who died instead of one of her personal assistants.

"Have you any word as to who Bragnar is working with?" Titus asked as soon as he closed the door to the conference room.

"No," Vox said grimly. "Pallu and Walkyr are going to scout the rebel camp to see if what

Eldora told me is true. She swore on her dying breath she was forced to do what she did."

"Do you believe her?" Banu asked as he activated the holovid in the center of the conference table. "The region she told you is thickly covered in mists and old growth forests. It is said even the trees there are alive. It is hard to believe that anyone could build a camp there."

"I believe her. Her family is from the forest clan. They would know how to live there. Plus, she had no reason to lie as she was dying. She knew there was nothing that could save her," Vox said, looking at the image of the thick mists that swirled into view.

The satellites could not penetrate the cloud cover. Maybe he needed to talk with Ha'ven or one of his brothers. Those damn Curizan loved a challenge when it came to technology. He knew his friend would have something within a few days that could probably tell them exactly how many leaves were on the trees.

"Have you linked him to anyone else? We know whoever Bragnar is working with must also be working with Raffvin. That damn Valdier has his fingers into everything," Titus grunted out. "Who did Bragnar associate with while he worked at the palace?"

"The handful of males and females he talked to have been cleared. None of them knew much about him. They all said the same thing—he kept to himself for the most part," Vox replied.

What was the connection? He knew it had to be related to the deaths of his aunt and her mate, the attempt on his mother's life, his kidnapping. Why would they do this? His thoughts turned to his aunt. She had been a gentle soul. His mind fought to piece together the clues. He looked at his cousins. They had taken Titus and Banu as well. Why was it important to take his father's side of the family? Titus and Banu were from his father's oldest sister. Maybe the clue was with her.

"Where is Illana?" Vox asked suddenly.

Both Titus and Banu started in surprise at the mention of their mother. "She is probably in her workshop. She loves working with her hands, and you know she creates some of the most beautiful bowls and vases with the mineral clay. Why?" Banu asked curiously.

"I am not sure," Vox murmured looking at the holovid again. "But something tells me we are missing something crucial, and she may have the answers we seek."

"I'm not following you," Titus said with a frown. "Do you want me to ask her to join us or would you like to go to her workshop?" he asked, puzzled.

"Let us go there," Vox replied suddenly anxious to see his aunt.

Titus and Banu stood up at the same time. Banu flipped the holovid off and shrugged his shoulder at Titus. He didn't understand either, but both of them had learned a long time ago to appreciate Vox's instincts. It had saved them more than once during their youth, not to mention during the war.

Titus led them through the huge palace. The gleaming pale walls changed color as they passed through them, reflecting the difference in the warmth of their bodies against the sensitive stone that picked up on their moods. The stone for the palace had come from the mountains surrounding the city. The tall arched corridors allowed an abundance of light through crystal clear windows that could be darkened with a single command. Workers moved on light feet, laughing as they went about their way. He could feel his aunt's touch among the workers. They enjoyed their duties.

Soon, they were entering a small building located on the west corner of the grand gardens. The small domed building was bright and airy on the inside and was filled with all different shapes and sizes of plates, bowls, and cups made from the special mineral clay found along the streams that ran down from the mountains.

"*Nënë,* how are you doing?" Titus asked, walking over to give his mother a kiss on the cheek.

"I'm fine," she replied with a raised eyebrow as she looked at her two sons before turning her gaze on Vox. "Hello, my lord," she said with a graceful bow of her head.

"Greetings, Illana," Vox said walking over and brushing his lips along his aunt's cheek. "How have you been?"

She smiled and shook her head. "I am well. Now, out with it. You three only came to see me when you were in trouble as cubs. What mess have you gotten into this time? You know your father isn't going to believe me if I try to cover for you, don't you?" she said, looking at Titus and Banu.

All three men chuckled as they stood back. "This time it is for a different reason we are here, *Nënë.* Vox thinks you might be able to help us piece together the attacks on our family," Banu said with a grin.

"Ah," Illana responded quietly before walking over to the sink to clean the mineral clay from her hands. "I knew this time would come," she murmured. "This must not go anywhere else," Illana said as she turned to look sternly at her two sons. "It pertains to Banu as well, but I hoped that I would not have to tell him for a while yet. It would appear the time has come to share a little of our family history that is known to few."

Over the next hour, Illana related a tale of four brothers who were the first rulers of Sarafin. One ruled the forest kingdom, one ruled the city near the ocean, one ruled the desert kingdom, and one ruled the ancient city as its guardian. The gods had divided their world so none was more powerful than the others, but together they would be practically invincible. To know who the true rulers were, they were marked with a symbol. Each symbol was unique to the warrior, but when placed together the symbols marked the location of the Heart of the Cat, a gem so powerful it had the power to either heal their people or destroy them. The four brothers, concerned that the gem would fall into the wrong hands, hid the stone in a location only known to them. As they buried it, the symbols formed on each, mapping the location so it could never be truly forgotten. Only the leader of each kingdom would have the mark. If that person were to die, then the mark would appear on the next ruler. But, if the line were to die out…

"...Then so would our people. Over time, legends built up about the location until it became more myth than reality. But, make no mistake, it is very real," Illana finished. "Vox, you wear the mark as will your son. Just as Titus does since his father passed the throne onto him. Banu, you also bear the mark since the death of your father." She turned sad eyes to her youngest son.

Banu's eyes narrowed in confusion. "I don't understand. My father still lives."

"No," Illana replied softly. "While your father and I consider you our son, your true parents died days after you were born. Your father was my younger brother. Your parents were murdered in their sleep. They had been drugged in an attempt to capture the desert kingdom, which is your true heritage. Your nurse stole you away in the night and brought you to us. Arimis went to avenge my brother and his mate's murders, but the desert had swallowed the kingdom. That is one of the many myths surrounding it. Only two of the kingdoms are known—the ocean and city kingdoms. The other two remain hidden until their rightful rulers return to the throne."

"Why? Why would you not tell me years ago about my parents?" Banu asked clenching his fists in disbelief and rage. "You let me think all these years I was your son. Why would you not tell me?"

"I have lost three of my siblings to tragedy. I could not bear to lose any more of you," she said calmly, looking at him intently. "You became our son the moment I held you in my arms. I loved you as assuredly as if I had given birth to you. If I had told you before the wars, you would have gone searching for the kingdom. You were too young to go. Then the wars took you away."

Banu swung around to stare out the window of the workshop, gazing blindly over the garden. "You said you lost three siblings. Who was the other, and who and where is the fourth member bearing the mark?" he asked harshly, turning to stare at the woman he had always considered to be his mother.

A tear ran down Illana's cheek, but she did not turn away from the harsh stare. "Mia," she whispered. "She was taken as a baby and never found. I have to believe she lived. She bore the mark of the hidden forest."

Vox listened in disbelief as everything he and his cousins had ever known came apart. His own fury with his father mounted as he thought of the information withheld from him. He was the King and should have been told of the legend and its effect on his family and people, especially now that he had a mate to protect.

"What happens if there is no one to bear the mark showing the hidden resting place of the Heart of the Cat?" Vox asked knowing deep down the answer.

"Sarafin will fall," Illana answered quietly.

"That is why Raffvin wanted me, Titus, and Banu. He knows about the mark, but how, and why didn't he just kill us?" Vox asked coldly.

"He needs us and Mia or any of her children who may bear her mark," Titus replied calmly, piecing the puzzle together. "He could not kill us if he wanted to find the Heart of the Cat and capture the power of the gem. He ordered our deaths when it appeared that he would not be able to find Mia or her descendants."

"We do not even know Mia survived or if she had any cubs," Banu stated in an emotionless voice.

"Yes, we do," Vox said with a sharp-toothed grin. "If she had not survived, then our world would have fallen already. We have family to find, cousins. Whoever is working with Raffvin must be aware of the legend as well. If that is the case, they may be working on their own agenda and not necessarily with Raffvin."

"Great!" Titus growled out as he ran his hand over the back of his neck in frustration. "So, is there anyone out there not wanting to capture or kill us?"

"My lords"—a guard burst through the door suddenly—"Lord Vox, your mate has been taken!"

Chapter 23

Riley laughed at Tamia, Bob's mate, as she related how she had captured the huge Gelatian's attention. Bob just chuckled and rubbed against the large peach-colored female. They enjoyed the afternoon as Riley teased both of her former "mates" about abandoning her while they told their mates how she almost blew everyone up, not once but twice.

"Doral and I need to go to the market. Would you like to come?" Tamia asked politely. "It is not far."

"I would love to go!" Riley said with an excited grin.

Vox had kept her practically a prisoner at the palace. Okay, that might be a bit of a stretch, but she hadn't been anywhere outside the ocean city and she wanted to see the beautiful ancient city. It reminded her so much of some of the pictures she had seen of the older cities in Europe and since she never got to see them, she figured she might as well enjoy this one.

"We will return shortly," Doral said, giving Fred a kiss on both lips with a blush.

"Very shortly," Fred's left head responded with a soft growl while he held onto both of her hands for a little longer than necessary.

All three women laughed as Doral pulled free with a vivid blush covering her face. They picked up the baskets by the door that they would need to carry their purchases. Riley adjusted her oversized purse over her shoulder and nodded to the two guards that Vox left. She knew better than to argue with them following her around. Vox should have been born a bulldog because he wouldn't budge on her wandering around without a couple of guards always tagging along.

"So where to first?" Riley asked as they stepped through the gate.

"There is a market where many different fruits, vegetables, and breads are sold. Bob does not eat meat, but Fred does. We will go to the market first. There is another market a few streets further where they sell beautiful cloth and other things," Doral replied as she moved rapidly through the crowded streets.

Riley followed the clipped pace Doral set. She might be small, but she was a bundle of energy. She was so happy her two friends had found someone to spend their lives with. Fred had told her that his older brother had been killed in a dispute over credits, and his father wanted him to return. He had talked at length with Doral and both of them decided that they did not want to raise their young on a fueling station. Bob had become a prominent silversmith in the small village he had settled in on Curizan. That was where he met Tamia who had also sought refuge after escaping captivity from a slave trader who made the mistake of challenging a Curizan warrior. The warrior had freed Tamia and brought her back to his world to live. She had been working as a seamstress in the village. Both men decided they wanted to start fresh and had already established their homes there.

"Oh my," Riley said with a huge grin as she took in all the different stalls selling their wares. "Do you think Vox has credit here?" she asked hopefully.

One of the guards chuckled. "You may purchase whatever you want, my lady. Lord Aryeh instructed us to make sure you had whatever you desired. He said he would deal with Lord Vox if he should have a problem."

"I knew I was going to love that adorable old hairball once he realized I was the best thing that ever happened to his son!" Riley declared with a royal wave of her hand.

Doral and Tamia dissolved into giggles while the two guards chuckled. Riley tossed her wayward curls over her shoulder and raised her arm. "Charge ladies! And I truly mean charge! We are going to do some major shopping. I swear I was going through withdrawal!" Riley said as she sashayed her ass right through the middle of the crowded market in excitement.

She spent the next half hour exclaiming over one find after another in the food market. It was when they continued onto the merchant's market that she thought she had truly died and gone to heaven. The silk scarves, unusual handbags, and other accessories outdid the little overpriced boutique Tina worked in during high school. Riley moved rapidly from one stall to another, picking up scarves, hats, bracelets, and handbags with a critical eye.

"How much is this?" she asked one merchant before turning to another and pulling another item up and showing it to other merchant. "And this? Tamia is that too much for this? Doral, what do you think? Does this make me look too pale? Oh my god, look at this! I have to have it! Do you think Vox will be upset? The guy says it is seventy-five credits. Is that a lot?" Riley asked, having no idea the worth of a credit. For all she knew, it could be the equivalent of a thousand bucks back home. "Damn! I should have had Viper tell Tina to clean out my account back on Earth. She has access. I might have been able to convert it or buy stuff at home to cash in here. I really, really want this bag. It will go perfectly with several of my outfits," she added, biting her lip in indecision.

"Lady Riley, seventy-five credits is very inexpensive," one of the guards assured her. "Lord Vox would not be upset at all if you purchased the bag, especially as you like it so much."

"You really think so?" Riley asked anxiously fingering the beautiful beaded bag with the tips of her fingers. "It is the most beautiful handbag I've ever seen."

"Please package the bag for my lady queen," the guard called out to the merchant.

Riley grinned at the merchant as he handed her the carefully wrapped purchase with a low bow. "It is a pleasure doing business with you, my queen. I will inform my daughter you admired her work."

"Tell her I have never seen anything as beautiful as this, and I will take very good care of it," Riley responded to the beaming man.

"Riley, there are only a few more stalls to go. Do you want to see them before we return?" Doral called out from across the way where she had found a scarf she liked.

"We might as well as I don't know when I'll get a chance to return," Riley answered with a contented sigh. "This has been the best day of my life—well besides the day I met Vox, even if I did knock him on his ass."

Tamia laughed and moved to the next stall. Riley felt a sense of unease as they approached the last stall. It was a little further away from the others, and there were only a few shoppers down this way. That wasn't what had the hair on the back of her neck standing up though. There was something else, as if she was being stared at. She let her eyes wander around the area, pulling on her skills as a bail bondsman to help her. In the shadows near an alley a cloaked figure was standing in the shadows. Riley stopped, focusing on the figure with a frown. There was something vaguely familiar about it. The frown on her face turned into a surprised gasp as the figure emerged from the shadows and lowered the hood covering its head.

..*

Antrox 157 stared with hatred at the female who had destroyed everything he had worked for. He motioned with his hand. Four figures converged on Riley's small group. The two guards went down with blasts to their backs as they moved closer to Riley when she gasped and froze. The other two females screamed in terror. Within moments, Riley's unconscious body was being carried past him. He stared in distaste at the limp pale figure as the mercenaries he had hired walked by him. He would receive a king's fortune in credits for the female. He had sworn he would make her pay for ruining his reputation within the Antrox mining operations. He would have been lucky to hire on as a pactor supply clerk after what she had done. Now, he would have enough to buy his own mine. It would be small, but it was a start. He quickly followed the mercenaries out of the marketplace, ignoring the calls for help from the women as they bent over the still forms of the guards.

"We need to get out before they shut down all leaving flights," the huge merc carrying Riley snarled. "You didn't tell us she was royalty."

"She is nothing but an escaped acquisition. You were given the credits to capture her. I will give you the other half due you once she is delivered," Antrox 157 replied coldly. "Otherwise, you get nothing."

"Damn bug," another one of the mercs muttered under his breath. "Move it, Garl. I don't want to stick around for any of these damn cat-shifters. They like to rip you open and watch as you try to shove your guts back in."

"Prepare the ship for liftoff," a third merc yelled out. "We leave hot and fast."

"Grun, go ahead and make sure the way is clear," Tril snapped at the husky red-skinned creature who sped away on four legs. "You better hope she is worth the credits you promised," he said as he shifted Riley over his shoulder.

"She accepted five mates; three were Sarafin warriors. I have no doubt she will handle whatever the pleasure house sends to her," Antrox 157 replied, hurrying down the narrow alley.

Nothing else was said as the five figures moved rapidly down the narrow alley and up several flights of stairs until they reached the top of one of the taller buildings in the city. Grun was removing the cover camouflaging the small transport. It was a tight fit, but all five plus an unconscious Riley piled into the small ship. Garl shoved at the controls, and the specially modified ship rose rapidly before turning and shooting up through the atmosphere. The group was used to retrieving difficult and dangerous merchandise. This mission was especially challenging because none of them wanted to be on the wrong end of the Sarafin warriors who were bound to try to retrieve what they had stolen. They were there to retrieve and deliver, that was all. After the delivery, they would disappear for a few months before regrouping in a different star system.

* * *

Riley came to slowly. Her head ached and her stomach churned. She could feel that she was about to lose what she had eaten for lunch.

Being pregnant sucks, she thought darkly, keeping her eyes closed and breathing steadily through her nose in the hopes of not tossing her cookies. *I think this should be a totally male thing since they are the ones who want to brag about how potent they are. What the hell do they suffer from? Puffing their chest out too far? They pop the load and sit back while I get to be sick, gain even more weight, and have bigger boobs to carry around while they strut like a damn peacock!*

Riley continued listing all the disadvantages being pregnant entailed, hoping it would help calm her wayward stomach. After several minutes, it appeared to work as she felt confident she could open her eyes without them being crossed.

She turned her head cautiously, studying where she had been taken. Her heart jerked at the idea of her friends or the guards with her being harmed because of her. Her eyes blurred with anger at the thought of the senseless act.

"I'm going to smash that oversized bug when I get my hands on him. I'm going to feed him to the first Venus flytrap I can find. Or better yet, I'm going to find a really huge spider and watch as he squirms in its web before it sucks all his guts out," she muttered out loud.

A dark chuckle drew her attention to the door of her cell. She stared in fury at the grotesque creature standing on the other side of it. "What are you laughing at, you overgrown fleabag?"

"Antrox 157 said you had spirit. I am glad he did not lie. You will bring more credits on the auction block. Many of the more selective guests like a female with a little spirit. They want to see how long it takes to break her," the snarly voice replied.

Riley slowly sat up, putting a hand to her head to still the spinning. She glared at the creature. It was shorter than she, probably about five feet eight inches, if that. It was covered in gun-metal gray scales and had two red, beady eyes, no nose, and thin lips covering small, sharp teeth.

"Who the hell are you, and what are you doing working with a scumbag like that dickless bug?" Riley asked. "Don't you have anything better to do than kidnap innocent, defenseless females?"

Pud laughed. It was a shame he needed to deliver the pale female so quickly. The owner of the pleasure house wanted to test her out before he put her to work. It appeared the owner was bored and had become intrigued by the story behind this particular female. He rubbed the front of his pants, wondering if he could chance having a sample before he delivered her.

"You make me hard, female," Pud told her with a nasty grin. "I like that. It has been a while since a female has done that."

Riley rose up enjoying the way the filthy creature took a step back when he realized she was taller than he was. "Don't even think of it, you little squirt. I'll rip your dick off and feed it to you before you even realized that little worm in your pants was gone," she snapped out.

Pud's beady eyes glowed in anger. "Shut your mouth, female. I can understand why Antrox 157 wanted to see you suffer. You have a big mouth on you."

Riley grinned nastily at the creature. "All the more to bite your head off, you miserable little rodent. You just wait until Vox gets here. He'll make you wish you had never been born."

"Vox?" Pud asked, taking another step back and turning pale. "Vox d'Rojah, the Sarafin king?" he asked hoarsely.

"That's right, you steaming pile of cow paddy. I am *Mrs.* Vox d'Rojah! You've messed with the wrong bitch this time!" Riley snapped back in triumph, exaggerating a little about her new status.

It was only a matter of time before it became official. She was wearing Vox's ring, so as far as she was concerned it was practically a done deal. They were just waiting for Tina and Pearl to show up before having the official ceremony.

The beady-eyed creature muttered a long string of curses as he turned and hurried down the corridor. She bet he was wishing he hadn't taken on this assignment now. She was going to make sure he and that bug-eyed walking stick paid for hurting her guards and taking her.

"That's right, you shitless piece of crab poop! You'd better run, but you'll never be able to hide!" Riley yelled out behind him before giving a cackling laugh that would have made the Wicked Witch of the West shit her pants.

She was just thankful the slimy little bastard couldn't see how badly her hands were shaking. "Vox, you better get your ass here soon. I am totally scared out of my mind, you adorable puddy cat."

Chapter 24

"Give me a status report now!" Vox growled out as he strode onto the bridge of the *Shifter*.

"We have five targets we are pursuing. From the reports we have received so far from our tracking station, a transport left the ancient city traveling at a high rate of speed. It docked with a trader ship on the outer rim of the star system. Four transports separated from the trader and headed in different directions. Battle cruisers have been dispersed after those. We are following the trader's ship," Tor reported as he came to stand next to Vox.

"Conference room," Vox growled out, feeling his stomach tighten.

Lodar and Tor followed Vox into the conference room located next to the bridge. As soon as the door closed, Vox turned and glared at his friends. He opened his mouth to speak but couldn't get anything past the lump that had suddenly formed in it. He cleared his throat and tried again.

"What do you have on the attack in the market and about the ship's identification?" he asked hoarsely.

"Tamia reported they saw an Antrox before the attack. She said Riley appeared to recognize him before the guards were shot," Tor responded.

"One of the men is in critical condition. The other is stable," Lodar added. "Neither one of the other females was injured. It appeared Riley was the target."

"The trader ship is registered out of the Guambian star system. I have a feeling we will find out the documents have been forged. There were no identifying signals from the other four ships that departed from it, more than likely the mercenaries who were hired to capture Riley. They typically use this type of method to escape. It is easier for them to escape and makes it difficult to catch more than one."

"The question is—what do they want with her?" Lodar asked, rubbing his hand down his face.

Vox's face was frozen in rage as he remembered Antrox 157's threat to sell Riley to the pleasure houses dotted throughout the star systems. He should have made sure that slimy insect had been dead before he escaped the mining asteroid. He had hoped that the cold-blooded insect had blown up. He would not make that mistake again. The Antrox had signed his own death sentence by taking Riley.

"He plans to sell her to a pleasure house," Vox said thickly.

"Gods!" Both Lodar and Tor exclaimed in horror at the same time.

Vox turned to look at them. "Get me to that damn ship. She had better be on it. I'm going to rip out the guts of any male who has touched her."

Tor looked at his friend and leader with fire burning in his own eyes. "I'll be there to help you, my friend," he said before turning on his heel and striding back onto the bridge, barking orders to the helmsman to give him everything the *Shifter* had.

Lodar walked over to where Vox was staring out into the darkness of space. He stood next to him for a few moments in silence, not sure what he could say to help his friend. His own mind was picturing Riley's infectious smile, the delighted twinkle in her eye when she was causing mischief, and her lush figure that affected every male she met.

"I want you near when we find her," Vox said quietly in a husky voice. "If"—his throat worked up and down—"If we do not get to her soon enough and...and she has been harmed, I need you there to help heal her," he finished thickly.

"Of course. You don't even need to ask," Lodar said, placing his hand on Vox's shoulder and squeezing it briefly in comfort. "You are not the only one who has fallen in love with her. She is a very special female."

Vox didn't respond. He simply stood rigidly, staring out into space. He knew the moment Lodar left. That was the moment the tears he had been holding back broke free, and his shoulders began to shake. Never in his life had he cried. Not when he watched men he considered his friends fall during the war, not when he was tortured—never—but the idea of his beautiful, delicate mate suffering the assault of another male was too much for him. He cried silent tears of rage, hurt, and fear before he ran the sleeve of his shirt over his eyes. He felt the chill of ice as it coursed through his blood. He would kill any and everyone involved in hurting his mate. The gods would have no mercy for them.

* * *

"Sir, the last of the four transports has been searched. Lady Riley is not aboard it. That leaves the trader's ship. We are almost within range," the helmsman informed Vox who stood rigid on the bridge.

"Hail the trader's ship. Tell him to prepare for boarding," Vox instructed in an emotionless voice.

Information about the trader had come from Adalard. His warship had intercepted one of the transports. After interrogating the merc on board, he had been informed the trader's name was Pud. Adalard had forwarded the translated information the merc had on the trader to Vox. It had not taken long for the Curizan to decipher the files. Mercenaries were renowned for having information on those they did business with in case they needed something to blackmail them with later on.

The information had almost driven Vox crazy. The trader was a known sex slave trader, stealing and sampling the females before he delivered them. The females were always physically alive when he delivered them, but their mental state was questionable. The information gave graphic detail about his sexual preferences. He knew his cub would not survive an assault by the trader. That was the first thing that came to his mind. The trader liked to use tools on the females to clean them out first before he sampled them—repeatedly. Lodar and Tor had reviewed the information as well, becoming quieter the more they read. Lodar excused himself shortly after the report was finished so he could prepare a bag with the items he would need to help Riley.

Vox straightened and clenched his fists tightly when the beady-eyed creature answered the *Shifter's* hail. "This is Captain Pud Rasp. State your business."

"Prepare to be boarded," Vox said stiffly.

"Why are you boarding me? I am not in the Sarafin star system. You have no call to board my vessel. I am a legitimate short-haul freighter," Pud said nervously.

"We are boarding you. Don't try to stop us," Vox said with a wave of his hand to cut the transmission. "Prepare the fighters. Take out his engines. I don't want to take a chance he has modified them. If he has any weapons, take them out as well but do not breach the hull. We do not know where he may have hidden Lady Riley."

"Raghu, you have the bridge. Do not let that bastard out of your sight," Vox ordered to the current first officer on duty.

"Yes sir," Raghu responded taking over command.

"Let's go get my mate," Vox bit out to Lodar and Tor.

* * *

Riley worked the cover off the control panel with the Leatherman she had in her purse. She flipped it around until it had the pliers showing after she tossed the cover onto the bed. She was not about to sit around waiting to be rescued. Hell, she thought, cold, dank, and ugly might decide to test her theory about ripping his dick off. The thought of touching him was enough to make her want to vomit.

"That is so not going to happen," she muttered as she studied the wires.

With a shrug, she snipped the red wires crying out in startled pain when she cut the back of her hand on a sharp edge of the panel when she jumped at the sparks flying out at her. She cursed and reached over to wipe the blood off on the cover of the bed before pulling a bandage out of her purse and covering the cut. When she was done, she quickly snipped the rest of the wires being more careful as the sparks flew. She breathed a sigh of relief when she finally heard the click of the door.

"At last," she sighed impatiently. "Now, to do the amazing disappearing act. And they thought Houdini was the only one who could do it." She giggled. "And now, ladies and gentlemen, the amazing Riley St. Claire-d'Rojah performing her 'I'm-getting-the-fuck-out-of-here act!" She said with a flourish of waves and smiles for her non-existent audience.

She slipped out the door and moved rapidly down the corridor. She would hide on a different level. She decided that to drive the spaceship you probably went up, so she would go down. After all, someone had to drive the damn thing, didn't they? she reasoned. So, as long as monster man was up top she wanted to make sure she was as far away from him as possible.

She quickly slipped down the ladder between levels and kept going. She wound up one corridor and down another. After half an hour she decided she was so lost that she wouldn't even be able to find herself. That must give her some advantage. She trotted down another corridor, skidding to a stop when she realized she was in some type of cargo area. There were huge crates everywhere. She looked up at one group and decided if she could get to the top of it, she could lie down and no one would be able to find her. She bit her lip before an excited grin crossed her face and she shifted.

In her four-legged form, jumping from crate to crate was easy. She was also warmer with the fur coat she was wearing. She turned in a circle several times before she laid down on the top container, exhausted. She opened her mouth in a huge, sharp-tooth yawn and settled her head down on her front paws.

Nap-thirty, she thought drowsily. *Escaping and getting lost is hard work.*

She rubbed the side of her mouth against her paw as her mind began to cloud over with sleep. She would just wait here quietly until Vox came. It shouldn't take him long, and she would be much more of a help once she was rested.

Baby makes us sleepy too, her cat yawned before the exhaustion they were feeling overwhelmed them both.

* * *

Vox stood frozen in frustration. The damn trader had released some type of fragrance bomb into the ventilation system. The entire ship smelled of oil and sweat. The two smells covered any scent he would have had of Riley. On top of that, the slimy bastard had rubbed the same stuff all over his clothing.

He turned when the lead of Team Three came up. The warrior shook his head. "Nothing, sir."

He turned back to the trader who was shifting back and forth on his feet between two warriors who were positioned on either side of him. He took a menacing step toward the sweating male. His face darkened as Team Two reported they had found nothing in the lower cabin areas.

"Where is she?" Vox snarled, letting his right hand shift until his sharp claws were extended. "I won't ask you again."

"I...I...I told you," Pud stuttered. "I'm just a short-haul cargo freighter. I don't carry passengers."

Vox roared, letting his teeth drop down and shifting partially in rage. He could smell the lie on the man, even over the oil and sweat. He raised his clawed hand and swiped it down along the trader's face, ignoring the male's screams as he collapsed and gripped his shredded cheek in his palm.

"You dare lie to me," Vox snarled out in rage.

"Sir! We've found something," Team One called out. "There is a cell with the panel disconnected."

Vox turned dark, thunderous eyes on Pud. "Bring him. If I find her on this ship, he will die a slow death."

He ignored the trader's pitiful begging. He moved down the corridors heading down to the level where Team One waited for him. His heart thundered in his chest as he approached the door where his men were standing. He stumbled when he saw Lodar, who was kneeling by the bed, look up at him with a tight, grief-stricken face. Tor stood rigid by the door, the muscle in his jaw working back and forth.

"Is she in there?" Vox asked hesitantly.

"No," Tor said looking coldly at the sobbing trader.

"What?" Vox forced out.

"The blood on the bed matches Riley's blood," Lodar said, standing up. "She was held here."

Vox heard the words "Riley's blood" over the thunder in his ears. He spun around, grabbing the trader by the throat and holding him up against the outer wall of the corridor. He ignored the blood running down the man's face onto his arm. He ignored the desperate gasps as the trader tried to draw in air from where Vox was crushing his throat. He ignored the men surrounding him as grief and pain unlike anything he had ever experienced washed through him.

"Where is she?" He roared so loudly the walls vibrated with his rage. He pulled the trader back and slammed him back against the wall again. "Where did you put her body?"

"I…swear. I…swear," the trader tried to say. "I…swear I didn't hurt her."

Vox's face twisted in pain and grief. Pulling his left hand back, he swiped the trader across his gut, slicing him almost to his backbone. He dropped the dying male who was trying to hold his internal organs as they spilled out. Vox stepped back from the gore with a look of disgust.

"Find her," he ordered quietly. "I will not leave her here."

Tor and Lodar nodded. They left Vox, spreading out to search the ship thoroughly. Vox stood standing in the empty corridor watching dispassionately as the slave trader finally quit jerking. A horrible wave of grief overcame him, and he roared as the pain swept through him in never-ending waves of agony. Pulling his fist back, he slammed it into the metal wall over and over, ignoring the pain and blood from the strikes. It was nothing compared to the pain in his heart and soul.

Chapter 25

Riley rolled over onto her side taking the weight off her expanding belly. She was having the most wonderful dream. She and Vox were chasing each other around the meadow near the ancient city, only this time the guards weren't looking. She felt her back leg jerking as if she was running. Suddenly Vox sprang out from behind a bush, tackling her and rolling her over and over. She moaned softly in her sleep as she felt him mount her from behind, his teeth buried in her neck and his cock buried deep inside her womb. Another low moan escaped her before a noise in the cargo area disturbed the dream.

Wake up! her cat hissed quietly. *I smell danger.*

What? Riley muttered sleepily. *Tell it to come back later. Vox and I are getting it on, and it is so amazing.*

You are bad as mate! All you think about is sex, her cat hissed back in aggravation. *Wake up!*

Riley rolled over with a silent grumble. *You're damn right all I think about is sex. Hell, I was good for the first twenty-four years, for crying out loud! Double hell, if you consider I'm a St. Claire and was a good girl. I think I totally get to think of nothing but sex for the next forty or fifty years at least!*

You have to be alive to have it, her cat reminded her with a huff.

Great! Just great! Everything has to have strings attached. You have to be alive if you want to have sex. Fine! I'm awake, Riley growled silently to her cat. *So, where is this danger?*

I not know. I just feel danger, her cat replied. *Funny smell makes my nose burn. I not smell anything right.*

Well, don't stick your big-ass head up like a target. Just keep quiet, lie still, and wait. That is what the cats on my world do. Then they pounce when the target gets close, Riley responded logically.

I wait, her cat promised.

Riley kept her head down, letting her ears flicker back and forth, trying to pinpoint where the sound that disturbed her came from. Everything appeared to be quiet, but the hair on the back of her neck was standing straight up telling her that she wasn't alone in the cargo bay any longer. Her ears flickered again, perking up when the door to the cargo bay suddenly opened. She froze, barely breathing as she heard the sound of footsteps entering the room. They seemed to echo overly loud in the silence.

"This is the last room that hasn't been searched," a deep voice whispered.

Riley shivered as she heard the footsteps divide before everything became silent again. Whoever was searching was very light on their feet. Riley curled up into a tight ball, trying to make herself as small as possible on the top of the crate. She heard the door open again, and the sound of heavy footsteps echoed through the cargo bay.

"Have you found anything?" a familiar voice called out harshly. "I want every crate opened and searched thoroughly."

Vox! Our mates! Riley and her cat both cried out in excitement.

Riley uncurled her huge body and stood up on shaky legs. Damn, she was a nervous wreck. She was so going to be a total crybaby when she got Vox's arms wrapped around her. She shook her body and moved over to the edge of the crate. At the same time, a movement between two crates a short distance away caught her attention. Antrox 157 stepped out, raising a laser pistol, pointing it at Vox's chest. Riley didn't even think about what she was doing. Her horror and fear for her mate overrode all thought. Leaping from the crate at Vox, she shifted as she fell toward him, screaming for him to look out at the same time as Antrox 157 fired the laser pistol.

Riley felt her body jerk when she hit Vox in the chest as he turned toward her scream. They tumbled down, rolling over and over until Vox lay sprawled on top of her. She gripped his shoulders tightly in panic.

"Are you okay?" she asked in a frightened voice.

"Yes, you…" Vox tried to speak over the sounds of laser fire.

"I'm good." She smiled up at him, brushing her palm against his cheek. "Go get that bastard," she gasped as laser fire barely missed them.

"With pleasure," Vox grinned, showing his sharp teeth.

Riley lay still as Vox rolled off her and called out commands to his men to surround the crate where Antrox 157 was hiding. She reached down and touched her side which was beginning to burn fiercely. Her eyes widened when her fingers came away covered in blood. From the feel of it, the damn Antrox hadn't missed after all. Riley coughed slightly as her throat filled, beginning to choke her as she tried to breath in.

We hurt, her cat hissed frightened. *I feel essence leaving. We hurt bad.*

Our baby? Riley begged.

Our poor baby, her cat moaned softly. *Our poor baby.*

No! Riley screamed as she struggled to draw in a breath. *No!* She cried out as darkness blurred her vision. *No, damn you! I won't lose them. I love them both too much,* she whispered, fighting against the pull on her to give up and let the pain go. *Never!* she thought as she felt the tug of hands and the cry of despair shattering the sudden quiet of the cargo bay.

* * *

Vox motioned with his hand for the four warriors on each side to circle around the crate. There was nowhere for Antrox 157 to go. He was dead, he just didn't realize it yet. Vox looked up and with a swift leap, he landed on silent feet on top of the crate. Running along the edge, he could see the Antrox jerking nervously back and forth trying to keep the openings to the crates in his view. He never looked up. If he had, he would have used the laser pistol on himself instead of worrying about the other warriors. Vox dropped down behind him when 157 turned again. He reached his hand around and gripped the thin creature's wrist, snapping it like it was a twig. Antrox 157's screams filled the cargo bay before they were silenced as Vox lifted the creature up and slammed him against the crate with a grin.

"Now, you die," Vox said letting his right hand shift. "Slowly," he added before he ran one razor-sharp claw across Antrox 157's stomach. "You will never harm my mate again," Vox said, dropping the Antrox when he heard Lodar's desperate cry for him.

Vox spun around, squeezing through the opening between the crates. He stopped in horror when he saw Lodar kneeling over Riley, his hands covered in blood. He moved with jerking, running steps toward her. Dropping down next to her, he cupped her face, turning it toward him.

"What have you done now?" he croaked out.

Riley tried to smile up at Vox as he stared down at her face with worry. "Guess I'm not okay," she whispered weakly. "This sucks."

"Yes, yes, it does," Vox said tenderly. "You are not supposed to get hurt. I do not like it when you are hurt."

Riley's eyes filled with tears. "Don't want to die," she choked out. "Thought I was the heroine this time."

"You are," Vox whispered as he stroked her cheek with trembling fingers. "You will always be my heroine."

Riley smiled softly before her eyelids flickered and closed peacefully. She looked so beautiful. Her hair was spread out in a curly mass of waves around her, making her look just like he had made love to her. Her eyelashes lay like crescents, begging him to kiss them until she woke up.

Vox looked at Lodar in panic. "Help her," he begged his friend. "You have to help her."

Lodar shook his head. "I would need to get her into a regen bed," he said. "There is none on this ship, and she won't survive if we move her."

Vox shook his head in denial. He couldn't lose her. He just couldn't lose her and their son. His shoulders shook as the magnitude of the situation flowed through him. Never had he expected to find his mate. Never had he expected to love someone so much she would become the very fabric of his existence.

"Sir, look!" One of the warriors exclaimed as he picked up the spilled contents of Riley's oversized purse that she carried everywhere. "She has everything in here!"

Lodar glanced up, his eyes widening when he saw the portable regen device the Curizan had developed and kept secret. His breath escaped him in a disbelieving chuckle. Only Riley would have a top-secret medical device the Curizan prized in her purse.

"Give that to me!" Lodar demanded, holding out his hand and waving his fingers urgently at the man. "What else does she have?"

"Everything!" The warrior laughed. "She has medicine in here that will take care of everything from a toothache to ulcers to internal bleeding," he replied, bundling up all the small vials of medicine Riley had taken from the medical unit on the asteroid.

Lodar pulled the portable regen open and attached the probes to her temples to keep her brain functioning before he used the scanner to start the healing process. He ordered one of the men who worked with him in medical to begin using the vials she had taken to stop her internal bleeding and prevent her from getting an infection. They worked steadily while Vox knelt beside Riley, talking to her about all the things he was going to do to her when she woke up.

Twenty minutes later, his voice was hoarse from relating every threat and punishment he could think of. He blinked furiously when Lodar told him Riley and his son would be fine. He looked at his friend's exhausted face and tried to thank him, but his throat was too tight to get the words out. He felt the dampness on his cheeks, and for once, didn't care that his men could also see it. He was going to have to punish Riley for this too. He had never cried in his life, and now she had made him do it twice in as many days.

"You can't punish me," Riley murmured huskily, her eyes still closed. "Your dad said you had to give me whatever I wanted. By the way, I spent a fortune of your credits at the market."

Vox's head jerked down to stare at his mate's beautiful, flushed face. "You did? What did you buy?" he asked in a husky voice.

Riley's brilliant, baby blue eyes open to stare up at him. "I bought the most beautiful oversized purse you've ever seen and the most god-awful jacket. You aren't allowed to kill this one. I love it."

Vox's relieved laughter echoed as he threw back his head and shouted with joy before he gently drew Riley up into his arms. "You can buy whatever handbag and hideous jacket you want. I promise not to destroy it."

Riley's eyes softened. "Can we go home now? I don't like this place."

"Yes, my mate. We can go home now," Vox promised.

Epilogue

"Where's my goddamn gun!" Pearl snarled. "I'm going to fill his ass with lead if he doesn't get it down here! Forget the salt. You damn creatures just lick that shit up, even if it's in your own ass."

Viper clenched his fists tightly at his side and counted to twenty backward. It was one of the few things that helped prevent him from putting his hands around Riley and Tina's grandmother's neck. Even so, it was still very, very tempting.

"He will be here for the ceremony," Viper growled out. "And I did not lick my own ass."

Pearl looked at Viper with an expression that clearly said she didn't believe him. Tina stood to the side, refusing to look at him, which was even more infuriating. He would have thought saving her life would have made her more receptive to him, but no! She kept a wall of ice so thick between them, he really did feel like his dick might freeze off. If it hadn't been for that one night…

Viper cursed again when Pearl asked for her shotgun. "I am not giving you that damn gun! You are dangerous enough without it," he snapped.

"Don't you dare talk to my poor, defenseless grandmother like that!" Tina said, glaring at Viper in anger. "If she wants her shotgun, you should give it to her. It *is* her property after all," Tina pointed out in a frigid voice.

"Yes—the one she keeps pointing at me every opportunity she gets," Viper snarled back. "Let her fill your ass with rock salt and see if you like it!"

Pearl chortled at the thought. "I bet he would volunteer to lick it off, Tina girl. Want to see if he will?"

Tina blushed a bright red and glared at her grandmother before sniffing and turning her back on both of them. "You're right, she doesn't need her shotgun," she muttered under her breath.

Aryeh, Rosario, and Illana chuckled as they watched Viper run his hands through his hair in aggravation. All of them stopped and turned when they heard the music of the wedding march begin. Vox rushed down the aisle to stand next to his brothers who were lined up, chuckling under their breath.

"Did you get it?" Walkyr asked quietly.

"Yes, she really, really wanted it," Gable added.

"She said she wouldn't marriage you without it," Qadir added with a huge grin. It had been his turn to come up with something for Vox to hunt down, and he had made sure it hadn't been easy.

"Guall's balls," Pallu muttered, trying to keep a straight face. "If Riley doesn't kill you, her grandmother will. You are late for your own marriage ceremony."

The four brothers laughed as they glanced at Pearl who was standing waiting for her granddaughter to walk down the aisle on Bob and Fred's arms. They had never seen anything like the slender older woman with white spiked hair. She was wearing more leather than all four of them put together. Pallu looked at his brother Viper who was staring—still—at the petite dark-haired female on the other side of Pearl. Viper was the only one who wasn't celebrating. Pallu's eyes widened as he saw the brief look of sadness in his brother's eyes as he gazed at the little human female before he covered it. There was more to the story than just Viper returning with Riley's family.

All eyes moved to the back of the room as Riley appeared dressed in a flowing white lace gown covered in tiny blue stones the color of her eyes. She glowed with happiness as she walked down the aisle toward Vox, who was smiling just as broadly. The swollen roundness of her stomach stuck out in front of her. Bob and Fred walked slowly as the music continued to play. Once they reached Vox, Bob and Fred held out each of her hands to him.

Vox growled loudly before he grinned. "I do. We marriaged now. I want to go back to our living quarters."

Riley's face creased into a frown, and she stamped her foot. "Oh no, you don't! You are not getting out of this. I want it done right," she growled back before turning to Titus. "Titus, get your ass up here and say the things I told you to write down. This big ox is going to agree with every one of those vows, or I want my Taser and pepper spray back."

"I've got a new Taser, Riley, if you need it," Pearl volunteered, pulling it from the waistband of her black leather pants.

"Oh gods, no, you don't! I thought I took all of those damn devices from you," Viper roared, reaching for Pearl.

"Don't you manhandle my poor, elderly grandmother, you jerk," Tina erupted in fury, grabbing the Taser before Viper could and pressing it against his chest in warning. "Now get back in line so Riley can have her wedding."

"Make me," Viper snarled menacingly.

"Okay," Tina said and pressed the button.

Viper jerked as the shock hit him, stumbling backward before collapsing onto the floor in a quivering jerking mass of twitching nerves. His loud curses filled the small chamber they had converted for the wedding. All four of his younger brothers stood around him with their mouths hanging open, trying not to laugh.

"Oh, to hell with it," Riley said in resignation. "I do. Let's go to the reception. Maybe it will go better than the wedding," she muttered over the noise of all the brothers suddenly asking Tina and Pearl about Tasers.

"How about we skip the reception and get to the wedding night?" Vox asked with a hopeful grin. "I have something for you."

"What did you get me this time?" Riley asked, rolling her eyes and chuckling.

Vox reached into his pocket and pulled out a small, squeaking animal. "A mouse!"

In a matter of seconds, a huge, very pregnant white tiger was knocking over chairs and tables as she chased the poor Sarafin replica of a mouse around the room. She wasn't alone, though. Soon Pearl, Tina, Bob, Fred, their mates, and a handful of other guests were the only ones left in their two-legged form. The other cat-shifters had joined in the fun, thinking it was part of the marriage ceremony to chase the mouse.

"Well, hell, I think that was the best damn wedding I've ever attended. I'm glad that boy chose my Riley girl. He'll keep her on her toes." Pearl chuckled. "Now, is anyone up for some grub?"

To be continued…Viper's Defiant Mate.

ABOUT THE AUTHOR

Susan Smith has always been a romantic and a dreamer. An avid writer, she has spent years writing, although it has usually been technical papers for college. Now, she spends her evenings and weekends writing and her nights dreaming up new stories. An affirmed "geek," she spends her days working on computers and other peripherals. She enjoys camping and traveling when she is not out on a date with her favorite romantic guy. Fans can reach her at SESmithFL@gmail.com or visit her web site at: http://sesmithfl.com. Join me for additional information about the books at http://pinterest.com/sesmithfl/s-e-smith/, http://twitter.com/sesmithfl, http://facebook.com/se.smith.5?fref=ts and at my new book discussion forum at http://www.sesmithromance.com

Additional Books:

Abducting Abby (Dragon Lords of Valdier: Book 1)

Capturing Cara (Dragon Lords of Valdier: Book 2)

Tracking Trisha (Dragon Lords of Valdier: Book 3)

Ambushing Ariel (Dragon Lords of Valdier: Book 4)

For the Love of Tia (Dragon Lords of Valdier: Book 4.1)

Cornering Carmen (Dragon Lords of Valdier: Book 5)

Paul's Pursuit (Dragon Lords of Valdier: Book 6)

Choosing Riley (Sarafin Warriors: Book 1)

Ha'ven's Song (Curizan Warrior: Book 1)

Hunter's Claim (The Alliance: Book 1)
Lily's Cowboys (Heaven Sent: Book 1)
Touching Rune (Heaven Sent: Book 2)
Indiana Wild (Spirit Pass: Book 1)
River's Run (Lords of Kassis: Book 1)
Star's Storm (Lords of Kassis: Book 2)
Jo's Journey (Lords of Kassis: Book 3)
    Rescuing Mattie (Lords of Kassis: Book 3.1)
    Tink's Neverland (Cosmo's Gateway: Book 1)
    Hannah's Warrior (Cosmos' Gateway: Book 2)
    Tansy's Titan (Cosmos' Gateway: Book 3)
    Cosmos' Promise (Cosmos' Gateway: Book 4)
    Gracie's Touch (Zion Warriors: Book 1)

Made in the USA
Lexington, KY
20 January 2014